the
RAVEN
ROOM

THE RAVEN ROOM TRILOGY
BOOK ONE

ana medeiros

DIVERSIONBOOKS

Diversion Books
A Division of Diversion Publishing Corp.
443 Park Avenue South, Suite 1008
New York, New York 10016
www.DiversionBooks.com

For more information, email info@diversionbooks.com

First Diversion Books edition November 2015.
Print ISBN: 978-1-62681-777-7
eBook ISBN: 978-1-62681-776-0

To Garfield.

I'm here. Again. How can I stay away?

As I walk down this narrow corridor, I caress the blood-red walls with my open palm and I can feel the energy of the place course through my body. This is the secret. The big secret all who come here have to protect if we want to die and be reborn through our desires. I'm afraid. Afraid I'm depraved. Afraid solitude is all I'm ever meant to feel.

It's dark. Warm. Sounds of pleasure, sounds of pain, echo around me and I close my eyes. The air in here is different from anywhere else. It's full. Heavy. I can taste it. The taste of unleashed sexual appetite. I kneel myself at the feet of it all, like a faithful lover. It energizes me. I don't have to pretend to be that other person anymore, the one who survives in the outside world. Here is where I come to forget. To let go. Here is where I come to be alive.

I enter the room and she's already here. Naked. While her body carries the scars we both have come to love, I carry her scars within me. In my soul. They are ours. The crimson glow of the light embraces her body like I never will. It comforts me. It makes her crave what's to come. I touch her and the sensation of her skin against my fingertips sends a shiver down my spine. Our eyes meet. A dark prelude. I'm inside of her and while we move together, gasps and sighs escaping our lips, we both know there's honesty in the gift we present each other with. She allows me to be myself, and I'm weak when I'm being strong. That's where the beauty of trust lies.

I hurt her. She hurts me.

I kill her. She kills me.

We have never met before. We are strangers.

CHAPTER 1

He still thought of them.

Julian woke up that morning covered in a thin layer of sweat, feeling like he couldn't breathe. He forced himself to inhale and sat on the bed with his head hanging forward between his tense shoulders. He kept his eyes closed, afraid to open them. Maybe he was still in the house. The fast pounding of his heart against his chest was making his whole body throb. It hurt. He ran his fingers through his hair and rested his damp forehead on his arm.

Julian opened his eyes. Unwrapping the covers from around his lower body, he got up and made his way to the window at the opposite end of the dark room. He drew the heavy, grey curtains and the dull, early winter morning light surrounded him. He squinted and the feeling of the hardwood floor against his bare feet brought him unexpected comfort. He had always liked the cold.

It was another snowy day in Chicago. Through the floor-to-ceiling bedroom windows on his eighty-fifth floor condo on North Wabash Avenue, he had full view of the eastern side of the city. Though it was early, the streets below were already hectic with traffic and pedestrians, all trying to move as fast as they could. To Julian they looked like scattered, lost toys. Sometimes he would concentrate, trying to hear the faint buzz of city noise, but that far up it was impossible. There was only silence. He felt detached from all the life unfolding at his feet, but he never got tired of watching it. The view was magnificent. It didn't matter how often or for how long he stared at it. The city skyline was a sight that never failed to move him.

Two years ago, when Julian first walked in with the real estate agent to check out the condo, he wasn't planning on buying it. The asking price was higher than he wanted to spend and he was looking for an older dwelling, something with an intimate atmosphere and a past; a home with a soul. But the instant he had stepped into the master suite he had been mesmerized. The sun was setting and the sky was bleeding in different shades of red, until all the colors drowned in sheer darkness. He had bought the condo on the spot.

The soft, shifting sound behind him made him turn.

"What time is it?"

Julian faced the bed. He tried to hide that he had forgotten she was there.

He smiled, "Seven-thirty."

"Come back to bed," she said, pulling the covers aside and opening her arms to him.

Meredith was beautiful. He had revered her healthy, toned body from the first time he met her, over a year ago. She exuded life and he had been naturally drawn to her. He appreciated that she never asked for too much. There were no demands or expectations. Their time together was fun, passionate, and carefree. Just what he needed. To Julian, that made her the perfect lover.

"What do you want?" he asked, moving his eyes from her face to her unclad breasts. He was no longer smiling and there was now a demanding, harsh quality to his voice.

Meredith bit her lower lip, delaying her reply. With an unabashed look, she stared at his naked body and touched herself. She arched her back and a sound of pleasure escaped her parted lips.

"I want to fuck you," she said.

Julian continued to watch her, not moving from his spot by the window. He knew she could see he was getting aroused. Locking eyes with his, she took her fingers to her mouth, licking them with abandon, and then placed them back between her outstretched legs.

"Please," she added.

He stroked himself slowly, but with purpose. "Get on your stomach. I want to take you from behind."

She turned around and Julian approached the bed. He covered

her body with his, spread her legs further apart and, with one single trust of his hips, entered her. She gasped and he closed his eyes. No words were exchanged. Meredith's frame wasn't fragile but he had her in a submissive position, emphasizing how much stronger than her he was. Using his strength to his advantage, Julian took full control. He didn't show her any gentleness. Moving her long brown hair aside, he bit the back of her neck. The sound of her breath catching in her chest brought him intense gratification.

Meredith buried her face in the mattress, yielding to the force of having him deep inside of her. Julian had learned her body; he knew she was close to climax. Taking in the clean scent of her skin, he wrapped her hair around his closed fist and, tugging hard, lifted her head off the bed. Sliding his free hand under Meredith, he stroked her with his fingers. Her moans grew louder as he caressed her. The feeling of her body convulsing, tightening around him, was all Julian needed. Bringing Meredith to her hands and knees, he allowed his desire to take over. They were both panting. Holding her by the waist, his head thrown back, the sound of his body slamming against hers with powerful force reverberated through the bedroom. Meredith continued to shudder and, though lost in his own lust, he was aware of how incredibly wet she was. Julian felt his release building and he leaned forward, his face in her hair. Spasms rocked his body and, as his gravelly moans mixed with hers, he spilled inside of her.

Julian pulled out of Meredith and rolled over, facing the ceiling. Fighting for breath, neither of them moved for what felt like a long time.

Meredith was the first one to speak, "You're ruining all the other guys for me."

He chuckled, absently touching her nipple with his fingertips. When they had first met, at the end of last summer, Meredith's body had been an alluring golden tone. Now he knew she was naturally very fair and he enjoyed the contrast of his swarthy complexion against hers.

He closed his hand on her voluptuous breast. "All I'm doing

is raising the bar. It guarantees you don't waste time on men who can't satisfy you." Julian brought his face closer to her and started to lick her nipple with his tongue. "Like the one you were sleeping with last month."

"Which one?"

"Mister Listerine."

Meredith groaned and slapped the side of his head. "His name was Theodore."

"He made you use mouthwash after you sucked him off." He continued to lick her nipple as he spoke. "You should have told him to go take a hike the first time it happened."

"He had OCD." She was staring down at him, her fingertips tracing the outline of his black and grey tattoo sleeve. "Jesus, you're being such a cunt."

"Is that the type of language they're teaching in grad school these days? If I was your dad I'd ask for my money back."

"Gross. Can you please not mention my dad as you suck on my nipple? It kills the mood."

"Figured it might turn you on."

At those words, she closed her fingers in his hair and pulled hard.

He laughed, wincing in pain. "Is this how you treat the man that just gave you an orgasm?"

"Yeah, one! You want me to be kind, you have to do better than that."

"Oh, I'm sorry. I didn't realize I'd let you down."

"You can make it up to me. Take me to The Raven Room next time you go," she said, resting her leg on top of his. "We've been talking about it for months."

Meredith wasn't demanding, but when she wanted something she was relentless. "I'll think about it," Julian replied.

Getting up, he walked toward the en suite bathroom. "I have to go. My first patient is in an hour and, with this weather, it'll take me twice as long to get there. Don't you have a lecture or seminar?"

"I'm skipping," she answered, hiding under the covers.

"No, you're not. Get up and get dressed. I'm leaving in fifteen minutes," he said from the bathroom.

Meredith sat up and moved her tangled hair out of her face. "Wow, I don't even get the chance to shower before you throw me out?"

Returning to the bedroom, Julian approached the bed and, grabbing both her ankles, pulled her roughly toward him. She was now sitting on the edge of the bed, with him standing between her open legs.

"I'm doing you a favor," he whispered against her ear. "You'll have my scent on you all day. You'll remember how good it felt to have me deep in you," he continued, noticing the mark he left below her collarbone the night before. He kissed the bruised skin. "You won't be bored during your lecture. You'll be soaking wet."

Meredith rubbed her thighs along the side of his body. "You're making me wet now."

When Julian pressed two of his fingers inside of her, she looked up, searching his eyes. He moved them in and out of her several times. Eventually he brought the damp fingers to his lips, watching her as he sucked them into his mouth.

Julian pulled away from her. He left the bedroom again, closing the door behind him. A few seconds later he was in the shower, feeling the hot water cascading down his head. Images from his nightmare came back to him and he lifted his face toward the water stream, hoping he could cleanse himself of the past.

Meredith had gotten out of bed and was standing by the expansive window. Her whole body felt sore but she enjoyed the satiated emotion that always followed. As she came to a decision, a smile formed on her lips. It was time for her to find out who Doctor Julian Reeve really was.

CHAPTER 2

Odetta's voice was Julian's companion every time he drove alone in his car. He knew the lyrics to most of her songs and on that Sunday, as he made his way to Peter and Grace's house in Lincoln Park for the birthday party of their one-year-old twins, he hummed along to one of her blues tracks. He looked relaxed and in high spirits but he couldn't shake the sense of dread every time he thought of the afternoon ahead of him.

The sidewalks were deserted. Chicago was in the midst of its hardest winter in over fifty years and the punishing weather was all one would hear being discussed across town. Constant snowstorms, freezing temperatures, dangerous driving conditions, persistent delays in public transportation—all of it was forcing the locals to hibernate. But the harsh weather was also having an invisible impact on Chicagoans. Julian had heard many of his mental health colleagues mention the spike in the demand for antidepressants and sedatives. Pills, he believed, in most cases caused more harm than good. He figured that by the time spring made an appearance everyone around him would have gone a little bit crazier. But for Julian it was different. He was secretly enjoying the savageness of the season. The cold lulled the city to a quieter pace and the stillness that permeated the air sharpened his instincts.

Julian wished he could have declined the invitation to the birthday party. But Peter was his oldest friend. They had met several years ago, while they were both pursuing their undergrad. In the beginning, Julian had been annoyed by Peter's sunny disposition but after a few months of attending the same classes, he had come to enjoy Peter's company. By their third year of university, Julian was considered a member of Peter's family. His friend would often voice that Julian had been adopted twice, first by Hazel, when he was sixteen, and second by Peter.

After graduation, Julian remained in the city to attend the Chicago School of Professional Psychology and Peter temporarily moved back to Toronto, where he had grown-up, to attend medical school. During that time they continued to visit each other often. Achieving academic success despite the constant drunken adventures and string of failed romances, Peter was the fun-loving friend Julian had learned to appreciate, support, but many times condemn. Their summer trips to Peter's cottage in Muskoka, called by many the Malibu of the North, were always the highlight of their time together. It was then, through witnessing Peter's interaction with his family, that Julian understood how his and Peter's lives would forever be different. The love of his family would always enable Peter to behave recklessly. If he fell, Peter knew that they would be there to catch him.

Julian parked on the street outside of Peter and Grace's three-story home. "Goodbye my friend, Odetta. Till next time," he said, turning off the music. He continued to tap his gloved fingers on the steering wheel. He was fighting the urge to turn the key in the ignition and drive away.

Julian was disgusted with himself. All he had to do was go into the house, socialize for a few hours and then leave. Instead he was hiding in his car like a coward. Looking for a distraction, he glanced at his phone. There was a text message from Meredith, reminding him of her desire to go to The Raven Room. He wanted to take her but the truth was that he was afraid of what might happen if he did. Sighing, he decided it was best to leave things as they were. It was safer that way.

He jumped out of the car, grabbed the boxes from the back seat, and walked to the front door. Grace greeted him with a warm smile.

"Julian! We were starting to think you were going to bail on us."

"You know I wouldn't miss the party."

Grace took the presents and his coat. "I'm very happy

you're here."

"Me too. Where're the boys?"

"They're down for a nap. Can you believe it? I'm sure you and Pete would love to catch up before we all start drinking to dull our nerves against screaming kids." As soon as she spoke, a high-pitched scream echoed down the hall and they both flinched. "See?" she laughed. "Peter's upstairs in his office. Go."

"Are you sure you don't need my help? Sounds like you might."

"No, we're fine. Just drag Pete downstairs in a few minutes to cut the cake."

As he made his way up the stairs, Julian heard the voices coming from the other end of the house. He was appreciative that Grace, knowing how much he disliked gatherings, saved him from having to greet a horde of talkative family members, yuppie friends, and shrieking kids.

He found Peter sitting in the middle of his disorganized office, smirking at his laptop screen.

"Hey man," Peter said, running his hand through his disheveled blonde hair. "Looking forward to eating some rainbow-colored cake?"

Julian fell into the big worn-out couch beside Peter's desk. He grabbed a small rubber giraffe stuffed between the seats and grinned. It belonged to the twins. "Everywhere I go I'm stalked by toys."

"Not just toys. You've got hungry pussy jumping at you like spider monkeys."

Julian lifted his eyes to Peter. His grin morphed into a smirk. "That fast, huh? No 'How are you doing, Julian?' No 'What's new at work, Julian?' Straight to living vicariously through my sex life. Envious?"

"C'mon man, my golden days of banging whores are behind me. You've become my premium spank bank supplier. Porn gets kind of boring, after a while."

Julian looked through the bay window. It had started to snow. "Did you tell Grace about Meredith?"

"Is that her name?"

Julian didn't waver. "Did you tell Grace?"

"Why do you want to know?"

"I want to know how ugly a picture of me you've been painting."

"Yeah, I told her. We both worry about you." He leaned forward and rested his elbows on his knees.

Julian faced Peter, his expression solemn. "Don't do that. I'm the psychologist here. I'm the only one allowed to sit like that while pretending to care about someone."

"I'm not pretending, jackass. That Meredith girl is what, twenty?" He frowned, "And you, forty?"

"Thirty-nine." From the corner of his eye Julian saw a large pile of toppled books on the floor. He wondered how Peter ever found anything in the midst of the chaos of his office. "She's twenty-three, an adult."

"I don't care if her pussy is a place where magic happens and dreams come true. Why are you wasting your time with her?"

"Wasting my time?" Julian repeated.

"Stop fucking vapid little things in your glass tower. Meet a chick in her early thirties. Get married. Have kids. You need a family, man. It'll do you good."

"Pete, you're a successful plastic surgeon. You've got a beautiful house in Lincoln Park, an amazing wife, two sons. It's great. I'm truly happy for you. Can't you do the same for me? Be happy for the life I have?"

"Hey, I'm happy. Like I said, permanent spank bank. But it's fucking depressing."

"Well, it works for me."

"This Meredith girl is going to catch feelings, if she hasn't already—"

"You're being presumptuous," Julian didn't let him finish. "Meredith's young and, yeah, she can be stubborn and entitled, but she's someone who doesn't wait to be chosen. She chooses. That's rare."

"You're giving her too much credit," Peter said, turning to

arrange the scattered papers on his desk.

Julian was still holding the toy in his hand. "I respect her enough to believe her goal in life is not to have me fall in love with her. There're women who happen to enjoy a man's company and sex just for the simple fact that they take pleasure from it."

"That's easy for you to say," Peter replied sourly. "Women go crazy for you, the brooding type."

"I'm not brooding. I'm congenial."

"What are you talking about, man?" Peter stopped organizing his desk and gave Julian a bemused look. "You're a standoffish motherfucker."

Julian set the toy giraffe on the arm of the couch. "How're you and Grace doing?" he asked, changing the topic of the conversation.

"As you said, I make fucking good money, I own a beautiful house in Lincoln Park, I've an amazing wife and two sons. I'm living the dream." There was a sneer in Peter's words.

"I asked how you and Grace are doing. Not how you're doing."

"Good. We're good."

Julian knew Peter well enough to catch him on a lie. Before he could say anything, Grace walked into the office with one of the twins in her arms.

"We're ready to cut the cake." Not bothering to ask if he wanted to hold him, she passed the boy to Julian. "And there's someone downstairs I want you to meet."

"Please don't tell me it's another one of your single friends," Julian said, feeling the boy's soft temple against his cheek. For a brief second he closed his eyes, inhaling the boy's scent. Julian fought the urge to kiss the top of the child's head. He hadn't seen Seth or his twin brother in more than two months and, right now, he was in awe of how perfect he looked and felt. It made Julian's chest hurt.

He caught Grace watching them.

"This one is great," she replied with forced enthusiasm. "You'll really like her. She loves to travel and she's an art director—"

"And she's not twenty years younger than you," Peter jumped in.

"Yes!" Grace nodded in agreement.

"Guys, guys! Last time I went on a date with one your friends she was wearing so much glitter on her face I was sparkling for weeks!" Julian stared at both Grace and Peter. "I'm not interested."

"You know what they say, glitter is the herpes of the make-up world. Once you get it on you, you can't ever get rid of it," Peter said, chuckling.

"Pete!" Grace shouted. "You're not helping."

Standing up, Peter stumped toward the door. "I'm out of here. I'll be downstairs with the damn rainbow cake."

Grace shook her head and joined Julian on the couch. He thought she looked tired, if not downright unhappy.

"Seth likes you," she said, watching him hold the boy. "Can't remember the last time I have seen him stay in someone's arms for this long."

Julian touched the boy's dark curls.

"Do you want me to get Eli so you can hold him too?" She caressed the neck of the giraffe Julian had placed on the couch. "I can leave the three of you here alone. We don't need to cut the cake just yet."

He took a deep breath, facing her. "Grace…I can't. They're Pete's kids. And they're so lucky," he paused, seeing his words were upsetting her, "they really are. Please don't ask of me something I can't give."

"Julian, I'm not asking you to give them anything." She rubbed her forehead with her hand, a sign of frustration. "I just want you to allow Seth and Eli to give you what you need."

"What would that be?"

"Love."

Grace's words made Julian think about the decision he had made earlier, while sitting in his car. If he were to allow anyone closer to him, Meredith would probably be the only one who could handle the reality of the man he truly was. He wouldn't share with her the whole truth, that was something he couldn't ever do, but maybe sharing a part of it would be enough.

"I don't want the boys to care for me. It's better if they don't.

Believe me," he replied.

"What happened to you?" Grace's voice was heavy with compassion and that infuriated Julian. Pity was an emotion he despised.

"It's not about what happened to me." Not wanting to show the depths of his feelings, he focused on sounding aloof. "It's about what I do to others. That's what matters."

"What do you mean?"

"Grace, please," he said, lowering his voice. "This was not part of our agreement."

Silent, she looked away. The twins resembled Grace, with their flawless dark skin and striking Eastern African features. The major differences were their green eyes and the freckles dusting their cheeks. Throughout his career he had met a lot of children, all different ages, and even though he enjoyed working with them, he rarely came across one he truly connected with. But now, being there with Seth, he wondered if he would feel different toward the twins. He didn't want to give himself the opportunity to find out.

He lifted Seth off his lap and passed him to Grace. She took the boy, not looking at Julian.

"I'm sorry, Grace," he said, barely above a whisper. "I really am."

"Don't apologize to me, Julian. Seth and Eli, no matter what, are a part of you."

Julian didn't reply. He left the room. But before he did, he put the little toy giraffe in his pocket. He couldn't leave it behind. He wanted to keep it forever.

Chapter 3

Meredith was running late to meet with her stepmother Pam at The Wormhole Coffee, which was not far from her apartment in Bucktown. She adjusted the wool scarf around her neck, glanced at the sky, and hoped it wouldn't start to snow. She couldn't remember the last time she had felt the warmth of the sun on her skin. Her mood always took a turn for the worse when she had to move around the city, dressed in heavy snow boots and a long jacket. It made her feel extremely unsexy.

She saw Pam sitting at one of the small tables behind her large laptop. Her father had married Pam four years ago. A federal judge and a homicide detective, they were, at first glance, an odd pairing but somehow made it work. When her father had introduced them, at her sixteenth birthday party, Meredith had been at the height of her rebellious stage and the last thing she had wanted was a stranger calling her out on her recklessness. Getting high in her friend's basement and getting into clubs with a fake ID was her idea of a good time. Pam couldn't have disagreed more.

Before she approached her stepmother, Meredith bought herself a large latte. The hipster behind the counter went all out with the latte art, forming a perfectly shaped heart with the milk foam. That granted him a wink and one of her charming smiles.

Meredith ran on coffee and cigarettes. She promised to herself she would quit smoking before she hit the age of twenty-five. After that, the plan was to spend the next five years eating a vegan diet and to lather her skin in overpriced serums made of twigs and seaweed.

"Sorry it took me so long to get here." She gave Pam a quick hug. "The roads are a mess."

Pam frowned, "Ugh, what's new?"

Meredith sat opposite Pam and started removing the layers of her winter clothes. "There's something I need to tell you." She ran her hand through her tangled hair. That was another reason why she hated winter. Farewell to shiny, bouncy locks.

"Oh." Pam raised an eyebrow. "Who is he?"

Meredith threw her head back and laughed. "Why do you think it has anything to do with a guy?"

"It's always about a guy. Or a girl. I don't even know anymore."

"Okay, fine. Maybe you're right." She stared down at the mug cradled between her hands. "It has to do with a guy."

"Please tell me this one isn't married."

"That stage is over. Too much drama. This one is definitely not married."

"But let me guess," Pam paused, pretending to think, "no less troubled?"

It bothered her that Pam knew her so well. They stared at each other for a few seconds. Eventually Meredith's serious face broke into a smile.

"C'mon, you know that's not possible," she said, scooping up a dollop of white foam from her coffee and licking it off her finger. "Besides, who am I to judge?"

"Enough with the buildup. Who's this guy? Where did you meet him?"

"Where else? At a bar." Before she continued, Meredith cleared her throat. "He has been around for a while, though."

She considered adding that he was also not the only man in her life but she decided that Pam didn't need to know that.

"What's the catch?" Pam asked. Due to her cop's mentality, she leaned in closer to keep their conversation private.

Meredith locked eyes with Pam. "I need your help."

"With what?"

"This guy is somewhat of a mystery. I need you to find out his story."

"What? Why would I do that?"

"'Cause you're my stepmom."

"What makes you think he has a story?"

"He won't tell me much about himself. I have tried asking."

"I don't have time to be doing background checks on your boyfriends."

"He's not my boyfriend and I don't need you to run a background check on him. I'm sure he has a clean record."

"So you want me to dig?"

"You got it."

"Why? You haven't given me a good enough reason."

"He's taking me to The Raven Room. He's a member."

As soon as she had heard the words Raven Room Pam sat-up straighter.

"Have you been?" she asked.

"No. Not yet."

"Meredith, listen to me. Please. It's no place for you."

"So you've heard of it," Meredith said, smiling.

"I have. But I don't know anyone who has been able to get inside. Who's this man, Meredith?"

"Exactly. That's what I want to know."

"What's his name, where does he work, where does he live?"

"Will you get me what I want?"

"How do you know he's a member?" Pam asked.

"I overheard a phone conversation between him and his friend. Afterwards I just asked him about it." Meredith took a sip of her coffee. "He made me promise I would never mention it to anyone. Refused to even discuss it. But then, with time, he became more open to the idea of taking me."

"Don't go."

"I'm a big girl. Now, will you help me?"

"You're a reckless, stubborn child. Is he pressuring you to go?"

"No," Meredith was quick to say, looking almost appalled by Pam's question. "He's not that type of man."

"I thought you didn't know who he was."

"No one forces me to do anything I don't want to do.

21

You know that."

"So, finding out more about him is worth you betraying his trust?" Pam asked.

"I have my reasons."

"Such as?"

Meredith didn't plan to tell Pam but she didn't see why she shouldn't be honest with her. "In less than a year I'll be done with my masters and I refuse to work for free at some shitty magazine. I'm going to have a great career as a journalist, so why not use this amazing opportunity to my advantage?" she said, excitement in her voice. "The Raven Room draws the most powerful people in the city and I'm going to write a piece about it and one of its members."

Pam looked taken aback. "Does he know?"

"He doesn't need to know. I'll keep his identity a secret."

"Don't tell anyone what you just told me."

Meredith had pitched her idea to the head of her program, and she had encouraged Meredith to pursue it. If she wrote a good enough investigative piece, her professor would connect her with a couple of magazines and newspapers that might be interested in publishing it. But after watching Pam's reaction to her plan, Meredith wouldn't be telling her that she had already shared it with someone else.

"I won't. And I'm trusting you not to tell anyone either."

"If I do this, your dad can't find out. He would be furious."

"The last thing I want is for my dad to know. This stays between you and me."

"I'm not happy about this, Meredith."

She didn't want her impatience to show but Pam was making it hard for her. "Are you with me on this or not?"

"Give me his name. I'll see what I can find."

Taking a folded piece of paper out of her bag, she passed it to Pam. Her stepmother unfolded the paper and read the information she had written down.

"A child psychologist at Lurie Children's Hospital and an Associate Professor at the Feinberg School of Medicine?" Pam glanced at her. "This man can't have people knowing he goes to a place like The Raven Room. Be careful."

Meredith knew what Pam was getting at. A man such as Julian would understand that maintaining appearances was pivotal to success. But Meredith had spent enough time with Julian to know he didn't value those things as much as one would expect. Julian was a loner. He kept everyone at arm's length. He didn't have a large social circle and he didn't have many close friends. The only one Meredith had heard of was Peter. She also didn't know much about the other women in his life. She assumed she wasn't the only one but, so far, she hadn't seen or heard anything to confirm her suspicions. She wasn't bothered by the thought of Julian having other lovers. She enjoyed talking about her own sexual experiences with him because, unlike everyone else, he never made her feel judged.

Meredith looked through the coffee shop window and realized it was getting dark. A small group of people walked in and the cold emanating from their bodies made her shiver. She wished she could leave Chicago every winter. There was nothing she enjoyed about the city during that time of year.

She felt her purse vibrate. She pulled her phone out and raised an eyebrow when she glanced at the screen. Julian had texted her. He wanted her to come over to his place on Saturday night, wearing only a black dress. No underwear. With Julian she never knew what she was going to get. Some women might be taken aback by it but Meredith craved it.

"I have to go," she said to Pam, drinking the rest of her coffee. "Call me when you find out something and we'll get together."

Meredith felt her stepmother's eyes on her as she put her jacket and scarf back on. There were more things Pam wanted to say but she was holding back. It was there, in her worried expression.

Chapter 4

Meredith's phone starting to ring and she peeked inside of her clutch to see who it was. She didn't answer.

"Aren't you going to take that?" Julian asked.

"It's my stepmom. She has been calling me all night."

They were sitting in the back seat of a cab. "I'm really excited," she said, glancing at him.

"You might be disappointed." It was dark inside of the cab but Julian knew she was smiling. He rested his open hand on her knee and the feeling of her smooth skin against his palm stirred memories of her naked body against his.

They had met at his place earlier and, after a few glasses of red wine, he had ended up deep inside of her. Seeing her stand in front of him with her chestnut-colored hair in a loose chignon, perfect red lipstick and in a simple but sophisticated black dress that complimented her body, he had found himself wanting her with an urgency he couldn't ignore. Aware that because Meredith would be there he wouldn't be able to engage in his normal activity at The Raven Room, fucking her on his living room floor had dulled Julian's need. It had been short but intense. Usually Meredith was quick to climax but he hadn't given her the chance. It had been about him. Not her.

"I won't be disappointed," she whispered, tilting her head back.

The cab was moving south along North State Street and the brightness coming from the streetlights reached Julian's face. Meredith recognized the expression she saw. He was still aroused. Without saying a word, she reached for his hand on her knee and covering his fingers with hers, guided them up her thigh. She had debated if it had been a good idea to wear a dress in the middle of a harsh winter without stockings or underwear, but Julian had requested it and now she was thankful the black dress was all she had on. She shifted on her seat and as his hand disappeared between her slightly open legs, she felt the remains of his orgasm trickle from inside her.

Julian was looking through his side window and Meredith closed her eyes, abandoning herself to the feeling of his warm and strong hand on the most sensitive part of her body. Suppressing every sound, she bit her lower lip. Briefly, she opened her eyes and glanced at the driver through the rear-view mirror. She couldn't tell if he was aware of what was going on between her and Julian but the idea of a complete stranger knowing that Julian had his fingers in her was exhilarating. She could feel herself getting wetter.

"Come for me," Julian said against her ear, breaking the silence inside of the cab. Hearing him speak, Meredith turned to face him and saw that he had again returned to look through his window. She wondered how he could be so close and at the same time so far away.

He moved his fingers in and out of her and Meredith stared at the passing store signs glowing in the night. It was warm in the cab and the familiar scent of Julian's cologne aroused her. Suddenly it all became too much. The relentless pressure inside her, the heavy silence full of unspoken words, her increasing desire. The outside world became blurry and the violence of her orgasm made her sway. She blinked, tears rolling down her face.

Meredith realized that, at some point, Julian had moved his hand away. He continued to sit beside her but no part of his body touched hers. He was not looking at her. Feeling more tears roll down her face, she didn't know why she was crying.

"Please drop us off at the corner of Madison Street," Julian said to the driver.

Gracefully, she dried the tears from her cheeks with the back of her hand. Standing on the sidewalk, as she waited for him to pay the driver, she wondered if The Raven Room was in the Loop neighborhood, the downtown business district.

"Is it around here?" she asked as Julian draped his long, wool winter coat over her shoulders.

"I told you to wear a dress and no underwear. I will keep in mind that I need to tell you to wear a jacket as well." He was trying not to smile. "There's a car parked on the other side of the street. We're driving."

Meredith frowned but didn't say anything. She was contemplating how she was going to walk through the snow with her high heels.

"Come here." Julian extended his hand to her. As soon as she took it, he scooped her up in his arms without effort and started walking.

"Aren't you a gentleman?" She wrapped her arms around his neck. "Sometimes you do manage to impress me."

Julian felt Meredith rest her face against the side of his neck. He could smell her fragrant hair amidst the cold air. It was Meredith's signature scent, a mixture of rose, fresh citrus, and sensual vanilla. It would linger on his bed sheets and pillowcases and, even though he had been bothered by it at the beginning, over time the scent had become comforting to him.

When they reached the parked SUV, Julian put her down and unlocked the doors. Meredith was fast to curl up on the passenger seat. As he turned the heat on full blast, she noticed the vehicle they were in looked brand new.

"Who owns this car?" she asked with curiosity as he merged into traffic. "Is it yours? I have never seen it before."

"Just borrowing. Consider this your private car and me your driver."

"A driver who also provides sexual services? I'm afraid to ask how much all this is costing me."

Julian looked at her from the corner of his eye and winked. "It's a mutually beneficial arrangement."

"Is sex our currency?" she asked, laughing.

"No, Meredith. Not sex."

"Then what is it?"

"You're a smart young woman. Sooner or later you'll figure out."

Meredith glanced at the dashboard clock. It was almost two in the morning and they were still moving south.

"What area of town are we going to?" she finally asked.

"Chinatown. We're almost there."

It had started to snow and Meredith moved her face closer to the window. She had heard the reports warning of another winter storm but she had hoped they had been wrong. It now looked like they were in for a rough night.

"The Raven Room's in Chinatown?" There was disbelief in her voice.

Julian turned into what looked like a back alley and stopped the car.

"Let's go," he said, killing the engine and jumping out of the SUV. He opened her door and helped her out. Meredith tried to look around but the snow was falling harder and it was dark. They made their way through a large, metal door and down a poorly lit, narrow set of stairs, the loud sound of her stilettos on the steps echoing through the small space.

"We're not allowed to take our phones inside," Julian said as they reached the bottom of the stairs. He opened the door and they entered an even darker area. Only after he took her phone and his coat did Meredith see the man in a black suit standing behind a tall counter. As Julian passed the items to him he also included a card. She leaned closer, trying to get a glimpse of it, but the man was quick to give it back to Julian, who put it in his pocket. Meredith almost groaned with disappointment.

He opened what looked like a warehouse sliding door. She felt him rest his hand on her lower back and gently direct her to walk through it. "After you."

The first thing Meredith noticed was the gentle crimson lighting. And the scent, rich and smooth. The underlying notes of burning wood reminded her of the small library in her grandparents' New England cottage where, as a child during Christmas vacation, she would sit looking at beautiful picture books as the damp, gloomy afternoons morphed into cold nights. There was a dark and sweet base to the scent that made her remember her grandfather smoking his favorite tobacco pipe while enjoying a glass of bourbon. The Raven Room's atmosphere was mellow, luscious, welcoming. Meredith felt right at home.

"What can I get you to drink?" Julian asked, taking her hand and leisurely moving toward the bar area.

"The usual." She enjoyed the feeling of his warm hand on hers. The music wasn't loud and she could hear the other people near them chatting softly. Everyone was dressed like they would be at any sophisticated city club and Meredith noticed she wasn't the target of any curious looks. That pleased her. The man standing behind the bar, probably in his mid-fifties, wore a grey vest over a black dress shirt that he had rolled up to his elbows. He shared a friendly hug with Julian.

"My buddy tells me this is your first time at our club," the man said, giving her one of the most handsome smiles she had seen in a while. He wasn't what she would call good looking, but he had more sex appeal than most men his age. "I'm Ben and," he glanced at the large collection of alcohol covering the wall behind him, "it'll always be my pleasure to serve you."

"Thanks, Ben. I'm Meredith."

"No matter how busy we are at the bar, Meredith, just come to me and I'll put a drink in your hand before you can look at me twice with those beautiful eyes of yours."

She winked at him. "As long as you're smiling I don't mind waiting."

After more casual banter, Meredith and Julian moved toward the middle of the room.

"So, how does it work?" she asked as he handed her a Bulleit Bourbon on the rocks. "Besides the fact that we took a cab, then jumped in a car that doesn't belong to you, and are now in the basement of a building in the heart of Chinatown, this place seems pretty normal."

"Surprised we weren't greeted by naked women walking around

with silver trays offering glasses of champagne?" He looked at her with mischief as he took a mouthful of his Sazerac. "Now that I think about it, me too."

"Yes, that's exactly what I was thinking."

"The members like discretion. A club that operates out in the open attracts a different type of individual."

Julian was standing close to her and her eyes fell to his chest. He was wearing a pristine white shirt under a midnight black blazer. As the color of the blazer matched his hair, the white shirt heightened his bronze skin tone, which in turn complemented his Eastern European features. Meredith thought it was a great look on him.

"Is it legal?" she asked, resting her hand on the middle of his chest. She could feel his body heat through the shirt's fabric.

"Meredith, your curiosity will be your downfall."

By the look on his face she knew Julian wasn't going to give her a straight answer. "How does the club work?"

"Like any other sex club."

"Be more specific."

Julian wrapped his arm around her waist and brought her closer to him. Lowering his head, he rubbed his lips against her forehead and continued down her temple, kissing her jawline. He took her lower lip between his and bit down. She gasped, not expecting to feel his teeth on her, and kissed him back. Meredith moved her free hand to touch his hair. Julian pressed her to him and the fact that he wasn't being gentle only made her want him more. Feeling his arousal against her body, she leaned on him.

"I could fuck you right here and no one would blink," Julian whispered, his breath mingling with hers. "Does that answer your question?"

Meredith caressed the back of his neck with her long nails. "How big is this place?" She wished she wasn't holding a drink. She wanted to fondle him.

"This is just the bar and lounge." He felt her shift and now he was nested between her slightly parted legs. "Not much happens down here. Upstairs is where you'll find most of the activity."

He ran his hand along her back, until he touched her below the waistline. Cupping her flesh, he undulated her hips, making sure the movement guaranteed him a good stroke.

"I see." She took her glass to her lips, trying to remain coherent. It was almost impossible when Julian was all she could feel and smell. "Does anything go?"

"Depends on your definition of anything."

"What's not allowed?"

"Everything is allowed," Julian answered, staring into Meredith's eyes. "As long as there's the consent of all parties involved and no minors."

"I'm surprised no one asked to see my ID."

"You're with me."

"So I'm your guest?" she asked, raising an eyebrow.

"Something like that."

"The card you showed when we arrived. What is it? Your membership card?"

"It's my key."

"Can I see it?" Meredith asked, smiling.

Julian reached inside his pocket and passed it to her.

He watched her flip the smooth, black card between her fingers a couple of times. He laughed when she frowned.

"It's blank. There's nothing on it," she said, confused. "No words, no pictures, no numbers, no magnetic strip. Nothing."

"That's where you're wrong. There's a lot on that key."

Meredith passed it back to him. "It has a chip inside?"

"No chip. These keys have a special touch to them."

He didn't continue and she lifted an eyebrow. "Which is?"

"Curious and impatient." Julian shook his head. "What am I going to do with you?"

"Spank me?"

"That wouldn't accomplish anything." He brought his lips to her ear and licked the contour of it. "Maybe I should have you volunteer at Lurie."

Meredith groaned. "I'd rather take it up the ass all night long."

Julian threw his head back and laughed out loud. He loved teasing her. "I'll show you what's special about the key. I promise."

"I'm holding you to that."

"I'd expect nothing less."

Meredith looked around. There were probably around fifty people by the bar, mostly socializing in small groups, men and woman of different ages. She was relieved she didn't recognize any of them. As she assessed her surroundings, a couple stepped into the room, their entrance revealing a black door in the corner hidden behind a heavy red curtain.

"Where does that door lead?"

"That's just another entrance."

Something in Julian's voice made her turn to face him. He was lying. She was sure of it. He was holding back, showing her only some areas of the club. But at that moment calling him out on it wouldn't accomplish anything. "I want to go upstairs."

He locked eyes with her as he drank the rest of his Sazerac. "Very good," he finally said. There was an air of resignation in his expression.

They rested their empty glasses on the bar counter and Meredith followed Julian to an impressive staircase at the opposite end of the room. As they walked up the stairs, Julian continued to hold her hand and that small gesture pleased her. It showed Meredith he wanted to make her feel safe. They had never held hands before.

Meredith's shoes sunk in the thick carpet runner, the same type of carpet her ex-boyfriend's parents had in their Streeterville home, the kind that costs more than hardwood flooring. The amber glow shining from the wall sconces concealed flaws and enhanced the smallest hint of beauty in the people passing them. Not concerned if she was acting like an awestruck girl, Meredith traced the intricate geometrical patterns on the red wallpaper with her fingertips. It created the illusion that the walls were pulsating. She pressed her palm to the wall, almost expecting to feel the sanguine warmth of a living creature against her skin.

When they reached the top of the stairs, she blinked a few

times, trying to break free from the hypnotic state she found herself in. The lighting was now a deep red and the rich scent she had noticed when they entered the club was stronger here. It seeped into her pores and she tasted it in her mouth.

"Is that perfume?" she asked Julian, taking a deep breath. "Where is that coming from?"

"The story is that, during prohibition, this used to be a bourbon distillery." He spun around, his arm around Meredith's waist. "Have you ever been to a barrel aging warehouse?"

Meredith glared at him. In response, Julian ran his hand down her back and ended the caress with a playful swat. "I'll take that as a no. Barrel aging warehouses don't smell like alcohol. If you ask anyone that has ever been to one what they remember the most, they'll all say the same thing. How amazing they smell. A mix of oak, burnt-caramel, smoke, spices. The barrels have been gone for a long time but the scent stayed."

"Is that a true story? I have never smelled anything like it." Meredith closed her eyes, taking it in.

"That's what they say, but it probably was just a yak-yak bourbon operation and what we now smell is nothing more than the scent of sex. Arousal," Julian said. "A bunch of rich assholes fucking each other like the animals they pretend to not be."

She wrapped her arms around Julian's waist. "I want to see everything. Show it to me."

"You won't find anything here that you haven't seen or done yourself." He brushed his thumb over her lower lip. "It's just sex."

"Show me your favorite area."

Julian took a while to respond and Meredith stared into his eyes. Julian was on the verge of telling her something but words never came. Instead, he led her to one of the rooms adjacent to the hall where they had been standing. Inside, there were people walking around, chatting, laughing. Some were naked, others wore black silk robes, and a few, just like her and Julian, were fully clothed. The atmosphere was of a lively party and when she saw smiles directed at her, Meredith smiled back.

They sat in one of the shadowy corners on a large, comfortable leather couch. "This is my favorite spot," Julian said, drawing imaginary circles on Meredith's shoulder. The movement of his fingers was slow and rhythmic, soothing.

Meredith was completely at ease.

"Why is it your favorite?"

"It's cozy. We can sit here and see everything that's happening, without being the center of attention." Julian leaned back, pulling her toward him. "And this couch is heavenly."

Meredith took off her high heels and folded her legs under her. Julian was right. She felt like a pampered voyeur.

"I can show you where the lockers are. There will be a brand new silk robe waiting for you. In fact," he tilted his head to a woman wearing expensive looking lingerie, "you can wear anything you want. Or nothing at all. It's completely up to you."

"Later. I'm enjoying just being here."

Meredith spent a few minutes admiring a very attractive, fit man, having what looked like a cheerful conversation with a couple, while he inserted a sex toy inside a man who was on his hands and knees in front of him. Occasionally he would remove the toy from inside the prone man and bring it to the man's lips, making him lick it before inserting it again. He was rewarded with loud, pleasurable moans from the target of his ministrations.

"They're very sexy together, aren't they?" Julian said, watching the same two men she had her eyes on.

"Are you turned on by them?"

"I'm not indifferent to them but, as a woman, you have the ability to be turned on by everything. We men, unfortunately, have more limitations."

She chuckled. "Everything?"

"Everything," Julian emphasized. "If I showed you a video of a lion and a lioness mating, the chances of you getting wet are much higher than me getting a hard-on. Alas, one of the many beautiful things about female sexuality. I'm deeply envious."

Meredith watched two couples who were the most vocal in the

room. They were moaning and whimpering, a pile of legs and arms, all moving with the intention of bringing pleasure to one another. She heard screams of sexual release coming from other rooms and her imagination ran wild. She wished she could be everywhere in The Raven Room at once.

"You'll like the dungeon," Julian said with a smile. "It's the only area of the club that, instead of being Art Deco, is completely Art Nouveau. You'll feel like you you're being gagged and tied up in Paris, your favorite city."

"I get to be a Parisian slut? My dreams have come true!" she chirped. "Isn't that your favorite city as well?"

"Stockholm is my favorite. I'm not as sophisticated as you."

Meredith rolled her eyes at his comment and they both laughed.

Julian glanced at his watch. It was almost three-thirty in the morning. In around one hour the club would start to empty out and that was something of a relief to him. He wished he could share Meredith's enthusiasm but nothing of what was taking place around them was new. The thrill of group sex, the anonymity of a sexual act with a stranger, the forbidden draw of kink—the appeal of what this area of the club had to offer him had faded a long time ago. What made him return to the club over and over again was hidden away, far from Meredith's eyes, behind the black door.

He spent a few minutes looking at the bodies in front of him. Julian didn't feel anything toward any of them. No lust, no appreciation, no envy, not even repulsion. The moans, grunts, and the erotic words exchanged were flat noises to him.

He turned his head to the far left of the room, where the lighting's red hue was particularly vibrant and he caught himself admiring the naked back of a female straddling her sexual partner. The male was sitting on a large chair and she was facing the wall. All Julian could see was her very long, tousled hair falling down her back, the curve of her buttocks, the soles of her bare feet and her arms, resting on the shoulders of the male under her. She was fully nude. And she was small. Julian could tell she was not only short, but also thin. Too thin. He had never been attracted to underweight women and, at that precise moment, he wasn't sure why she had caught his attention. Maybe it was the way she was moving or how delicate her waist looked under the man's oversized hands. Or that despite her very small frame, she was well shaped. She owned her body, Julian thought. She embraced it and was in charge of her sexuality. To him, that was what made her so incredibly alluring.

Her partner got up and carried her across the room with her legs wrapped around his waist. The man was still inside of her and if she hadn't rested her forehead on his shoulder, Julian would have been able to see her face. They sat on one of the several low benches in front of him and he now had almost a full view of her.

She was aroused. She was enjoying herself but she was detached from her partner. Maybe she didn't know him or maybe he didn't matter that much to her. She was sharing her body, nothing more. Her pleasure was her own.

Julian was lost in her experience. Suddenly, she lifted her eyes to him and his breath caught in his chest. He couldn't tell what color her eyes were or the exact shade of her hair but it didn't matter. As she continued to move with her partner, her lips were slightly parted, her hair in disarray, but those were details in the periphery of his awareness.

It was all about her. And in Julian, for the first time in his life, there was stillness. Pure tranquility. She was near. Julian could see it on her flushed face, on her erect nipples, on her tense body. And in her eyes locked on his. She was sharing her approaching release with him through her unfaltering gaze.

Julian felt it. When she quivered and tilted her head forward, as her orgasm took her in its fold, he had to close his eyes. The intensity of her pleasure was devastating to him. Never before had he felt someone else's emotion as his.

When he opened his eyes she was still watching him. The feeling radiating from his chest was so genuine that Julian wasn't surprised by the burning sensation of unshed tears. He took a deep breath.

"Are you okay?" Julian faintly heard. "Julian?" He turned his head and faced Meredith.

"Did you hear me?" she asked.

"Sorry?"

"Are you okay?" she insisted, resting her hand on his forearm.

"Yes." He swallowed hard and stared at Meredith with a disoriented expression. "Why do you ask?"

"Just want to make sure. I was talking to you for a while." She narrowed her gaze on him. "What happened?"

"Nothing happened. I'm just tired."

Meredith smiled. "Do you want to fuck?"

Julian faced the room and realized the mystery woman had left. Her partner was also gone. He felt the urge to get up and search for her, not sure with what intent, maybe to speak with her, find out her name, or to just continue to admire her from a distance. But now that feeling was slowly being replaced by a need to attend to Meredith.

He leaned closer to her. "I want to watch you being fucked by another man."

"Which one?" she asked.

He scanned the room and he could tell several men were giving her lustful glances. "Your choice."

Meredith looked at one man who had been glancing at her since they had sat down.

"Him. He's attractive," she said, not removing her eyes from the naked man lounging with a woman.

"I think they're a package deal." He looked in the same direction as her. "I've seen them here a few times."

The couple smiled at Meredith and she smiled back. When the woman made a gesture for her to go join them, she looked at Julian with some uncertainty. She was turned on. She could feel the unleashed desire coiled within her but she wasn't sure how to react to their invitation. Since entering the club a couple hours earlier, Meredith's perception of reality had shifted and everything around her was unfolding within the dense haze of a primal sensuality she had never experienced before. It made her feel powerful. Alive.

"I want to watch you being fucked by both of them," Julian

said to her, his voice commanding.

He saw Meredith get up and, with no rush, walk up to the couple. She was younger than them and it was clear to Julian that they wanted her. The man gave Julian a quick glance, an unspoken request for permission, to which he answered with a small nod. Julian wanted to concentrate on the scene unfolding in front of him but his mind kept going back to the woman who had left so suddenly. He was attracted to her, that was clear, but there was another basic urge that he hadn't felt in a very long time—a need to possess.

Julian forced himself to focus again on his surroundings and his eyes met Meredith's. Resting on the day bed, she was naked with the other woman's face between her open thighs. Julian saw her hooded gaze, the one that always told him she was close to orgasm, and he smiled at her. Never was she as beautiful as she was now. Several people were admiring Meredith, her strong body in full display, arching her back with abandon every time the other woman's tongue touched her sensitive core. She reached for the woman's partner, who had been stroking himself while watching the two of them together, and Julian knew what Meredith wanted. Having a man come on her face, on her body, truly aroused her. While the woman was simultaneously pleasuring herself and indulging on Meredith, pushing her to climax, the man leaned closer to Meredith's body. He couldn't take his eyes away from both women prone before him, no one in the room could. Meredith closed her fingers on the woman's hair, her legs quivering as her lower back lifted from the couch. The man, while holding himself in his closed fist, came on Meredith's convulsing body. Some met her chin, pooling in her collarbone, but most of it landed on her nipples, and now was running down the side of her breast.

Meredith had her eyes closed as she absently rubbed it on her skin. She felt its warmth, the delicate texture against her palm. When she opened her eyes Julian was crouching by her. The red glow of the room accentuated the inscrutable expression he wore so well and that made Meredith touch his lips with her fingertips.

"You're changing my whole existence," she whispered, showing him a sad smile. "I don't even know who you really are."

"You're the one changing your own existence, Meredith. I'm just the man who'll make sure you get home safely."

Julian kissed the inside of her wrist.

"She knows who you are, though."

He frowned. "Who?"

"The woman who was here earlier," Meredith answered, continuing to look at him. "And you know that she does."

Chapter 5

A very serious eight-year-old boy was staring at him. Julian was staring right back but his mind was elsewhere. Like Julian did whenever he felt restless, he was drumming his fingers on his knee. He didn't know how long they had been in that room, maybe thirty minutes by then, and they had barely said a word to each other. The night before, after leaving the club with Meredith, Julian had dropped her off at her place and had gone home. He hadn't slept. Even if he had wanted to sleep, he would have forced himself to stay awake. It had been one of those nights when the thought of doing a line of cocaine had crossed his mind several times but, as usual, he had opted for a couple of energy drinks instead.

The boy leaned back and, balancing himself on the back legs of the chair, started to teeter back and forth. That went on for a few minutes before it caught Julian's attention. He had taken the boy as a patient because the other psychologists in the department had complained about heavy workloads and how close they were to burning out. Julian saw their complaints for what they really were—excuses. He lectured at the university twice a week and he had the highest number of patients. In his line of work saying no to a child was not an option.

He needed to focus.

"Were you happy you got to see your sisters today, Harry?" Julian asked, closing his hand into a fist. He had to stop drumming his fingers. He forced both of his hands to remain on the table. Holding the notepad and a pen helped.

"I guess," the boy replied. His chair continued to wobble back and forth.

A month earlier Harry had lit a couch on fire, while his two younger sisters slept on it. Now, as Harry sat in his weekly session with Julian, his sisters were two floors down recovering from third-degree burns.

"I'm sure they were happy to see you," Julian added.

"I guess."

Harry had yet to show any emotion about what had happened and that's what had brought him and Julian together. One of Julian's colleagues had said he was a lost cause—a kid from Englewood, being raised by his elderly grandmother while the mother served a life sentence for murder. In Harry's file Julian had read that, years before, the father had been shot dead during an altercation with the police.

"When was the last time you visited your mother?"

"A while back, I guess."

Julian almost sighed. Harry wasn't making it easy for him, of course, on today of all days, when he was so off his game. He watched the boy's chair sway back and forth a couple more times. It had started to make a squeaking sound and Julian knew he had to do something. Otherwise he would go mad, trapped in a room with a boy too young to understand what he was up against. Over the years, Julian had been repeatedly warned by the head of the department about his approach to his patient's issues. He was directed to act as he had been trained, not just do what he felt was right. Julian's reaction was to simply ignore such warnings. He followed his instincts, not a script.

"I know you miss your mom. When I was your age all I wanted was to have my mom back, too," he said, staring at the pen in his hand. "You want to tell her what you've been learning in school. Or how sometimes you're confused and, just like a shaken can of soda, you are so angry inside that all you want is to let it out. Break something because you know you'll feel better afterwards."

"Where was your mom? In jail?"

"I don't know. I didn't have sisters or a grandmother to take care of me. I was all alone, and, let me tell you, it was scary." Julian rested the notepad on the table and started to draw on the blank page. "South side, just like you."

"What about your dad?"

"I never met him. Do you remember yours?"

"A little."

"I remember my mom would tell me stories about enchanted cats, wizards, giants."

"Stories about enchanted cats?" Harry asked. "Sounds stupid."

"Yeah, they were pretty stupid." Julian continued to draw. "Do you ever feel scared, Harry?"

"Sometimes."

"Were you scared when your sisters got hurt?"

There was a pause. "A little," Harry finally said.

"I know you were." Julian hadn't looked at the boy for a while. The smooth sound of his pen strokes across the paper was almost loud in the small room. "And I bet you still are."

Harry had stopped teetering on his chair. Curious to see what Julian was drawing, he had inched closer to him. "Are they going to be okay?" he asked.

Julian turned his notepad upside down and started to use the top half of the paper. "Why do you want to know?"

"Because."

"You're afraid they're going to stop loving you."

Harry didn't reply. His eyes followed every line Julian drew.

"Why are you afraid they're going to stop loving you?" he continued.

"Because I did something bad."

"Why do you care, Harry?"

"It was an accident," he said, cautiously touching the corner of the notepad.

"You did something you didn't mean to do and your sisters ended up getting hurt because of it." By now Harry was sitting so close to Julian that both of their heads, bent over the sheet of paper, were almost touching. "Why didn't you mean to hurt them?"

"Because I love them."

"Sometimes we do things that hurt the people we love. Your mom, your dad, have done things that hurt you. I'm sure you got angry but did you ever stop loving them?" Julian asked, moving the pen faster across the page.

"No."

"I know you're scared but your sisters are scared too. Do you want them to be scared?"

"No."

"So, what are you going to do?"

"I don't know," Harry said shyly.

"C'mon, yes you do."

"Tell them I'm sorry?"

"That's a good start."

"I won't play with matches anymore?"

"That's good too. What else?"

The boy was quiet.

"Listen, Harry," Julian said, after a while, "I'll teach you a little trick. When you do something that hurts someone, apologizing is important, but is not enough."

"So what do you do?"

"You do something just for them. Something that doesn't benefit you. You let them choose what cartoons to watch, even if you'd rather watch different ones; you let them eat the last mouthful of chips in the bag, even if you're so hungry your stomach hurts; they call you a fool but you don't call them a fool back because you know they're just having a bad day, like you do sometimes." Julian turned the notepad again, finding a blank spot to draw on. "And you do it again, and again, and again. You never stop. It's like playing ball. Talent alone is not enough. You train hard until you're good at it."

"I can try, I guess."

"I'll be here to help you." Julian looked up and smiled at him. "I got your back, Harry."

The boy nodded. "Why are you drawing?" he asked, when Julian turned his attention back to the notepad.

"It's something I do when I'm sad and scared. I draw characters from the stupid stories my mom used to tell me."

"Why are you sad and scared?" Harry asked.

"Because, sometimes, I remember that I have also hurt people. But, unlike you, I can no longer do anything for them."

. . .

After leaving the hospital, Julian was on his way to visit Hazel but Peter convinced him to meet for a quick dinner at Top Notch Beefburgers on Beverly. While growing up, Julian had promised to himself that if he ever had more than twenty dollars to his name, he would eat there once a week. So during his first year of undergrad, Julian had introduced Peter to Top Notch. It became one of Peter and Julian's hangouts where they would gorge on burgers and fries that had been fried in beef tallow.

"You look like shit, man."

"Piss off, Pete," Julian said, taking a long sip of black coffee. "You always say that."

"That should tell you something." Pete bit into his burger. "Why aren't you eating?" he asked as he chewed. "All you do is chug down coffee."

Julian didn't respond. His mind was on the woman he had seen at the club. He wondered if he would see her again and that only made him think about her more. The night before he had sat in front of his bedroom window and, while staring at the city below, gone over all the details of her he had been able the absorb during their brief encounter. She looked young, maybe the same age as Meredith. He wanted to know more about her. Meredith had said the woman had known who he really was. That's exactly how Julian felt. She knew the man who hid the scars under a tattoo sleeve; the one who kept returning to the heart of The Raven Room because it was the only way he knew how to control the need that threatened to consume him. Whoever she was, she had seen that man. She had recognized him. To Julian, that meant she was just like him.

Julian brought the mug to his lips and enjoyed the burning

sensation of the bitter hot coffee on his tongue. "How are Grace and the boys?"

"Good," Peter started to say but then paused, "you know what?" He dipped a french-fry in a mountain of ketchup. "Kids are a lot of work, really."

Julian chuckled, shaking his head. "You've always wanted kids."

"I know, I know," Peter replied, mildly exasperated.

"The boys are not the problem," Julian continued. "What's really going on, Pete?"

"What're you talking about?"

"When I was over for Seth and Eli's birthday, you were acting cagey. I can see there's something eating at you."

"What?" Peter frowned. "I say you're looking like road kill and you turn the conversation around and make it about my behavior?"

"Don't fuck with me. What the hell is going on?"

Peter didn't answer but he didn't try to avoid Julian's unfaltering gaze.

The restaurant was almost empty. Besides the low humming of the music filling the place and the occasional laughter from two men sitting closer to the door, there was a poignant stillness in the air.

Peter finally spoke and when he did his voice barely carried across the table. "That day I was chatting with someone online."

"Who?" Julian asked, his attention on Peter. "A woman?"

"Yeah."

Julian waited for him to continue.

"I have tried. God have I tried." Peter ran his hand through his hair, something he did when he was feeling frustrated. "But I need more."

"Any others besides this woman?" he asked, his voice as low as his friend's.

"No."

"What are your expectations? Is it just sex?"

"Yeah, of course."

"I know you've never been able to just fuck one woman for long. You crave diversity, I get it. Most people do. But you also have two young children who depend on you. You have to think how your actions might affect them."

"I'm not happy," Peter revealed, shoulders slouched.

There was fierceness in Julian's eyes. "I don't care. Seth and Eli have to come first."

"Man, who are you?" Peter asked, with a mix of disbelief and anger. "You've avoided the boys since the day they were born. It's like you're afraid of them or something. They're my kids. I know what's best for them."

The bright florescent lighting, mixed with the smell of fried onions and greasy bacon, was making Julian nauseous but he fought the urge to get up and go outside for fresh air. "I just want them to have the father, the family I never had. That's all Pete," he finally said.

"I know. Listen, I'm just having a bit of fun on the side. Nothing to be worried about, okay? My family is completely separated from it."

"Are you planning to leave them?"

"Grace and the boys? Don't be fucking crazy, of course not."

"If Grace finds out you're sleeping with another woman she'll leave you. She was devastated the first time around. Don't make her go through that again."

"She won't find out. I'm being very careful."

"Everyone says that."

Crumpling up the napkin he had been holding tightly in his hand, Peter threw it on top of his leftover fries. "I have to get home. Grace is working and the babysitter can't stay late," he said, buttoning up his jacket. "I'll call you about tennis."

As he got up, Julian saw him reach for his wallet. "Don't worry about it. It's on me. Just get home to the boys."

Peter left angry and Julian remained seated, staring into the blank wall. Eventually the waitress came over with the bill and told him they were closing for the day. Julian glanced at his watch and realized he had been sitting there, by himself, for almost an hour.

Chapter 6

"What do we have here?" Pam asked, entering the bedroom. There were no windows in the basement apartment and because none of the light fixtures worked, they had to bring in extra lights to be able to see. Pam didn't need to take off her jacket to know there was no heat either.

"The same fucking thing we always have," said the young detective sipping coffee in the corner. "A dead body." He raised his head to see past Pam. "Can someone tell the landlord to turn on the damn heat? We're fucking freezing down here."

"Forensics won't let us. Something about unwanted fluctuation or some shit," someone shouted back from the other room.

"Assholes."

Pam got closer to the bed, her attention on what was in front of her. "Don't be a pussy, it's not that cold."

"Says you who just waltzed in. I've been in this meat locker for over an hour."

"That's 'cause I have more to do than just stand around holding a spiked cup of joe."

"Hey—"

"I don't give a shit, Colton," Pam said, interrupting him. "Just stop whining."

She looked down at the naked woman on the bed. She was pretty but there was nothing memorable about her. The harsh glare from the lights made the floral sheets look faded, like they had been left in the sun for too long, and if she were to touch them, she knew how they would feel—threadbare and delicate.

"Who found her?" Pam asked.

"The landlord. She was late paying rent so he shut off the power and the heat. When that didn't work, he came down to kick her out. The door was unlocked."

"She hasn't been dead long. Less than twenty-four hours."

"Who knows? The cold might have kept her fresh."

Pam glanced at him and the expression on her face made him put his hand up in the air. "Just saying."

She crouched by the bed and brought her face closer to the woman's. She put on a pair of gloves and lifted the woman's hair from her body, revealing her breasts. Pam noticed the series of faint cuts below one of her nipples. The cuts weren't deep and they had already started to scab. Were she still alive, they would have completely healed in a couple of weeks, leaving no scars.

"Why are we wasting our time here?" Colton asked. "This ain't no homicide." Pam continued to ignore him. "Fuck, Sung, I'm telling you, no hand but her own had anything to do with this chick's death."

An officer peeked into the bedroom, carrying a messenger bag. "Is this yours?" he asked Pam.

The ringing sound coming from inside of it made her glance at her watch. It was probably Meredith, wondering where she was. They were supposed to meet thirty-minutes ago. "Colton, can you pass me my bag?" She was removing the woman's hair further away from her neck when the messenger bag landed by her feet and some of the folders inside of it spilled into the floor. "What the hell is your problem?" she asked, angry.

"You asked me to pass it at you."

She reached for the folders and put them back in her bag. If she hadn't been working she would have punched him in the face. He was just the type of detective she despised, incompetent and arrogant. Pam was about to stand up when she stopped herself. "Colton, come here."

"Why?"

"I need you to come here."

He walked around the bed and stood not far from her.

"Closer."

"Are you kidding me?"

"Just do it."

Cursing under his breath, he kneeled on the carpeted floor beside Pam. He still held his coffee cup.

"Get closer to her," Pam said, looking at the woman on the bed.

He opened his mouth, ready to say no, but after some hesitation he did as Pam asked. "What do you smell?"

"A corpse?" he answered, scowling.

"Don't be a smartass. You're no good at it. What do you smell?"

He tilted his head toward the woman. "Fabric softener?" He turned to Pam. "I don't know, she smells nice. It's her hair so maybe it's her shampoo."

Pam got up and, removing her gloves, reached for her bag. "I'm out of here. I want the preliminary report on my desk by end of day tomorrow. And have the coroner call me with the cause of death."

"Why'd you want me to smell her?" he asked, watching her leave.

"I didn't want you to smell her, Colton. I wanted you on your knees."

Pam called Meredith back. She was upset that Pam was so late, so Pam offered to pick up some food on her way to Meredith's place.

She was certain her stepdaughter wouldn't be happy to hear what she had to say about Julian Reeve. For weeks now Pam had been trying to tell her to distance herself from Reeve, but headstrong and rebellious, Meredith was ignoring her.

"You look distracted," Meredith said, watching Pam across the small kitchen table. They were done eating and now all that was left from their meal were the bottles of cold beer in their hands.

"Just work. I wish I could take a break from it all."

"You love your job way too much to do that."

"Only crazy people love their jobs." Pam drank her beer. "Your job will never love you back."

"I'm so glad that I'm past the age of having to bring you to school on Career Day."

"Me too."

Pam's phone was on the table and started to ring. Both she and Meredith looked at it. "Who do you have saved on your phone as a Christmas tree?" Meredith asked. "You hate Christmas."

Reaching for her phone, Pam stood up. "Work. I'll be right back."

Meredith watched her make her way into her bedroom and shut the door behind her. Pam had always made her career a priority and that's why Meredith had shared with Pam her reason for wanting information on Julian. Her investigative piece on The Raven Room was the type of journalism that would open doors for her. She wanted to succeed on her own merit, not because her father had made a call to his powerful friends. She figured Pam would respect that. But Pam had been leaving her voicemails and sending her texts, telling her to distance herself from Julian. She didn't know why, but wasn't naïve—something that Pam had uncovered must have concerned her; that was the reason Pam had asked to come over.

Her apartment had finally reached a painful level of cold. Meredith went to turn up the thermostat, and as she stood outside her bedroom door, she leaned in to listen to Pam.

"It's him. He killed her."

There was a pause and Meredith moved closer.

"I'm sure. I just came from there. She matches the profile," Pam said to the person she was on the phone with. "No, not yet, but I bet any money the coroner's report will come back confirming what everyone, besides you and I, thinks is the cause of death."

Meredith couldn't hear what she said next.

"Listen," Pam added, speaking louder, "I got to go. We can talk tomorrow."

As soon as Meredith heard her say that, she tiptoed back into the kitchen. When she was younger, Pam would often catch her eavesdropping and she would become furious.

"You look pissed," Meredith said from her chair, glad Pam hadn't caught her.

"It has been a long day. Before I got here I was at a crime scene with my new partner, Colton. I hate that I need to deal with idiots like him. He just wants to live long enough to get to enjoy his pension. He said the smell on the woman's hair was shampoo, for Christ's sake," Pam continued, lost in thought.

Meredith decided it was better to remain silent.

"He acts like an asshole because I'm a woman. A non-white woman with more seniority than him, nonetheless."

Colton might not like having a woman telling him what to do but Meredith could only imagine how hard it must be for anyone to work with Pam.

"Speaking about men…you know why I'm here, don't you?" Pam asked.

"If it's about me and Julian, you're wasting your time."

"You asked me to dig into his past. He's not the type of man you want to be with."

"Why? You haven't given me any good reason. What did you dig up on him?"

"You're using him to benefit your career but it's not worth it, Meredith, believe me. Sleeping with a rich, older man is not the way to go."

"You'd know."

As soon as she spoke she saw she had hit a nerve. Meredith knew Pam and her father cared for each other, but if to shut her up she had to say what others thought, she would do so without remorse.

Pam fumbled with the contents of her messenger bag. "Fucking Colton! Because of him all of my things ended up all over the crime scene." Eventually she passed Meredith a manila folder. "Here's what I found on Julian Reeve. I hope that once you read it, you'll understand why I want you to stay far away from him."

Pam left and Meredith remained seated, holding the folder in her hands. She opened it, flipping through the stack of documents. They didn't include any information on his life prior to being adopted and all they revealed was that at sixteen years of age, Julian had been a juvenile offender and a drug addict.

She closed the folder and rested her chin on her hand. That's when she noticed it. It wasn't her imagination; the scent was on her hands. Reaching for the folder she brought it close to her face. Meredith took a deep breath and images of blood red walls, amber lighting and naked bodies flooded her mind.

CHAPTER 7

Julian was the only one clothed. The walls, the ceiling, the floor—all were black. The scarce, tear-shaped light fixtures bathed the darkness with the hue of rubies and made the bodies around him glow, like they were burning from the inside out. It was warm and sweat pooled on his lower back.

The ice cubes inside his whiskey glass were long gone, making the drink taste less than perfect, but he didn't care. He was happy to be drinking something. From the corner of his eye Julian saw a man approach and sit beside him. The man was clad in a three-piece suit and like Julian, the man must have felt as if he were on fire. But as he had just lit a Gurkha Black Dragon cigar, Julian wasn't surprised that the man's poise wasn't giving anything away. Julian reasoned that people who casually sat back while burning over a thousand dollars in tobacco were unlikely to give others a glimpse of their discomfort.

"Was not expecting to see you up here," the man said.

"Needed a change of scenery."

"Don't we all?"

Julian remained silent. He had seen the man before but he didn't know his name. Various desires motivated people to frequent The Raven Room but once there, sexual gratification was the only reason to stay. That made all of them unenthusiastic to discuss their lives outside of the club. Even when they shared their names, it was usually an alias.

"The first time I came to the club was with my wife," the man continued, holding his cigar between his fingers. "We were regulars and there isn't much we didn't do." His gaze was lost in the smoke dancing in front of him. "When she passed away I was here every week. It made me feel closer to her."

"Is that why you came upstairs? To be closer to her?"

"Yes. Only after she died did I make my way down. I changed. You?"

"I'm looking for someone but it doesn't look like tonight is my night." The cloud of smoke reached Julian's face and he breathed it in. The rich tobacco notes, mixed with a hint of coffee, relaxed him.

The only reason Julian was sitting up there was because he had been looking for the woman. He couldn't stop thinking about her and he wanted to see her again. If he did, Julian wasn't sure he would speak to her or, if he went as far as approaching her, what he would say.

"Is she one of your girls?" the man asked with a knowing smile.

"She's not."

"Not yet," the man added.

His words made Julian gulp almost all of his whiskey.

"It's okay, you don't have to look so uncomfortable," the man said, amused. "Down there people talk. There's no way we can keep our predilections a secret."

Julian didn't reply and the man turned his attention to what was happening around them.

"I always get a kick when I sit here and I watch." The man said with a chuckle. "They call themselves hedonistic; they believe they're so debauched merely because they come to a sex club. If they knew people like you and I were right here, among them, they would be appalled, wouldn't they?"

"We are no different from them," Julian replied, watching two women who were kissing.

"How can you say that when you're sitting here, surrounded by people fucking, bored out of your mind?"

Julian saw the man summon a woman who had been lying on the floor, between two men who were more interested in each other than her. She crawled across the black hardwood floor and came to rest her hands on the man's knees with a large smile on her face.

Julian glanced at her and he noticed her dilated pupils.

"Isn't she beautiful?" the man asked, caressing the woman's long hair. "Imagine what we could do with her, you and I, together."

"She's high."

"So?"

Julian reached toward the woman and touched a lock of her dark hair. He stared at the thick strands, rubbing them between his fingers. Not long after, he shook his head as he let go of her hair.

"Because she's high?" the man asked.

Julian didn't reply and he took Julian's silence as a yes. The man burst out in a howl of laughter that made his whole frame shake. His eyes became moist with tears from laughing so hard. "But that's half of the fun."

The two men faced each other. He was older than Julian by more than a decade and, for a brief instant, Julian believed he was staring at his future self.

Julian stood up and walked out of the room. As he made his way down the hall, the vivid color of the flower arrangements made him want to stop and touch them. They stood, fragile and doomed, amongst people intoxicated with lust. Julian passed a small group who was drinking champagne and singing happy birthday to a woman who was surrounded by men only wearing large bows over their crotches. Had Julian been in a good mood he would have laughed. He entered one of the bathrooms, turned on the tap and splashed cold water on his face. He was drenched in sweat. The thought of using the large communal showers on the other end of the club crossed his mind but he needed to leave. He had been coming to the club every week since seeing the woman and even though it was still early, he couldn't spend the next four hours wandering its rooms and halls. He would be tormenting himself.

Reaching for a clean towel, Julian dried his face and stared at his reflection in the mirror. He looked old and tired. It was his belief that he only had three things going for him: his build, a head full of hair, and a large cock. At the rate he was aging, though, he wouldn't be surprised if soon his body started to let him down and, with that, came the inability to be a good fuck. Then, his large cock would be of no use to him and he would have even less to offer.

Julian exited the bathroom and walked down the stairs. The club was filling up, cheerful voices and laughter could be heard above the full notes of the background music. Some nights the whole place would turn into one large orgy. Sighs, screams, the sharp sound of flesh meeting flesh—combined with copious amounts of alcohol, tobacco, and drugs—would incite a prolonged state of widespread euphoria. He looked around at the growing crowd and, to Julian, they were like a bunch of eager children waiting for the gates of an amusement park to open for the day. The restlessness in the air told him tonight would be one of those nights.

Among the crowd, Julian spotted the man with whom the mysterious woman had been. They locked eyes. Maybe they had passed each other before but until seeing him with the woman, Julian had never noticed him. At The Raven Room, a person's body was more important than his face. After a moment, the man returned his attention to the people he was with. Julian stood, searching for her one last time. She wasn't there.

CHAPTER 8

The next day, when Julian finally managed to leave his home, he was late for his first patient consultation. It was snowing and the drive to the hospital was slow and hazardous, the roads full of frustrated drivers who were constantly honking and glancing furtively at the screens of their phones.

"Good morning Dr. Reeve."

Julian turned and managed to smile at Clementine, the department secretary. People loved her because she looked like the quintessential grandmother—a plump, sixty-year-old woman who always wore her hair in a Heidi braid. Julian was convinced Clementine knew that everyone saw her as the department matriarch and that she used that knowledge to her advantage. She was more disorganized than all the doctors she was meant to support and her computer skills were limited to sending emails. Clementine didn't know how to book a flight or a hotel. Many times he had been close to demanding she be replaced but every time he stopped himself. He had a soft spot for Clementine. She always made sure there was a fresh cup of coffee in his office waiting for him.

"Should I send Lily in?" she added.

"Please." He couldn't be happier that today Lily's mother wasn't attending their session. His dislike for the woman was too strong and he didn't know if this morning he would be able to hide it.

Two minutes later, he was sitting across from a thirteen-year-old girl who was wasting away. Her anorexia was winning and after several months of therapy, Julian didn't know if Lily was going to make it. Losing a patient to their illness was never easy but he suspected losing Lily would haunt him. He needed her to live.

"Can I have some coffee?"

Julian saw the way she was staring at the mug he held in his hand. "I think that's a bad idea, Lily."

"It helps with the hunger."

"I know."

She didn't try to argue with him. She turned her face to the window. He watched her. She had been released from the hospital a week ago and being back at home wasn't helping. Lily was even more withdrawn than the last time she had been in his office.

"I'm glad your mom is not here today."

"Me too."

"She's hard on you, isn't she?"

"I hate her."

Julian wished he could tell her he shared her feelings. "Could you go live with your dad for a while? I was told he's doing better."

When Lily spoke her voice showed no emotion. "He's still a drunk."

Julian stared at his coffee mug. He needed to tell her the truth. "Lily?" he said, his tone gentle. He now had his eyes on her and he waited for her to face him. She took her time but when she did, Julian held her gaze. "While you're sitting here with me your friends are out there hanging out with each other, chatting about who they have a crush on, shopping, listening to the music they love, making plans for the summer. Not only are you missing out on all of that, you're going to die. Not several years down the road. I'm talking in a couple of months. Before all that snow outside even melts. I'm not trying to scare you, Lily. I'm being honest with you. Your body is shutting down."

"I'm not scared."

"Think about all the things you could do but you won't have a chance to because you'll be dead."

She left her chair and went to stand by the window, her back to him. Julian didn't know how she was managing to hold herself up. He joined her.

"I don't want to talk...not right now," she said.

He put his hands in his pockets, watching the traffic on the street below. "Is it okay if I just stand here with you?" He saw her nod. "Seeing the cars…the people…it always brings me peace," Julian continued. "The noise in my head goes away and I feel better."

"It makes me forget everything that hurts," Lily added.

"And I feel less alone."

"And I feel less alone," she repeated.

Neither of them spoke for the rest of Lily's appointment. They stood, side by side, watching life unfold through the dirty window.

By the time Julian left the hospital it was dark outside. It hadn't been a good day. After making a few phone calls and strategically avoiding his colleagues, he had left feeling powerless.

Julian decided to walk to his usual coffee shop, enjoying the harshness of the cold wind on his face. Caffeine had always helped him and he knew as soon as he was able to smell the robust and intense notes of an espresso, he would start to feel like the man he needed to be.

He wished he wore weather appropriate clothes rather than tailored slacks, a merino wool jacket and dress shoes. His clothes made him look like he should be strolling the streets of a European capital, not sinking his legs into large piles of grimy snow and sliding on patches of ice. By the time he entered the coffee shop, half of his body had gone numb, and he spent some time wiping his feet on the large rug by the entrance. He needed to warm up.

The place was rugged, faintly smelling of decay—the usual character of a rundown building—something he tended to secretly enjoy. As he ordered his much needed espresso and prepared to leave, Julian suddenly came face-to-face with the person who, for the last several weeks, hadn't left his thoughts.

"Hi," said the young woman standing in front of him.

Julian blinked several times, forgetting the espresso in his hand. Timidly smiling at him, she was waiting for him to reply, but all he could do was look at her with a combination of awe, relief, and surprise.

"Hi," he finally said.

Neither of them spoke but they continued to stare at each other. She shifted on her feet. "Hi there," she said again. "Do you remember me? Last time you saw me I had less on."

Julian continued to look at her. Never before had someone he had seen at the club approached him.

"Am I breaking one of the rules by speaking to you?" She started to back away from him, suddenly more interested in Julian's shoes than his face. "Sorry, I didn't know."

As she turned away, Julian reached out to her, stopping her. "Please, don't go. I wasn't expecting to see you here, that's all." He knew he couldn't be handling that moment more ineptly. "I do remember you." He smiled. "And you weren't wearing anything."

She laughed. "I was sitting over there," she paused, pointing at her things on the back corner table, "when I saw you come in. I thought to myself—now he's underdressed."

Julian laughed with her. She had looked shorter at the club. He wished her hair was down and not up in a loose ponytail. He remembered her long, untamed hair and how enticing it had been to him.

"I'm Julian."

"Alana."

She had approached him but she was shy. He could see it in the way she stood by him and by the light blushing on her cheeks as she said her name. Before glancing away, her eyes lingered on his. Julian didn't feel the same visceral emotion he had experienced at the club, maybe it was because she wasn't showing the same self-possession. But, in that moment, he recognized in himself a sentiment he believed he was no longer capable of feeling—affection. It made his hesitation vanish.

"Do you want to sit and chat for a bit?" Julian asked as he moved away from the small group of people waiting for their coffees.

"Would love to." She took a step back as he got closer. "Want to sit at my table?"

He took note of her reaction to him. "Sounds perfect."

They made their way to her table and he sat across from her. He noticed the pile of books. "What are you reading?"

"I'm a drop-in youth worker volunteer at the Howard Brown Health Center," she picked up a tea mug that looked huge between her small hands. "Have you heard of it?"

"The organization that supports the LGBTQ community? I have. They're very large."

"So, I met this fifteen-year-old kid and I promised him I would help him improve his reading and math skills," she continued. "I'm trying to find some good books for people with low literacy and I need to refresh my memory of eighth grade math."

As Julian removed his jacket, he placed his gloves and scarf on the table.

"I guess I should mention I failed eighth grade math," she added.

He grinned, appreciating how her face lit up when she smiled. "I'm sure you'll do well. Both of you can commiserate over your math woes."

They casually chatted for a while. Julian became aware that, beyond the piece of information about her volunteer work, she was hesitant to share details about herself. After some gentle and strategic probing, all he was able to find out was that she worked at a bookstore in the Logan Square area, Bucket O' Blood. On the other hand, she was visibly curious about him and enthusiastically asked as many questions as he thought possible. She had a youthful, easygoing quality to her and he felt relaxed in her presence.

She was wearing a thick sweater that hid all of the subtle, feminine curves he had seen at the club. The memory of her small, well-shaped breasts was now all too vivid. His eyes lingered on her neck, the only area of her body besides her face that wasn't engulfed in oversized clothing, and he felt himself react to it. She had an erotic neck.

"Well, we've established you're a geek," Julian said in a friendly tone, after listening to her explain why Dune was her favorite book series.

Alana chuckled, sipping her tea. She looked at him over the brim of her mug. "I have been told that before, Julian."

There was something in the way she pronounced his name that made all the hairs on his body stand up. It felt like she had opened up the door to a place deep within him. It simultaneously frightened and calmed him. In that moment Julian knew he wanted her.

The coffee shop had emptied out considerably. There were only two other people sitting by the window, busy working on their laptops, and the woman behind the counter, entertained by her phone.

Alana looked at his hands and when she lifted her eyes to him, he saw she desired him as well.

"You're blushing."

She licked her lower lip. "I guess I have been caught."

He heard the subtle hint of mischief in her voice and that encouraged him. "What shall we do about it?" he added, not hiding his intent.

She gave him an elusive smile. Julian noticed the small speckles of yellow in her brown eyes and he was amazed at how she was gradually transforming right in front of him. At first she came across as a pretty young woman, not much different from the average female one would see walk down the street. But then there were those slight details about her that, once noticed, made her enthralling—her eyes, the elegant curve of her neck, how her smile enhanced her high cheekbones.

Getting up, Alana excused herself and walked toward the stairs that would take her to the bathrooms below. Before she made her way down, she stopped and locked eyes with him. Julian took that as an invitation.

He waited a few minutes and then followed her down the stairs. He found Alana standing in the small hallway. Without hesitation he closed the space between them and, as he backed her into the bathroom furthest away from the stairs, slammed the door shut behind them. His hungry lips found hers and he pushed his tongue into her mouth. Tasting the peppermint tea on her tongue, Julian couldn't stop himself from moaning. As he pressed Alana's back against the door he felt her holding onto the front of his dress shirt, her lips just as demanding as his. They were kissing each other savagely. Breathing hard, making blatant sounds of carnal desire, they were fueling each other's lust with abandon. The refreshing taste of her mouth together with the feeling of her slight body pressed tightly against his, led Julian to think she was almost unearthly, about to vanish from his grasp. That only deepened his desire for her.

He pulled her heavy winter sweater over her head and the warm feeling of Alana's soft skin against his palms made him kiss her with renewed urgency. As he undid her bra and his hands found her breasts, her sounds of pleasure intensified. Her hair had come loose, falling over her shoulders, down her back. Julian wildly ran his hands through it, getting a small whimper out of her. He couldn't resist the urge to close his fingers on the long strands.

"I want your mouth on my cock," he said, breaking the kiss.

Alana nodded in response and in one fluid movement she sunk to her knees. Unzipping his slacks, he released his erection. When he felt her soft lips, her wet tongue moving in circles, his legs bent slightly with the wave of sexual hunger that overcame him. For several long minutes he didn't move, allowing it to build.

"Look at me."

Alana's eyes shot up and he saw in them the need to please.

"Deeper, take me deeper." He slid further into her mouth. "Relax your throat."

She did what he said and the tension slowly left her body.

"That's it," he whispered. "That's it."

Holding her head, Julian forcefully pushed forward. Then he felt it, the rush of lodging himself deep within Alana's throat. He groaned, aware he had to pull back so she could breathe. Lost in the power play taking place between them, Julian tried to hold on to that unique sensation for as long as he could.

As he moved, Julian felt Alana take a series of frantic, deep breaths. Not wasting time, she took him back inside her very wet mouth.

"Oh fuck." He closed his eyes, his whole body shaking. "I need to come."

Julian closed his fingers on her nape, and as he thrust he felt the back of her throat open up again. Her hands reached for him, closing on his straining thighs.

"I got you, Alana. I got you," Julian said, glancing down at her. Their eyes met briefly.

Her body surrendered to him and he was now almost squatting over her. With his mouth open in a silent cry, her face now flush with his body, he was able to slide in deeper. Soon his release was overtaking him and Julian held on to the back of her head as his body convulsed. He was coming straight down her throat. The feeling was overwhelming. For a few seconds, everything outside of him faded into emptiness.

With his orgasm still washing over him, Julian took a step back. Sliding down the door, he met Alana on the floor. With red, bruised lips, mascara smudged around her eyes, and matted hair, she watched him as he tried to steady himself. He could swear his heart was trying to rip through his chest. Julian caressed her hair and as he brought her face close to his, he noticed the scar on her shoulder.

Forgetting they were on the dirty, cold bathroom floor of a small coffee shop on North Wells Street, Julian kissed Alana's scar.

CHAPTER 9

"I'm trying to remember here, but I think, you know, innocent-looking."

"Wait," Meredith said, scrunching up her nose. "Was she underage?"

She was at Carol's Pub, a dive bar in Wrigleyville, pounding back beers with homicide detective Luke Colton. She could handle her alcohol but, if she wasn't careful, she would pass out before getting what she came for.

"Not underage, dummy." He laughed, finishing his beer. "But like a schoolgirl, you know what I mean? It was hard to tell 'cause she was naked on the bed but that's what I thought when I first saw her. It was a fucking waste of our time, though. Even before we heard back from the coroner I knew she had just OD'ed. Don't get why your stepmom was so obsessed."

Meredith was laughing too but in her head she was thinking that Pam had been right. Colton was an idiot.

"Was the girl beautiful?" She leaned toward the table. Her low-cut top barely covered her breasts.

"I don't like blondes. I prefer brunettes, just like you," Colton openly stared at her cleavage. "And your curves."

His eyes were glossy, a sign that he was tipsy and, holding the back of her neck, he pulled her to him. Meredith didn't stop him. Colton was a good kisser and they kissed until her jaw started to hurt. She was ready to call it a night; she had learned everything she wanted to know about the dead woman. There wasn't much more she needed to get out of that man's brain.

"You smell nice," she said, licking the side of his neck. "Do you think I smell nice?"

"You smell fucking amazing."

He was looking at her like he wanted to devour her and that made Meredith chuckle. A part of her felt superior to him. Another part of her felt filthy just by being there with him. That aroused her.

"My stepmom kept going on and on about how good that girl's hair smelled. I know she's dead but the thought of her smelling that fucking good and you were there is making me jealous." The words coming out of her mouth were so ridiculous she wanted to bang her head on the bar countertop.

"Babe, you're unbelievably hot. That dead skinny bitch has nothing on you. I still can't believe I'm here making out with you."

"Neither can I," she said, burying her face in his chest.

"When I think about it she just smelled like she had been fucked, you know? It was a man smell. You, on the other hand, smell like a woman begging to be fucked."

"Do you want to fuck me?"

"Do you even need to ask? When you agreed to meet for drinks I almost came in my pants."

Meredith wrapped her arms around his waist. When she had stopped at the station it had been easy to find out what detective Colton looked like. While being careful not to run into Pam, all Meredith had to do was say she was detective Pam Sung's stepdaughter and that she was looking for Colton. The officer had pointed to a young man who, in that moment, was walking out of the station. Meredith had followed him to the coffee shop across the street and waited for a good moment to approach him.

"Do you want to get out of here?" she whispered by his ear.

Soon they were inside of his dark car, which was parked on a side street by Carol's Pub.

"My place?" Colton asked, sitting behind the wheel.

She had to decide. By the time they would get to wherever it was he lived, she would have long stopped wanting to be touched by him. "No. Fuck me in the back."

"Babe, it's like the North Pole in here. Wouldn't you rather a warm bed?"

"You'll keep me warm." She fondled him. "C'mon, your cock is rock hard. You're so ready. And so am I."

"Let me get my wallet. The condom is in there."

They fumbled toward the back of the car and Meredith straddled his legs.

"Fuck," she cried out when he entered her. What he lacked between his ears, Colton made up for with what he had between his legs.

Meredith still wore her top but when he managed to free her breasts and circle her hard nipples with his tongue, she closed her eyes. It was good but not enough to push her over the edge. She needed to concentrate on having Colton inside of her; on being fucked in the back seat of a car by a man she couldn't stand.

"Damn, babe, your pussy is clenching my cock like crazy. I'm going to come soon."

She moved up and down on him. "I want you to come on my face."

"Are you sure? I don't—"

She clamped her hand over his mouth. "That's what I want."

Shortly thereafter she was belly up on the fabric seat and Colton was trying to balance himself over her. His car was small and there wasn't enough room for both of them. Her bent knees were pressed against one of the windows and she was gasping for air, his body too close to hers.

Meredith spread her legs and touched herself. Her fingers knew exactly how much pressure, how fast to move and in no time she was close to experiencing the pleasure she sought. Eager to get him there as well, she lifted her head and brought him into her mouth. The taste left behind by the condom wasn't pleasant but she didn't care.

"I'm coming babe."

As soon as he spoke, Meredith moved her face away from him. Her body tensed up and release started in her core and expanded through her limbs. Warmth showered her face.

She didn't let Colton drive her home. She took a cab straight to

Near North Side, Julian's condo. They were supposed to go to The Raven Room that night.

"Wasn't expecting you so early," Julian said, closing the door behind her. It was only ten o'clock and she had told him she would come over around midnight.

"Just felt like it."

The living room fireplace was lit and the curtains were drawn back. Chicago stood, beautiful and resolute, as far as she could see. Sitting on the couch she picked up the open book and smiled. "*Straw Dogs: Thoughts on Humans and Other Animals*," she read out loud. "How boring."

"C'mon, I can't always be exciting."

Feeling his stare on her, she looked up. "What?"

"You have dried come on your hair and your mascara is half down your face." He didn't move away from her. "Was it good?"

"Was okay. My eye hurts." She made a face and they both laughed. "I need a shower."

In Julian's en suite bathroom Meredith undressed and stepped under the stream of hot water. She sighed, the heat on her skin allowing her to take a moment to reflect on all the things that had been going through her mind for the last week. Meredith decided she wasn't going to tell Julian about Colton. She also couldn't discuss with him the information she had learned through Pam. It was difficult for her to reconcile the Julian she knew with the teenager the files portrayed him to be. One thing she was certain of—it didn't dissuade her from spending time with Julian and writing her piece on The Raven Room. On the contrary, now she had more interesting material for her article. More than she had ever dreamed of.

She returned to the living room wrapped in a thick bath towel. Julian was on the couch with his feet up on the coffee table and when he saw her he passed her a large mug.

"You've had enough alcohol."

"Hot chocolate?" she asked "Do you think I'm five?"

"Just try it."

She sat beside Julian, giving him a suspicious look. As she

brought the mug to her lips and sipped it slowly, they kept their eyes on each other.

"So? What's the verdict?" He was grinning.

"Fuck, this is good."

"I made it myself. From scratch."

Meredith didn't believe him.

"I swear," Julian said, proud of himself. "If you go into the kitchen you'll see the ingredients on the counter and the dirty pot on the stove. I make a killer hot chocolate."

"We've known each other for over a year and only now you pull this out of your bag of tricks?"

"I save it for special occasions."

"What's the special occasion?"

"You showing up at my place covered in come."

Meredith laughed, drinking more of her hot chocolate. It was rich, hot, and not overly sweet. It couldn't have been more perfect. "Before you run to get yourself checked out I want you to know I used protection."

"I'm not worried, Meredith. We've talked about this before. If you have unprotected sex with someone you tell me. And if I do I'll tell you. It's very straightforward."

"Do you think I'm dirty?"

He ran his eyes over her wet hair and leaning closer, sniffed her. "You smell pretty clean to me."

"On the inside."

"Do you feel dirty on the inside?"

"Don't talk to me like a shrink."

He was quiet for a while and Meredith sipped her drink. She didn't want to gulp it down. She wanted to savor it.

"No, I don't," he finally said. "Is this about what happened tonight, before you got here?"

"Why did you make me hot chocolate?"

"Because you looked stressed out and were acting restless. Wasn't thinking you felt guilty for having a man come on your face. I didn't make you hot chocolate to lessen your self-disgust."

"Sometimes I fuck guys I can't stand. I do it so I can get off on the disgust I feel toward myself for being with them." Her wet hair was dripping down her arms and she shivered. "I don't feel ashamed. I feel ashamed for not feeling ashamed about it."

Julian took her feet and placed them on his lap. He cradled them between his warm hands.

"Well, you asked me not to talk to you as a shrink and I won't." When he massaged the sole of her foot, Meredith sunk further into the pillows around her. "I'm going to talk to you like a man who respects you—don't feel ashamed. We all fuck people for the strangest reasons. At least you're aware of yours."

It was a Saturday night and by the time they arrived, The Raven Room was full to the point that it was hard to move around. The music was loud and people were talking even louder so they could be heard. When Julian went up to the bar to order them some drinks, Meredith made her way upstairs. Before she stepped away, she had noticed that Julian had showed the card, which he had called his key, to Ben. She would have to remind him to share with her the card's special touch, like he had promised he would.

When she walked past a large mirror Meredith stopped and adjusted her hair. After showering at Julian's she had tried to style her hair but without her curling iron her hair hung flat around her face. She looked far from her best.

"Don't worry, you look just fine."

Meredith turned around and standing there, before her, was a woman in a black silk robe.

"Thanks," Meredith replied, tucking a piece of her hair behind her ear.

"One of the great things about the red lighting in here is that it covers all of those pesky flaws we agonize over."

The woman appeared to be in her mid-thirties. She was holding a cocktail glass in one hand and a cigarette in the other.

"How many times have you come here?" she continued, smiling.

"This is my second time. I'm still trying to find my away around."

She put her glass down. "Can I borrow your lipstick?"

Meredith had been about to touch up her makeup when the woman had spoken to her and had forgotten she was still holding her go-to lipstick, Passion by Chanel.

She passed it to the woman and watched her draw on the mirror with it.

"Just imagine the club as being a large mansion with three floors," she said, adding a third line to the square. "The staircase is in the middle of every floor. The rest is just halls that lead to different rooms."

"What's on the third floor?"

"More of what you see around you. None of the rooms at the club have doors but there's one, right here," she tapped the mirror with the lipstick, "on the third floor, which has a door. It's all black inside. We call it the Black Dragon."

"Because it's all black?"

"Because there's an old guy who sometimes shows up there but never fucks. He just sits and watches as he smokes Black Dragon cigars. Every room has a name. All animals."

"Why is the club called The Raven Room? Which one is the raven?"

The woman giggled. "Damned if I know. There isn't a raven room at the club."

Meredith didn't miss a beat. "I saw a door downstairs, on the main floor, behind the red curtains. Is that another entrance?"

The woman stopped drawing and shrugged. "I think so."

As she returned the lipstick, Meredith felt the woman's stare on her. Meredith didn't know why she was bothering to put it back in her purse. The lipstick was ruined.

"I'm Meredith," she said, pleased to be meeting another person at the club.

The woman took the cigarette from her lips and blew the smoke up in the air. "I'm Nina. You don't remember me, do you?"

Meredith looked at the woman more closely. She had no idea who she was. "Should I?"

"Not really." She laughed, again holding her glass. "You fucked me and my husband. I went down on you."

Letting her head fall forward, Meredith covered her eyes with her hand. "I'm so sorry—"

"No one remembers anyone here," she said, cutting Meredith off. "The only reason we do is because we hadn't fucked a girl like you in a while. We nicknamed you the blue unicorn." She leaned closer to Meredith. "Blue because of your eyes."

Meredith tried to smile.

"And unicorn because every couple dreams of having a girl like you join them in a threesome—hot bisexual babe," Nina added.

Starting to feel like she had fallen through a rabbit hole, Meredith excused herself and went to see where Julian was with their drinks. She needed one.

When she returned to the ground floor she couldn't find him so she took the opportunity to investigate what was behind the door she had asked the woman about. Both Nina and Julian had said it was another entrance to the club but Meredith didn't believe them. She crossed the room and, pulling the heavy curtain aside, pushed the door open. There was a set of stairs leading down. Looking over her shoulder she looked for Julian one more time. She still couldn't see him in the crowd. His absence convinced her to see where the staircase would lead her. After making her way down the stairs, she found another door. As soon as she opened it she found herself face-to-face with a man wearing a black suit.

"Your key?" he said, assessing her with an impassive stare.

He didn't look like any of the nightclub bouncers she was used to seeing when going out with her friends. His demeanor was too subdued, which made him appear menacing. Meredith doubted that man would believe any excuse she might come up with.

"I think I'm lost. I've no idea where I'm going. Can you help me?" She gave him her most innocent smile.

He didn't reply. Instead, he spoke into his earpiece in Mandarin. Without wasting time, he got hold of her arm and dragged her up the stairs.

"Hey, c'mon, no need to fucking touch me." Meredith was no

longer scared. She was outraged.

The man didn't reply. He continued to hold onto her arm.

"'I told you I was lost. Why the fuck are you manhandling me?" Wearing her stilettos, she almost tripped on one of the steps. "Let me go!"

Soon they were back on the main floor and even though the man released her, two others dressed like him joined them.

"What's wrong with you people?" Meredith shouted, rubbing her arm. She would have bruises. "Do you even speak English?" she continued. "I was lost."

She skimmed the room. There were more than fifty people standing around but no one appeared to be paying attention to what was happening. One of the men in the black suits took a step closer and she put her hand up. "Stay the fuck away from—Julian!" she cried out when she saw him walking toward her. Meredith was so relieved she almost ran to him.

"Where were you?" he asked, his voice clipped.

"I got lost and—"

Julian didn't bother to hear what she had to say. He turned to one of the men and, to add to her confusion, started to speak in Mandarin as well. He and Julian were having a heated conversation. She didn't need to understand it in order to know it was about her. They both kept pointing in her direction. She noticed another man, leaning by the bar, who was staring intently at the interaction between Julian and the man in the black suit.

Ten minutes later Julian and Meredith had left The Raven Room and were in the car, driving away.

"Julian, what the hell was that all about?" she asked, rubbing her arm.

"What were you doing? Why did you go down there?"

"I got lost."

Julian glared at her.

"I swear."

"You don't go down there, do you understand me? You don't even look at that fucking door again."

"What's down there?"

"Enough, Meredith!"

Never before she had seen him raise his voice and she was surprised he was speaking to her in such manner.

"Who were those men? Security guards? They fucking look like gangsters." He was angry with her but she wouldn't allow him to intimidate her.

Julian didn't answer her.

"Do you know them?" she continued.

"It doesn't matter. Just stop asking questions."

She had been roughly grabbed by a man she had never met before and now Julian, with his shouting and dismissive tone, was adding to the whole abusive experience. It didn't matter that she was snooping and had lied. They still had no right to treat her like she didn't deserve an explanation or an apology.

"Is this about the woman?" she blurted out.

He turned to look at her. "What woman?"

She hadn't planned to tell Julian but now she couldn't take it back. Maybe it was a good thing. He might know something. "The dead woman," she repeated.

"What are you talking about?"

"The woman who showed up dead a few weeks ago."

"Meredith, I don't know what you're talking about."

"I found out through my stepmom. The woman had the club's smell on her hair. Just like we do after we leave."

"How did she die?"

"Drug overdose."

Colton had told her that the cause of death had been ruled an accidental drug overdose but, by overhearing Pam's phone conversation, Meredith knew that's not what had really happened.

"And her death is connected to The Raven Room because of the way her hair smelled?" He frowned. "That's ridiculous."

"It's not ridiculous. Maybe she was at the club when she was killed. Maybe she had just left the club when she was killed."

"And whoever killed her did so by drug overdose?"

"Probably."

Julian shook his head. "And this is what the police believe?"

Meredith wasn't going to reveal to him she had been the one who came up with some parts of that theory.

"What's down there, Julian?" she asked again.

"I told you before—just another entrance. I need you to stay away from it and forget what happened tonight."

He had his eyes on the road and they were both silent. After a few minutes of sitting beside each other without talking, Meredith realized they had passed his neighborhood. They were also still in the car they had picked up on the way to The Raven Room.

"You don't have to drive me home. I can take a cab," she said, looking through her window.

"It's three in the morning. I'll drive you to your doorstep."

When they arrived at their destination, Meredith couldn't wait to leave the car. As she was about to step out, he grabbed her elbow. "Did you tell your stepmom you've been going to The Raven Room?"

She gave him a sarcastic smile. "Julian, you're not the only one who knows how to keep secrets."

CHAPTER 10

Julian was thinking of Alana when he picked up the day's newspaper from Hazel's porch.

He hadn't seen Alana since the evening at the coffee shop a week ago and the memory of their encounter in the bathroom only intensified his desire to be with her again.

The bold behavior he had seen at the club, together with the shyness she had showed in his presence, gave Alana an insidious magnetism. He had to be careful around her. Most of his lovers were like Meredith, malleable but with firm boundaries they wouldn't allow him to cross. If he pushed too far they would push back. In that resistance he felt safe. Alana wasn't like that. He couldn't remember the last time he had oral sex as punishing as what he had experienced with her. He had bruised her and as it was happening Alana hadn't stopped him. She had enjoyed it.

The interior of the house was dark, only lit by a small lamp next to the stairs, and Julian took the time to remove his shoes before he made his way upstairs. Hazel no longer stood by the kitchen door, arms crossed over her chest, with her eyes on him to make sure he remembered he wasn't allowed in the house with his shoes on. Many times he had cursed at her, turned around and banged the door behind him as hard as he could. Hours later he would return and she would be again waiting for him. He would always end up taking off his shoes.

When he had first met Hazel, she had been a fearless social worker in the most violent part of town, dealing with the children her co-workers avoided. To this day Julian wasn't sure why she had decided to adopt him. He believed she had done it because she knew she was his last chance for survival. In recent years, together with dementia, Alzheimer's disease had robbed her of her independence and replaced it with a crushing vulnerability—it was his turn to do anything he could for her.

As he walked up the stairs, he saw the shape of several picture frames and he didn't need to turn on the light to know of whom they were. Aware that Hazel's family had turned their backs on her when she had refused to return to her abusive husband, at whose hands she had suffered a miscarriage that left her unable to conceive, Julian had always wondered why she kept pictures of them on her wall. If he had been her he would have burned them all.

For the last twenty-three years no piece of furniture, no shade of paint had changed inside of Hazel's home, but one thing was gone—the smell of a warm meal. After he had moved in, Hazel hadn't adjusted her cooking habits to accommodate his obsession with pizza and corn dogs. When she had served him Phoenix claws, Julian had given them one look before gagging all the way back to his room. Now, if Hazel were to walk out of the kitchen, stained apron tied around her waist, and put a plate of steaming Phoenix claws in front of him, he would happily have gnawed them to the bone.

Julian sat by the elderly woman on the bed and reached for her hand. "How are you feeling?" he asked in Mandarin, caressing the top of her hand with his fingers.

She faced him. "I'm waiting for my son."

"I have a message from him." Julian tried to show some semblance of a smile. "He wants you to know he still feels sorry for forgetting to feed your Halfmoon Betta while you went on your trip. He has been looking for one to replace it but he hasn't found the right fish yet. But he will."

"He's looking for one?" Hazel asked delighted. "Mine was a beauty."

"He also wants you to know he misses when the two of you used to watch basketball on TV together on Sunday afternoons. That was always his favorite time."

"He hates watching the game on the black and white TV. Can't buy a better one, we need the money for his school."

"He knows that. And he didn't hate watching the game on that TV as much he pretended to."

"When is he coming to see me?"

Julian looked at her fragile hand on his, how brittle her skin had become. He had been a witness to the slow deterioration of her health for years now but, every time he saw her, he was taken aback by how difficult it was for him to accept it.

"Any day now."

"Who are you?"

He paused. This was always the hardest part. "Your son, Julian."

"You're not my son," she replied, confused. "He's a young boy."

He saw Carla, Hazel's caregiver, walk into the room carrying a dinner tray. He took the distraction as the perfect opportunity to cease further upsetting her.

"I made carrot soup, Miss Cheng, your favorite," Carla passed the tray to him. "Julian will help you. Would you like that, huh?"

As Hazel gave a small nod in agreement, he caught himself exhaling with relief. When antagonized, she would usually lash out in anger and it would take hours for him to be able to calm her down. He moved from the chair to the bed and, sitting beside her, carefully spoon-fed her dinner. She no longer recognized him but she appeared to enjoy his company.

Hazel didn't speak for the rest of the evening and Julian took refuge in the silence that descended upon them. Opening the newspaper he had brought in with him, he flipped through it without reading any of the words printed on the page. He liked holding it in his hands; taking pleasure in the feeling of the paper against his skin. He was about to put it aside when a picture jumped at him. The article was about a recent change in the Tax Increment Financing to assist private redevelopment projects. The picture was of the mayor and some of the Chicago Community Development Commission members. Standing by the mayor there was a man the article identified as Steven Thompson, an entrepreneur. Julian recognized him—Steven Thompson was the man he had seen with

Alana at the club.

It was past six in the evening when Julian left Hazel's. He had received text messages from Peter but he put his phone back in his pocket without reading them. After seeing Hazel he felt tense and he was unwilling to deal with his friend. As he drove through town, he remembered Alana telling him she worked at an independent bookstore on Logan Square. He knew he should stay away from her when he felt the ominous side of himself so close to the surface but she was the only person he wanted to see.

Julian stood by his car, unbothered by the sharp cold, waiting for Alana to leave work. When he saw her walk toward him, wearing a pair of thick black-framed reading glasses and a plaid jacket two sizes too big for her, he smiled. She looked homely.

"What made you come this way?" Alana asked, not hiding her surprise.

"You."

She struggled with the large bag she was carrying and he feared she would drop it at any second.

"Here, let me help." Julian took the bag from her. "This is heavy. What do you have in here?"

"Books."

"Why am I not surprised?" They both laughed as he put the bag on the back seat. It had started to snow and he saw a light dusting of white covering her hair. "Are you hungry?"

She rubbed her arms with her hands as she tried to stay warm. "Starving."

"Get in. It's too cold for you out here." After joining her inside, he started the engine and turned up the heat. "I need to ask," he paused, running his gloved hands over the steering wheel, "how old are you?"

It was dark inside of the car but he could see her silhouette, a small bundle attempting to fight the shivers assaulting her body.

"Do you really need to ask?"

He heard the amusement in her voice. "I do. Every time I see you it appears to me you look younger and younger."

"I'm thirty," she said, removing her reading glasses.

"If you had said you were twenty I would have believed you."

"I know. I'm every pedophile's dream."

She tried, unsuccessfully, to hold back a laugh. Soon Julian was laughing with her.

"I've had a very long day," she finally said, a deep sigh escaping her lips.

"So have I." He rested the back of his head on the car seat. "Why are we laughing?"

"No idea."

"After our encounter at the coffee shop I thought you were shy. Now I'm reconsidering."

Alana looked shocked by his assessment of her. "Did you really think I'm shy?"

He nodded. "Uh-huh."

"The first time you saw me was at a sex club. Then, within two hours of running into each other, I'm sucking your cock in a bathroom. If you think those are the actions of a shy woman, I wonder what kind of company you keep."

"You also have no decorum." Julian added.

"You're the one waiting for me outside my work. I think you like my lack of decorum."

"No, I just like how you give head."

His comment made Alana laugh harder. "You're lucky I'm not uptight."

"Very," he agreed, grinning.

Julian leaned toward her and, as soon as his lips touched hers, all he wanted was to remove the layers of clothing Alana was wearing. He craved the feel of her skin. She ran her hands through his hair and he couldn't get enough of her touch. Julian deepened the kiss and she matched him with as much ardor.

"The things I want to do to you," he whispered, moving his lips from her mouth to the curve of her neck.

"Tell me." Alana tilted her head back. "Tell me what you want to do to me."

He took her earlobe between his teeth. "I want to make you stand in the middle of my bedroom and have you undress for me as I watch," Julian continued, running his mouth along her jawline. "I want you to do it very slowly, keeping your eyes on mine the whole time. You'll sit on my bed, naked, with your legs open, completely bare to me." He felt her close her hand on his nape, gripping his hair. "Will I kneel between your legs and lick you until you're so wet you'll be able to smell yourself all over my face? Will I get on top of you and fuck you slowly, kissing your beautiful neck? With my hands on your hips, on your hair, will I flip you over and enjoy your tight grip on me until I come deep inside of you?"

Alana inhaled sharply and he heard her make a soft sound of satisfaction.

"I want to do all of those things to you," Julian said. "I want to watch you. Hear you. Feel you. I want you to surrender your pleasure to me, Alana."

Holding his face between her hands, she ran the tip of her tongue along his lower lip. "I want something in return."

"What do you want?"

"You."

"I can't do all of those things to you unless you have me too."

She smiled. "I don't want your body. I want you."

"I can't give you something I don't know how to give."

She didn't reply and he felt a creeping sadness weighing on her. "Let's get something to eat." Julian caressed her cheek. "What are you craving?"

With her eyes closed she pressed her cheek into his palm. Seeing Alana seek out even the smallest gestures of tenderness he was willing to show her, brought back the feeling of affection he had experienced when he had seen her at the coffee shop. The knowledge he was, in that moment, helping to keep her warm made him happy.

"Cheese fries and a Nutella milkshake with whipped cream. That's what I'm craving."

"Sugar overload and grease coma it is. Do you know of a place?"

"Pick Me Up Café? It's in Wrigleyville."

"I know where it is."

"Really? You don't look like the type of guy who would go there."

"What does that mean?" he asked, amused.

"You look like you go to Magnificent Mile to get dressed in the morning."

"I do?"

"C'mon, you must know that. Your dress shirt probably cost more than everything I have on me right now and you drive around in this fancy Mercedes."

"I guess I never thought how I would come across to someone like you."

Alana didn't say anything for a while. They sat side by side and Julian continued to watch her, letting the pleasant sensation of her fingers move through his hair in a rhythmic cadence spread through his whole body.

When she spoke her voice was playful. "Someone like me? You mean someone who makes close to minimum wage, shops at Village Discount Outlet, eats at Pick Me Up Café and happens to think you must be an unusually well-paid psychologist and Associate Professor?"

Their faces inches apart, Julian felt her breath on him. In that moment the silence inside of the car was as full of meaning as any words they might say to each other.

"To someone as smart as you, Alana," he finally said.

Julian drove them to Pick Me Up Café and soon they were sitting down with a large plate of cheese fries between them. He wasn't hungry but he was enjoying watching her eat.

"Wondering how I can possibly eat this much?" she asked, laughing.

"Do you even have to ask?"

"I have a high metabolism."

"And the normal aging process the rest of us mortals are subjected to appears to have skipped you," he said, shaking his head.

"Most women I know would hate you."

The café was full of locals, and Julian thought what an odd pair they must look—an overdressed man watching a younger, quirky-looking woman eating ravenously. Julian glanced at the wall covered in customer drawings and pictures and then at the colorful LED outdoor lights on the ceiling.

"What part of town do you live in?" he asked, hoping she would slowly start to share more about herself.

"South side."

"South side?"

"Yeah, south side." She continued to eat, not making eye contact with him.

"Do you mind being more vague?"

Alana finished drinking her milkshake and gave him a slanted look. "There are things in my life I would like to keep private. I'm sure you can understand that."

"The guy I saw you at the club with, the one with the grey hair, how do you know him?" Maybe they were strangers, randomly having sex with each other at the club. It happened all the time. "I know his name is Steven Thompson," he added.

She had stopped eating and was now looking straight at him. Julian had to lean back in his chair, her expression so fearful it felt as if someone had kicked him in the chest.

"Alana, I understand you don't know me. I'm a man you saw at a sex club and to whom afterwards you gave a blowjob in the bathroom of a coffee shop. I get that. Asking you to trust me might be too much right now, but you can talk to me."

Julian watched her demeanor change. From being witty and cheerful, Alana shrouded herself with the remoteness he had only seen in people who had suffered in ways he hoped would never be known to her. Tears started to form in her eyes.

"I need you to promise me something," Alana said, trying to regain her composure. "When you see me at The Raven Room, don't approach me."

"What?" he asked, taken aback by her request. "Why?"

"I can't tell you why. You can watch me, but don't talk to me."

"Because of Thompson?"

"It goes beyond him."

Julian rested his elbows on the table. "When will you be at the club next?"

"I don't know."

He reached for her hand. "Listen, Alana—"

She didn't allow him to continue. "As you said we're strangers. Please don't get close to me at the club. It'll save me a lot of trouble."

Julian remained silent. Alana's hand was still on his and he felt her rapid pulse from her wrist against his fingers. She was afraid. "I'll do as you ask. I won't approach you."

As they got ready to leave, she wouldn't let him pay for the bill. She only agreed to let him pay for half of it when he jokingly threatened to drive away with the bag of books she had left in his car. He sensed Alana wasn't used to having someone do things for her or go out of their way to please her.

"Come over to my place." Julian had his eyes on her as he spoke. He wasn't ready to say goodnight to her.

They were standing outside of the Pick Me Up Café. It was no longer snowing and the sidewalk was covered with a thick layer of clean snow, something that didn't last long in the city. She agreed by giving him a short nod. They walked side by side, to his parked car.

"I love the sound of walking on loose, fresh snow," she said, hands in her pockets.

"Do you like winter, Alana?"

"I love winter."

Julian heard the joy in her voice. He looked up at the night sky and smiled. "Me too."

Soon after they were entering his warm, softly lit condo.

"You have such a beautiful home." There was wonder in her voice. "It's perfect."

"Thank you. I spent over a year putting the place together. Art Deco is a weakness of mine."

He watched her admire his favorite painting.

"This one doesn't belong…why do you have it?"

"I don't have a good answer for you. I saw it and I fell in love with it. Maybe because I can't decide if the woman in the painting is dead or alive."

"That's not why you have it."

"No?"

"No."

"Then tell me why, Alana."

"It's her eyes. You stand here, you stare at her, and you hope she'll raise her eyes and look at you. You want her to see you."

"Maybe she has already seen me."

"Then I would say she's dead."

Julian winced and his reaction made Alana chuckle. She gravitated toward the large built-in bookshelf running along one of the living room walls and he noticed she was still holding the bag of books against her chest.

"You know, it's safe for you to put the bag down. I promise I won't harm them."

She stood with her back to him, running her fingers along the spines of his books. "You have several books written in Hungarian. Do you speak it?"

"I do. It's my first language. Thanks to my adoptive mother I also speak Mandarin. But I'm dreadful at it."

Usually, when Julian revealed that about himself, most people would want to know about his past, asking more questions than he would ever feel comfortable answering. But when Alana didn't probe further, he was intrigued. It would be a good opportunity to casually make the conversation about her but, if he did, she would refuse to give him any information and the non-threatening atmosphere he was trying to build would be ruined.

Leaving her to enjoy his collection of books, Julian made his way to the bedroom. Sitting on the edge of the bed, he pulled his phone from his pocket and quickly texted Meredith. They hadn't seen each other since that night at the club.

He looked up and saw Alana standing by the bedroom door. She was still wearing her oversized jacket. When they had arrived he was about to ask her if he could take it from her but her body language told him she didn't want to part with it. She was in his territory and Julian believed she felt vulnerable, not yet sure it was safe.

Alana walked in and stopped a few feet from him. "That must be the largest, most comfortable looking bed I have ever seen in my life."

"When you have as many orgies and threesomes as I do, you do need a big bed."

"Do you like it?"

"Group sex or the bed?" He wasn't sure if she had realized he had been joking.

"Group sex."

"I prefer threesomes. You?"

"I have never had one."

He lifted his eyebrows, not hiding his astonishment. "Really? What else haven't you done?"

"Anal sex."

He had to stop himself from saying he didn't believe her. The more time he spent with her the more mystified he was. "I love anal sex. A favorite."

"Why do you love it, Julian?"

Alana took off her jacket and placed it, with her bag, on the reading chair in the corner of the room. She sat on the edge of the chair, staring at him with vivid interest. The light coming from the nightstand lamp bathed the room in a golden glow and softened the dark masculine décor. It complimented Alana, giving her an aura of serenity and, somehow, diminished her apprehensive demeanor.

"I love looking down at a woman's body and seeing the anticipation on her." As he spoke, the smoky quality of his voice became more apparent. "I love covering her with oil, massaging it into her with my hands, feeling the heat of my palms warming her up. Admiring her glowing skin come to life." Julian didn't take his eyes away from Alana. "Dripping more oil directly into her, using my fingers to caress her closed entrance, moving in gentle circles to coat her well. Slowly pressing forward, watching her open up to take one of my fingers."

Immersed in his description, Julian spoke from a place he usually didn't share with others. "I love watching my finger move in and out of her, feeling her soften under me. She knows that's me tricking her body to trust me, to let go, and right there and then there's a bittersweet note in the pleasure she's feeling. She knows this is where I need her to be so I can take my pleasure. It's both incredibly selfish and giving. She knows it. I know it. The perfect understanding of human nature."

He imagined he was doing to Alana what he was describing and a surge of heat started at the pit of his stomach and spread through his torso. "When I pull my finger out and I bring myself to her opening. When I press forward, forcefully, but with no rush. Enough to get inside of her but stopping close to bringing her harm. When she takes me and she starts to feel the burn…that burn, that deep bite that knocks the air out of her lungs and makes her body desperately fight me is beautiful. And it is beautiful because she's allowing me to do that to her. She's choosing to be vulnerable with me and that's pure intimacy."

Alana remained perfectly still, giving him her full attention.

"When I hold her hips more tightly, encouraging her to give in, to surrender to the pain, there's nothing beyond her," Julian continued. "As she embraces it and I feel myself move deeper into her and the tightness is so wonderful it almost makes me lose control, all I can think about and feel is her. When I'm all the way in I don't move. I savor it. I cherish it. I know she has surrendered to me and I can choose to make that fucking mine, hers, or ours."

Julian saw Alana lick her bottom lip and, at that point, he was so aroused that the touch of his clothes against his own skin was painful. "The feeling of being in control is unique. Intoxicating. That's why I love anal sex, Alana. The act, like only a few other things in life, feeds a need in me."

He waited for her reaction, knowing she was trying to understand what type of person, what type of man he was. Julian stood up and went to her. For the first time since he left Hazel's house, he realized he no longer felt tense, afraid of his own emotions. In a tender gesture, he lowered his head and kissed her. There was desire in their kiss but more than anything else there was a newfound intimacy.

"Going to take a quick shower. I'll be back soon," he said, with a last caressing touch to her cheek.

When Julian got into the shower and felt the hot stream of water hit his body, he wondered what to do. Everything he had seen and heard from Alana since their encounter at the coffee shop confused him. She appeared to be sexually experienced and at the same time disarmingly innocent. He didn't believe it to be an act, but that innocence hadn't been there when he had seen her at the club. That had been a raw, commanding, sexual Alana. He felt it in his core. This new side of her brought a nuance of gentleness to that attraction, which caught him off-guard. He had never met anyone like her before.

When Julian returned to the bedroom, wearing only a towel around his waist, he found Alana curled up in the middle of his bed. He stood for a while, watching her sleep. The plush comforter had molded itself to her sleeping body, like a large cocoon, trying to protect her from the outside world. Maybe it was trying to protect her from him, he thought. In only a pair of black leggings and a t-shirt, her colorful socks stood out. Usually in his bed, women were naked. But not Alana. She had rainbows on her socks. That made Julian smile.

Moving carefully, so as not to wake her up, he grabbed a blanket from the closet. Removing the towel from around his waist, Julian lay on his side, beside her. Adjusting the blanket over them, he wrapped an arm around Alana. Feeling the cadence of her breathing against his body, he inhaled deeply. Her proximity was making it impossible for him to ignore his state of arousal. One of the first things he noticed in a woman was her scent, the inimitable element that characterized her to him. Alana didn't wear perfume. Julian detected the fresh notes of the laundry detergent she used on her clothes and traces of her plain shampoo. His instinct was telling him to wake her up, pull down her leggings, and moving her underwear to the side, bury himself in her. No words. No eye contact. Just her warmth, her scent, her breathing, her heartbeat. But Alana was sleeping so soundly that Julian couldn't get himself to disturb her. His body relaxed against hers and he remembered the last time he slept beside a female, when the act was about truly caring for someone.

· · ·

Julian sat up in the bed, his heart racing. It was dark. For a brief moment he didn't know where he was and it took him a while to recognize his own bedroom.

He had dreamt about them.

"Who's Tatia?"

He heard the voice and Julian turned, startled. Narrowing his eyes, he saw the shadow by the window. It was Alana. She was sitting on the floor, facing away from him.

He got out of bed and, on unsteady legs, made his way across the room. Naked, he sunk to his knees beside her. At some point throughout the night she had undressed and now, only wrapped in the blanket he had used earlier to cover them, she was gazing at the city's night sky. He rested his forehead on the ceiling-to-floor glass and took several steadying deep breaths.

"It's beautiful," Alana whispered, still not looking at him. "Do you ever sit here and wonder what's going on down there?"

Julian followed her gaze. After a few minutes of staring at the tall buildings, the lights coming from them blurred into a swatch of varied shades. Even by the window it was too dim in the bedroom for Alana to see his tears and Julian was thankful for that.

"You were apologizing to someone in your sleep. Tatia. You kept saying her name over and over again."

Without the ill-fitting, mismatched clothing he had seen her wear, which worked almost as a distraction from the woman in them, Julian could now focus on her. Alana was a classic beauty. And that sad demeanor of hers, which was so hard for him to witness, made her beauty look almost tragic. In that moment he knew Alana felt as lonely as he did.

"Sometimes I can't sleep either. I have all of these nightmares. I guess it doesn't get better, huh?" she asked.

"It never does."

Her eyes were on his arm. "That's an unusual tattoo. Why a raven?"

He ran his fingertips along the wings of the raven. "It's a long story…maybe one day I can tell you." He looked up. "Who are you, Alana?"

She didn't cower from his intense gaze. "Who is she, Julian?"

The blanket had slipped off her shoulder, exposing her breast, and he moved her hair away from her neck. Slowly, with his eyes following his hand, he caressed her nipple. His touch was light, almost revering. Alana covered his hand with hers and pressed his palm to her breast. Enjoying the softness of it, Julian lowered his head and took her nipple between his lips.

Alana had her hands on his hair and she arched her back against him. Without warning, Julian trapped her nipple between his teeth. He bit hard. She gave a small cry, holding on to him. He moved away from her breast and licked her stomach, continuing past her navel. He took pleasure in unhurriedly indulging in every inch of her that his lips could find. The taste of her arousal on his tongue made him moan. So enthralled by it, he didn't know how long Alana lay open to him. With his eyes closed, Julian savored her blindly. That only made him more aware of her scent, of her taste.

The sounds of gratification escaping her lips, the way Alana gripped the hair on the back of his head, the undulation of her hips told him she was close. He slid his finger inside of her and her body readily welcomed it. He wanted Alana to experience as much pleasure as her mind and body would allow her to. He wanted her to lose herself. As her thighs trembled around him, Julian felt her tense up. Alana's body lifted off the floor with the intensity of her release and he rested his hand over her stomach, holding her tightly.

The dim light coming through the window allowed him to see

the desire she still harbored in her eyes. "Say it." His tone was firm. "Never hold back with me."

Before she responded, he watched her chest rise and fall, like she was trying to find the courage to speak. "I want you to do to me exactly what you described earlier. I want you to fuck me like that."

With her slightly parted lips and fast breathing, there was a hint of bashfulness in her voice. He got up and a few minutes later, as he was returning to her, he took in the image of Alana on the floor—naked, sex-tousled hair spread around her, arms resting above her head. Julian didn't want to ever forget such an image.

"Get on your hands and knees," he ordered, standing by her. "Face the window."

He knelt behind her and, moving her hair to the side, he closed his hand on the back of her neck. Up until then, his movements had been sensual and languorous but now Julian wanted to feel Alana submit to him. He squeezed her neck, loving how fragile it was under his fingers. Opening his hand, he massaged it for a while. Her neck was quickly becoming one of his weaknesses.

Alana hadn't said anything but her body was showing him that she was apprehensive. Julian grabbed the bottle he had gone to find and slowly dripped the oil on her. She jerked, startled by the liquid touching her warm skin. He watched as it trickled down her thighs and the back of her legs. Pressing his fingers hard into her flesh, Julian smeared it all over her body. He spread her open to him and, inserting the neck of the bottle into her opening, poured a large amount inside of her. Alana rested her forehead on the floor and she remained very still, aware of all of his movements.

"You're beautiful," Julian said, bringing his lips closer to her ear. "And the sight of you on your hands and knees, ready for me, is beautiful."

Gradually, without much resistance, Julian's oiled finger entered her. He moved it around, enjoying how well coated she was. Some of the oil was flowing out of her and Alana was responding to the pleasurable sensation of it. With his finger buried in her, Julian placed his other hand between her outstretched legs. He knew the heightened sexual tension created by the looming act he was preparing her for, joined with the feeling of both of his hands on her, would make Alana come undone. It happened fast and her body bowed with the intensity of it.

Watching her become lost in a wave of pleasure, Julian grabbed the condom he had brought back with the oil and rolled it on. He gripped her hips and brought himself to the small entrance. Julian steadily pressed forward. He didn't stop until he was deep inside of her.

With her palm pressed against the glass, Alana was now closer to the window and she was panting. He leaned forward, covering her body with his, and he wrapped one of his arms around her. She was too tight. She was lost in the burn.

"Breathe with me, Alana," he whispered, remaining very still inside of her. "Breathe."

He inhaled through his nose and exhaled slowly, through his mouth. "With me," he repeated, feeling her try to match her breathing to his. "That's it, Alana. With me."

"I don't think I can do this."

For a moment Julian wasn't sure if she was referring to what was happening between them or something else entirely.

"Can you feel me in you? How hard I am?"

She nodded.

"Let go, Alana." He wrapped both of his arms around her. "Into my arms, into me." She continued to steady her breathing and her body gradually softened in his arms. "You're opening up." He gasped, closing his eyes. "Feels so fucking good."

He straightened his back and placed both of his hands on her hips. He looked down and watched as he slid out of her. He pushed forward again and the feeling of her taking all of him made Julian's whole body shudder.

The rhythm of his thrusts became more demanding, rougher, and her moans louder. Holding on to her he could see by the angle of her back, the way her head dropped between her shoulders, that she was nearing her threshold.

"Stay with me, Alana." He leaned forward again, wrapping her with his body. Julian placed his hand under her chin and lifted her head up. She made a pleading sound. With their bodies covered in a mix of oil and perspiration, Julian felt his overextended muscles ache with the need for release. He couldn't hold back any longer.

Straddling her lower body, he planted his feet on the floor, on each side of her knees, and with a couple of powerful thrusts, held her as she swung forward with the force of it. The intensity of Julian's orgasm made him bear down into her, like he was trying to absorb all of Alana into himself, and his groans of pleasure came deep from within his chest.

Pulling out of her, Julian discarded the condom. He felt shaken. They lay side by side, on top of the blanket she had been using earlier, and he brought his face to the curve of Alana's neck. His hand was resting on her chest, between her breasts, and she laced her fingers through his. Remembering the terrified expression on her face when he had mentioned Steven Thompson, Julian gathered her closer to him.

CHAPTER 11

Meredith decided not to attend her last lecture of the day. Walking along South Ellis Avenue, she searched for a cigarette and a lighter inside of her oversized purse. It had been a dreary winter afternoon, without a hint of sunshine, and the cold had showed itself to be tenacious, not wanting to release its grip on the city.

As she held the cigarette between her lips, Meredith scrolled through her text messages. There were a few from friends suggesting drinks at Rainbo Club, her regular hangout, one from her father telling her he wanted her to join him on his upcoming trip to Aspen, and a short text message from a guy she had slept with at a house party the week before, wondering when he would be seeing her again. She chuckled, shaking her head. They both had been drunk and high on weed, which was probably why she didn't remember much about that evening. Yet, despite the gaps in her memory, Meredith was confident the sex had been bad enough that she didn't want to give it a second go. She kept promising to herself she would stop indulging in casual sex with men that saw her pleasure as the last item on a long grocery list. She blamed Julian for her dissatisfaction. He had shown her a different world, a hidden world where her body and mind were embraced by his genuine desire to celebrate her sexuality. Being Julian's lover gave her a glimpse of the woman she could become—confident, fulfilled, strong. Now that she had felt it, the possibility of not reaching that potential made her critical of any sexual experience that was less than what it could or should be. She was still angry with Julian for what happened at The Raven Room but keeping him at bay wouldn't give her what she wanted. Besides being her sexual game-changer he was the only one who could grant her access to the club.

She dialed Pam's number and left her a voicemail telling her she had decided to go over for dinner. She wondered what her father would do if he found out his only daughter had gone to an underground sex club with an older man. Meredith always expected to have fun during her university years. The perfect opportunity to drink, experiment with drugs, have plenty of no-strings-attached sex, fall in love, have her heart broken a few times, and break many more hearts in return. That's what her friends were doing and even though she definitely had her share of it, and enjoyed it, Meredith had outgrown it. Her last ex-boyfriend, a real trustafarian, was still in the picture. He would pop up now and then, visits that led to hours of happy-go-lucky sex. But Meredith knew he wasn't the type of man who could subdue, or even start to comprehend, the ever-present restlessness she felt within her.

Meredith parked in the driveway of her family home. She hadn't been over in several months but no matter how long she stayed away, every time she saw the gardens, now covered by thick layers of snow, she thought of her mother. She had been a talented gardener, spending hours tending to the flowers and trees she loved so much. Meredith missed her. When she was nine years old her mother had died after a long, painful battle with breast cancer and despite the brave face she had put on, losing her when she was entering the age she needed her most, left Meredith struggling to make sense of the world around her. If her mother was still alive she was sure they would be close. Her father would always say she reminded him of her mother and called Meredith a heap of beautiful foolishness.

One of the last memories she had of her mother was when she had showed her the Chagall Windows at the Art Institute of Chicago. At the time the blue cast of the stained glass had made her think she was a mermaid swimming in the ocean. Now, as an adult, when she was having a particularly difficult day, she would buy a ticket to the Art Institute so she could stare at the stained glass for hours. It was her refuge.

She caught herself sitting inside of her dark, cold car. Groaning with frustration, Meredith quickly dried her wet cheeks with the backs of her hands. She wouldn't get anything out of crying for a mother who had been dead for fourteen years.

As she ran toward the front door, she felt the salt sprinkled on the icy ground dig into the soles of her boots. The only person she had told where she went when she needed to get away had been Julian. He had joked, saying only a wealthy girl like her would think to pay over twenty dollars to stare at stained glass as a way to unwind. At the time that made Meredith think that he must resent people like her, born into comfort. Julian still perceived himself as being one of the have-nots and Meredith wondered if he would ever feel differently.

"M, so happy you could make it for dinner," her father said as she entered his library. He was sitting on his favorite chair, reading a book, and Pam was on the couch, several papers and folders scattered around her. The fireplace crackled between them.

"It's been a while," Meredith replied, walking up to him and giving him a hug. "I thought I was overdue for a home-cooked meal."

"Couldn't agree more." Pam joined the conversation, also receiving a hug from Meredith.

She sat across from her stepmother and noticed the glasses both she and her father were holding, "What are you drinking?"

"A well-deserved scotch," Samuel said with a smile. "Your stepmom and I need to fuel ourselves. May I offer you one?"

"I'm good, thanks. I wouldn't say no to a beer, though."

"I'm sure we can arrange that."

"Good. I'll go grab one."

"No need," he said, getting up. "I have to make a quick phone call before dinner anyway. I'll bring you a nice cold beer."

"Thanks, dad." As soon as the sound of his heavy footsteps faded down the hall, she turned to Pam.

They stared at each other. Meredith was the one to break the silence. "Why did you think the information you gave me would make me want to stay away from Julian?"

Pam sighed loudly, resting her head on the back of the couch.

"Someone is in a mood."

"Don't play games with me, Meredith. I've been pulling sixteen-hour days and I have a case on my hands that, every day, inches closer and closer to a dead end."

"No, you stop playing games with me. Why didn't you give me any information on him prior to him being adopted? You wouldn't have tried to get a hold of me for almost two weeks straight and then show up at my place with your panties in a bunch, asking me to stay away from him, if you hadn't found something important." She shifted to the edge of her seat, leaning closer to Pam. "What are you not telling me?"

"I don't know anything that I haven't shared with you. I still don't have the earlier documents but I will. It's only a matter of time."

"Bullshit, Pam. What's going on?"

Pam glanced at the door, visibly nervous her husband would overhear them. "Keep your voice down."

When Meredith spoke she was almost whispering. "I don't want to fight you on this. I understand you're trying to protect me. I do. But I need to know the truth."

"Have you been going to the club?"

"I have."

"Damn it, Meredith. Stay away from that place." Pam was struggling not to raise her voice.

"Tell me why."

"I don't know what else I'll find when I dig deeper into his past but Julian Reeve is not a man you want to betray. What do you think he'll do when he finds out you used him to get into the club with the intention to write a piece about him and The Raven Room?" They both heard a noise coming from outside the library. Pam stopped talking, waiting to see if it was Samuel. When she was certain they were still alone, she continued in a hushed voice. "Throughout the years there have been times I've wanted to gain access to the club. I've heard about other cops who also tried. Guess what happened? Nothing. You don't get to go near it unless someone from inside wants you to."

"He'll only find out after the piece is published. Even then, only he, you, and I will know he's the man in it. I'll deal with Julian when that time comes."

"Don't you understand? You're going to get into trouble and I won't be able to help you."

"Get me the rest of the information on him." She wasn't going to change her mind about writing the piece. To her, what had happened the last time she had been to the club only confirmed that the death of the woman was linked to The Raven Room.

Hearing her father's approaching footsteps, she forced herself to smile.

"Look at that, you brought me my favorite beer," she said, taking the bottle from him.

Samuel laughed, getting comfortable on his chair near the fireplace. "Now you're just trying to please me."

Meredith winked at him as she drank her beer.

The three of them chatted for a while, discussing how her studies were coming along, and the possibility of her joining him on his trip.

"This city is going through a rough patch." She heard her father say when she tried to focus on the conversation unfolding around her.

"Tell me about it." Pam pitched in. "We're completely underfunded."

"What do you expect with Matheson as our mayor?" Samuel asked.

Pam turned to Meredith, rolling her eyes. "Your dad can't stand the man."

"I still can't believe you voted for him," he said.

"You did?" Meredith accosted Pam.

"He was the best candidate," she said to Samuel, ignoring Meredith's question. "Don't understand how you still can't see that. But he needs to get rid of his crew, especially that mangy lap dog of his, Thompson," she continued.

"You have it wrong. Matheson is Thompson's fluffer."

Meredith was about to enjoy another sip from her beer but stopped, holding the bottle midair. Her father rarely spoke so strongly about people. "Who?"

"You wouldn't know who he is," Samuel brushed the question off. "I think he should run for mayor, though. He has the vision that could turn this city around. The man is brilliant."

"Don't listen to your dad. He lives in a bubble."

Meredith shrugged. "I couldn't care less about politics. I don't understand it."

"There's only one thing you need to understand," Samuel said. "In politics there's always a reason for every action. Nothing is arbitrary. And that reason, even though it might not be apparent because nothing in this life unfolds in a straightforward fashion, is always about getting something that you want. That's it." Samuel smiled at her. "You should apply this same rationale to your every day. If you do, you'll be ahead of everyone else in the room."

Later that night, when Meredith was back at her apartment, she sat in front of her laptop and added several new paragraphs to her research material on The Raven Room. She was keeping Colton within reach, with the hope she would get him to tell her the name of the woman that had been found dead the day Pam had come over to her apartment.

A noise over her shoulder made Meredith look up and she saw her housemate, Tess, walk out of the bedroom, enveloped in an invisible bubble of expensive smelling perfume. "Didn't know you were home," she said, admiring the animal print of Tess's dress. "Where are you going looking so glamorous?"

"I have a date," she said with a broad smile. "We're meeting at the bar of The Peninsula hotel."

"Okay…who's this guy?"

"A friend." Tess shrugged. "A friend who takes care of me."

Meredith couldn't even pretend she was surprised. One of her other friends had a man who flew her down to Miami every year, paying all her expenses, including her stay at the one of the most luxurious hotels in the city. A friend of a friend had a man in her life who paid for her apartment in West Loop, while she finished medical school. They were sugar babies and Meredith wondered if she didn't have a wealthy father who paid for her tuition and rent and gave her spending money, if she would be like those girls at Viagra Triangle, on the hunt for a private-jet–owning sugar daddy.

"I hope you're charging at least five hundred dollars a pop."

"Oh, believe me," Tess said as she put her jacket on. "Tuition isn't getting any cheaper…neither is the Celine bag I have been drooling over since October. M, I went to Barney's last week and I held it in my hands. And I just smelled it. I swore I heard violins in the background. I'm telling you, that's what you call love."

Meredith thought her friend looked breathtaking. She had put a lot of effort into curling her long blonde hair, applying barely there makeup that perfectly enhanced her girl-next-door features and selecting a tasteful combination of timeless accessories. "When you get it, we'll go out and celebrate," she said to Tess with a smile.

"You better believe it, honey. All night long."

"Just be careful out there. Text me if you need anything."

"Will do," she said as she closed the door behind her.

The apartment was quiet again. Looking at the time on her computer, Meredith wondered what she could possibly do with herself on a Thursday night that didn't involve going out. She had received a text from Olivia, whom she had met last year through friends, asking her if she was up to joining her to watch a local band perform at Empty Bottle, in the Ukrainian village. Meredith replied asking her if she wanted to come over instead. After a few minutes of texting back and forth, Olivia said she was on her way.

Meredith changed into a pair of yoga pants and a plain t-shirt, her favorite attire to lounge around the apartment. A few days ago she had looked at her reflection in the mirror and was taken by surprise when she realized she was only twenty-three years old. She shouldn't feel so weary.

Soon she heard a soft knock on the door. She smiled to herself. It was time to unwind, forget all about The Raven Room and Julian.

• • •

It was past one in the morning. Only the nightstand lamp was on. Olivia lay down naked on the bed, staring at the white ceiling of Meredith's small bedroom.

"It's so quiet in here."

Meredith didn't move. Her body was still recovering from her last orgasm.

"Does it bother you?" she asked, her eyes closed.

"I like it."

She stretched her arm and touched Olivia's ankle, caressing it.

"Why don't we do this more often?"

Olivia lifted her head from the bed and met Meredith's eyes. "Maybe because you're always too busy worshiping the cock?"

The comment caught her by surprise. She chuckled.

"Ready to finish that joint?" Olivia asked.

Meredith propped herself up, her head and shoulders resting against the bedframe. Like Olivia, she was naked, and the touch of the soft sheets against her skin made her shiver. To her, not too many things felt as good as Egyptian cotton sheets. On her last birthday Julian had surprised her with a set from D. Porthault, with beautiful full-blown red dahlias floating on a pristine white background. Not too many women she knew would have been thrilled to receive sheets as a gift from a man they were sleeping with, but she loved them and it proved to Meredith that Julian had come to know her well. The message he had included with it—*"So you and every one of your lovers can feel like royalty in your bed"*—was the perfect finishing touch. Right now, that's exactly how she felt.

"Here you go, greedy kitten," Olivia said, placing the joint between her lips and lighting it with one of the matches Meredith had for the candles in her room. "So what's new? Do you have a boyfriend?"

Meredith exhaled and the smoke lingered around her face. "No boyfriend. You?"

"I'm seeing this guy."

"Hmm…do you ever plan to tell your family?"

"Tell what?" Olivia asked, stretching her arm toward Meredith. "Pass it to me." She grabbed the joint, holding it between her thumb and middle finger, and took a deep pull from it.

"Hello?" Meredith slapped her thigh. "That you prefer women?"

"Definitely not. It's harder for us, black people, to come out."

"Does he know?"

"Jesus, honey, this bud must be strong. It's muddling your brain."

"Are you going to cheat on him forever?"

"Yup."

"That's wrong."

"You know what's wrong?" Olivia asked, playing with a strand of Meredith's hair. "Thinking a guy is down with his girl liking pussy. I mean, for real liking pussy. And not him just believing it's something she does to please him when he's hitching for a threesome."

"I don't think I'm with you on that."

"If you're smart, you would be. It shrivels their ego, sweetie. Soon enough he will packing up and looking for some chick who has wifey written on her forehead."

Taking the joint from Olivia, Meredith inhaled and held her breath for as long as she could. She felt the heat in her lungs.

"Do you prefer cock?" Olivia continued.

Putting out what was left of the joint, Meredith gave some thought to Olivia's question.

"I don't think I do. It's all about the person in question. I know for a fact I couldn't go the rest of my life without touching a woman." She moved closer to Olivia and ran her fingers down her arm. "Or tasting a woman."

Meredith kissed Olivia, gently at first, her lips caressing hers like the prelude to a much-cherished pleasure. Olivia intensified the kiss; a sound of satisfaction escaped her and filled the silent room. Deeply relaxed, her senses heightened, Meredith abandoned herself to Olivia's erotic touch. Their legs intertwined, their stomachs touched, she almost screamed when she felt Olivia's mouth close on her sensitive nipple.

"You're so wet." Olivia's words sounded like they were being torn out of her.

Lying down between Olivia's legs, all Meredith wanted was to pleasure her. "Gorgeous pussy." She didn't stop kissing and licking her until she felt Olivia pull her hair and tense up against her face.

Meredith loved watching Olivia climax. She found it inspiring. Enjoying the body of a woman was instinctual to her. It felt like she was finding a long lost piece of herself outside of her own body. Thinking of the way Olivia moved, feline and melodious, the beauty of her dark hair, the strong and simultaneously elusive feel of her full, heart-shaped lips, and her touch—admiring, fiery, but so tender—made Meredith relate to men in their love for the feminine.

"What are you going to do when you're done with your Master's?"

By now they had been lying side-by-side, chatting for hours. Meredith had lit several of the candles scattered throughout the room and their aroma, mixed with the earthy notes of the burning incense, was reminiscent of an autumn campfire. She yawned, trying to remain awake. She had to be up in less than three hours. "Have a career. And travel as much as I can."

"Where do you want to go?"

"Everywhere. One day I'll be a respected journalist and I'll live in Paris. In a beautiful historic house with a view of the Eiffel tower."

Olivia laughed, covering her eyes with her forearm. "Are you serious?" Her usual girly voice now sounded raspy, a sign she was also tired.

"I'm dead serious."

"You're so fucking crazy."

"Because I want to live in Paris?"

"Yeah."

"I'll find myself a couple of French lovers. Pussy on Monday. Cock on Tuesday."

Olivia had a large grin on her face. It slowly faded, giving way to an inquisitive frown. "Are you still sleeping with that guy?"

"Which one?"

"The old one."

Meredith guessed she was referring to Julian. "He's not old." She had to be the only woman in her early twenties who believed a thirty-nine-year-old man wasn't old. "He's still in the picture." She hadn't wanted to talk about him, or even think of him that evening, but that was proving to be impossible.

"Married? Kids? Hot-looking girlfriend with starfish syndrome? What's his story?"

When she heard Olivia mention starfish syndrome, Meredith laughed. She had no idea where the term originated from, but it described a woman who expected the man, for whatever reason, to be the one to do all the work during sex. Like a starfish, she would just lay there. Meredith felt sorry for anyone who went through life experiencing their sexuality in such a passive manner.

"Nothing like that," she answered, shaking her head.

"Oh God, please don't tell me he has mommy issues?"

For several long minutes Meredith didn't reply. She didn't know much about Julian's childhood. When Olivia didn't press her to answer the question, Meredith turned and looked at her. She had fallen asleep.

Meredith watched Olivia. There was a tranquility to her expression that Meredith hadn't witnessed in another human being in a very long time. Gently, so she wouldn't disturb her, she caressed her hair. Maybe she would invite Olivia to visit her in Paris. They could be young and carefree in the city of light. As Meredith rested her head back on the pillow and closed her eyes, she suddenly realized who could tell her more about Julian—Hazel, his adoptive mother. Once, when they were on their way to dinner, he had received a frantic call from Hazel's caregiver, saying she was having one of her episodes and he needed to come over as soon as possible. Reluctantly, he had taken Meredith along and after Hazel had calmed down, Meredith had chatted with her for a while. They had become fast friends. Hazel had an air of pragmatism that was compelling to Meredith. It was their common ground.

That had been less than two months ago. It was time for Meredith to visit Hazel.

Chapter 12

"I can't believe we're eating ice cream inside of your fancy car in the Whole Foods parking lot."

A splatter dripped down Julian's hand. He quickly licked it off. Alana tried to not smile. "I can't believe I'm not eating this ice cream off of your naked body, inside of this fancy car in the Whole Foods parking lot."

This was the first time they were seeing each other after she had spent the night at his place. The next morning, while he was still lying in bed, she had quietly gotten up, picked her clothes off the floor and dressed herself. Not even pretending to be asleep, he had kept his gaze on her. Alana had known he was watching her. Their eyes had met several times but her expression hadn't allowed him to guess what she was thinking. The one thing he had been certain of was that Alana's behavior hadn't sprung out of anger. When she had finished dressing and had grabbed her bag of books from the reading chair, Julian had asked her if he could drive her where she was going. She had refused. When he had asked her for her number she had said she didn't own a mobile phone and that he could call her at the bookstore. After that brief exchange of words, Alana had turned around and walked out of his condo.

It was hard, if not impossible, for Julian to guess what was going on in Alana's mind. She was extremely skilled at concealing her emotions. The few times he thought he had seen a glimpse of her true self it was when she was talking about books. Julian wasn't sure if she was being sexually submissive because she wanted to please him or because she was being loyal to her nature. He wondered how far he would have to push her to find out. Or even if he wanted to. It was dangerous to use sex as a medium to lift the veil into someone's mind.

Julian couldn't get the image of Alana on her hands and knees out of his head. It haunted him—her on the floor, facing the city night skyline through the large window, her body covered in a thin layer of sweat and oil, her long hair sticking to her face, her neck, as he entered her from behind amidst her soft whimpering. That had been one of the reasons Julian had called her at the bookstore and told her he wanted to see her again. The other reasons were less straightforward. He should keep his distance from her. There was her connection to Steven Thompson and her secrecy when it came to sharing anything about herself. There had been two emotions Alana hadn't been able to hide from him; pleasure and fear. He had wanted to give her all of that pleasure but he couldn't turn his back on her when fear seeped through every single one of her words and actions.

Julian had picked her up after she was done with work and when he had asked her what she was craving she had said ice cream. He wondered if Alana would ever let him take her out for a proper dinner. After some insisting on his part, she had finally revealed that her favorite ice cream was Mint Galactica by Luna & Larry's Coconut Bliss. That's how they had ended up at the parking lot, sitting in his car, each holding a pint of ice cream and eating it with plastic spoons.

Not wanting to ruin the feeling of intimacy they were experiencing, Julian didn't start the car, even though they had been done with the ice cream for some time.

"You should wear your hair down." He took in as much as he could of her. "You have stunning hair."

Alana turned her body toward him. "My best feature?"

"That would be your eyes."

Upon hearing his comment, Julian noticed she looked away. "Does my compliment make you feel uncomfortable?"

"Why are you doing this?" The cheerfulness was gone from her voice.

"Doing what?"

"Trying to be nice."

"You don't think there's kindness in the real me?" He wasn't sure why he had asked her that. He wished he hadn't.

"You're a kind man but not a nice man, Julian. The first time we spoke I said I wanted you. I meant it."

Her voice was so calm and rooted in self-confidence that he felt, at that moment, absolute respect for Alana.

"And I said I couldn't give something I didn't know how to give."

"When you held my head with both hands and you fucked my mouth, hearing me gag on your cock over and over again, seeing the tears falling down my face, you gave yourself to me. When you fucked me in the ass on the hardwood floor of your bedroom, you trapped my body under yours as you heard me cry out every time you forced your cock deep inside of me, you gave yourself to me. There's a thirst in you. You try to suppress it but you can't. You take pleasure in inflicting pain...in hurting me. You love it," she continued, her eyes on his. "That's why I want you."

He sat up straighter and closed both hands around the steering wheel. Looking through the windshield at the vacant parking spots around them, he had to coerce his body to exhale. He was now so attuned to Alana, he felt her body heat hitting him in steady waves. Her breathing was the only sound he could hear.

Turning the keys in the ignition, Julian accelerated out of the parking lot. "Put your seat belt on," he said, not taking his eyes off the road.

She didn't ask him where he was taking her but she glanced at him every couple of minutes. Julian didn't break the silence.

Around twenty minutes later he parked the car. "When I need to get away from everything I come here. I want to share it with you."

They were at the Music Box Theatre on North Southport Avenue. Julian purchased two tickets for a screening that had started five minutes ago. They sat in the last row of the almost empty theater room.

"Do you know what this movie is about?" Alana whispered by his ear.

"No idea."

"It's never about the movie, is it?"

Julian removed his coat, tilting his head toward her. "It's about me doing whatever I want to you." His lips were so close to her neck they brushed her skin as he spoke. "It's about me sliding my hands under your sweater and tugging hard on your nipples. It's about me kneeling between your legs, pulling down your jeans and fucking you with my tongue."

When she swallowed, he felt her throat move against his mouth.

"It's about having you straddle me as I'm all the way inside of you, enjoying your tight grip, your warmth," Julian continued, reaching for her hand and placing it on his crotch. He wrapped his fingers around hers and held his breath when she cupped him. "It's about you keeping your eyes on the screen, not being allowed to make a sound, as I bite your neck and kiss your lips until they are red and swollen. It's about us knowing I'm yours and you're mine."

His erection, heavy and hard, pressed against his slacks. It throbbed with her touch. He wanted to be inside of her. Alana kissed him. Her kiss was gentle, a light caress, but he could taste the hunger in her. It was the same hunger he carried within him, slowly roaring, always searching for release. Julian moved to his knees, between her legs, and soon she was pulling fistfuls of his hair, arching her back off her chair. Julian didn't care that there wasn't enough room between the rows of seats to fit his tall body; or that he was kneeling on discarded popcorn and the floor was sticky with soft drink stains and dirt carried in by the winter shoes of strangers. Julian bit the inside of her thigh with primal abandon and Alana cried out. He was vaguely aware of someone in the audience, possibly the man sitting a few rows ahead, shushing them.

He moved up along her torso and brought his face close to hers. Julian felt her breath mix with his. The scent of her arousal on his lips and on his cheeks was slowly driving Julian to lose control. The savageness of his raw masculinity coursed through his body.

Soon nothing else would matter. He forced himself to take several deep breaths. He needed to command his basic nature. Shuddering under him, Alana was so warm she felt almost feverish to him. He stroked her face with his cheek and hoped the softness of her skin would lull his heartbeat to a less agonizing pace. Trying to move as quietly as possible, he sat back on his seat. Reaching into his coat pocket, Julian grabbed his wallet and found a condom inside of it.

"Take your jeans off but keep your panties on," he said to her, his face in her hair. "I want you to sit on me, facing the screen."

Alana made no noise as she followed his instructions, her body moving easily among the seats. As the scenes changed on screen, the theatre switched between shadowy, almost complete darkness, to vivid brightness. As Alana lifted herself up and straddled his thighs, facing the front of the theater, a daylight scene came up. Julian thought, there he was, late on a Saturday night, in the back row of Music Box Theatre, with no idea what foreign movie was playing, fucking a petite blonde who was a complete riddle to him. That thought only made him grow harder.

He heard Alana make a small sound of distress and, if all of his attention hadn't been on her, he would have missed it. Because of the position they were in, Julian wasn't sure she would be able to accommodate all of him.

Moving her underwear further aside, he held her by the waist, steadying her. Part of him just wanted to force her body to take him. But that wouldn't achieve his goal. Julian knew that pain, simply by how it's enacted, could transform itself from a soul-breaking force to a catalyst of the most powerful pleasure. He didn't want to simply hurt Alana. It was about satisfying them both. For that, she needed to feel he was coercing her to accept the pain he was giving her.

He placed his fingers on her and stroked her in small circles. Hearing her gasp, Julian closed his hand on her nape and, taking a firm hold on her hair, pulled her head back toward him. He wasn't gentle. He enjoyed the sight of strain on her neck.

"Shhh, Alana…quiet. We don't want to be caught." He wrapped his free hand around her neck. He did it slowly, feeling each of his fingers press down on her fragile throat. Julian used just enough force to capture her wild heartbeat through his open palm. The weight of it would make Alana aware of each breath she took.

"I want to be all the way inside of you," he paused, struggling not to move, "fuck you the way you crave to be fucked." Her body was beautifully arched over his. "Feel my hands on your hair? On your throat? I'm not letting go until you come."

She gradually took more of him, but at a pace that made Julian open his mouth in a mute scream. He tightened his hold on her. Julian had to remove his hand from around her throat. He didn't want to. But he had to.

"Fuck," he whispered against her ear. "What are you doing to me?"

He looked up and saw she had her eyes closed. The expression on her face was a mesmerizing picture of ecstasy.

Julian started to move. He couldn't take his eyes away from her. The changing images on the screen were bathing her body in various shades of light and darkness, as if revealing the different facets of Alana. He wanted her body, her pleasure and her pain. He wanted Alana in all of her complexity.

She convulsed on top of him and he covered her mouth with his hand to muffle the moans escaping her lips. Julian's release followed hers and he had to press his face to the curve of Alana's neck to smother his own cries of pleasure.

• • •

Julian woke up.

It was still dark. He felt Alana's sleeping body beside him and, wrapping his arm around her waist, he brought her closer to him.

They had driven back to his place and it was past three in the morning when they had fallen asleep, exhausted, after they had subjected each other to several hours of pure visceral sex. No part of Alana's body had been left untouched by Julian and now, only a few short hours after the last time he had been inside of her, he wanted her again.

Alana had her back turned to him and, moving her hair out of the way, he brought his lips to the small area between her shoulder blades. He felt her steady breathing. Running his palm along the curve of her waist, he turned her to face him. It was too dark for Julian to be able to see and he used his touch to explore as much of her as he could. Rubbing the tips of his fingers along her ribcage, he thought she felt fragile. Too fragile. As if she would break under his hands. Not at all the type of woman he normally found himself interested in. However, the more he told himself that he shouldn't be attracted to Alana the more his desire for her grew. His fingers found the scar on her shoulder and he ran the tip of his tongue along the ragged line. To him her scar was beautiful.

Julian lifted himself over her and parted her legs with his knee. Letting his head hang forward, he took in her scent. Alana smelled like sex. He smelled like sex. The sheets and the pillows around them smelled like sex.

He shifted his body weight to his elbow, his torso meeting hers. It was the first time he felt her without a condom on and her body was reacting to his caressing strokes. Julian brought himself to her entrance, nudging inside of her. He knew he was playing with fire. Being careless. He took a deep breath, forcing himself to remain completely still. The tension was so great his whole frame started to tremble. Drops of sweat ran down the back of his neck. If she moved he was done for.

"Julian…" Alana's voice sounded hoarse and she whispered his name almost like a question.

"You feel so good," he said through clenched teeth. "So good."

She touched his face. For a short, meaningful, moment they didn't speak or move. In the darkness Julian could only feel and smell Alana. Nothing else. She raised her hips off the bed, just slightly, but enough for Julian to know he couldn't change what was about to happen. He entered her and then he stilled, using his own weight to press Alana down into the mattress. He didn't tell her why, but he wanted to capture that feeling—the first time her warmth, her slickness enfolded his flesh.

Alana inhaled sharply and Julian closed his arms around her. "Sore?" he asked, aware of the rough sex they had the evening before and throughout the night.

She nodded.

He brushed her hair away from her face and brushed his lips along her forehead. "I'll be gentle." He couldn't remember the last time he had said that to someone.

Julian started to move in and out of her and when Alana wrapped her legs around his waist, making him slide in deeper, he said her name almost as a plea. He rocked his hips, grinding his pelvis into hers, and the pressure of it made her dig her short nails into his back. Their kiss was languid and Alana caressed his tongue with hers until they were both moaning.

He broke the kiss. "Finish me off with your mouth." Julian crawled over her body, straddling her face.

As soon as her mouth closed around him and he hit the back of her throat, he tensed up with the pull of his orgasm. He reached down, closing his hand on her nape, and his breathing became more laborious. All he could do was hold on to her.

"Fuck…I'm coming…don't stop." As Alana swallowed him, Julian's torso bent forward and a loud sob escaped his chest.

Panting, he collapsed beside her. He felt her curl up and tuck her head in the crook of his arm and Julian kissed her hair. He needed to physically distance himself from Alana. He was still aroused, craving more stimulation.

He glanced at the clock on the night table and saw it was six-thirty in the morning. "Stay here," he said, getting up. "I'll be right back."

He got dressed in a pair of track pants and a sweater. Without turning on the lights, he made his way to the front door and put on his coat. He hoped she didn't leave while he was gone. He needed her to be there when he returned.

Not long after, Julian was back with hot coffee, a peppermint tea and a bagel in his hand. He was relieved to see that Alana was still in bed, under the covers, just as he had left her.

He opened the heavy window drapes to another cold, overcast winter morning. It was still dark enough that he needed to turn on the nightstand lamp.

"Wake up, Alana, I brought you something to eat." He sat on the edge of the bed, the mattress dipping under his weight. "We need to talk."

He watched her peek from under the covers and slowly sit up, pulling her knees close to her chest. "What time is it?" she asked with an apprehensive look.

Julian blinked a few times. He wasn't sure what he was seeing was real. "What the hell happened to your lips?"

She took her hand to her mouth, appearing confused. "What do you mean?"

Julian moved around the bed, closer to her and, taking a hold of her chin with his hand, turned her face toward the light. Her lips stained purple and red, it looked as if she had eaten wild berries. Her lower lip was especially bruised. Holding her face up, his eyes traveled down her elongated neck, and that's when he saw the marks.

He stood there, taking in the vision of her—naked, messy hair falling around her shoulders, waiting for his reaction with an anxious stare. Julian touched her swollen lower lip with the pad of his thumb. "Did I do this to you?" His voice was hushed, asking her a question he didn't need an answer for.

"Yes…does it look bad?"

"Uh-huh. Very."

"It doesn't hurt."

Julian let go of her chin and sat beside her, resting his elbows on his knees. "Seeing those marks on you, knowing I did that to you—"

"Is making you hard?" she asked, finishing his sentence.

He closed his eyes tightly, an expression of shame in his face. "Yes."

"Does it bother you?"

"I can't change what arouses me."

"I know."

He turned to look at her. She was staring at the rumpled bed covers, lost in thought. "Here, I brought you something to eat." He reached for the tea and bagel he had left on the nightstand.

"I'm not hungry."

"The last thing I saw you eat was ice cream," he stopped speaking, aware he was letting his frustration take over. "Please, Alana?" he continued, softening his voice. "Eat as we talk."

She took the food from his hand.

"Thank you," Julian said as he watched her take a small bite from the bagel.

They sat side by side, quietly, for a while.

"Yes," Alana said, looking at him with a weary expression.

He raised an eyebrow, not understanding what she meant.

"I'm on the pill," she clarified, sipping her tea. "And yes, I'm clean of STIs. You?"

"Same. To the STI part," he said, in a lighter tone.

"Isn't that what you wanted to talk about?"

"That was part of it." His eyes didn't leave her face. "The police think a woman's death is linked to the club. I want you to be careful."

She widened her eyes at his words. "I'm careful."

"Are you?" he asked, not bothering to hide his skepticism. "I'm a member of The Raven Room. I just did that to you," Julian paused, glancing at her neck and lips, "how do you know I'm not involved?"

"I don't."

"Is that all you're going to say?"

"I don't know what you want me to say."

"For reasons beyond my understanding, you won't tell me much about yourself, how you know Steven Thompson." He no longer sounded angry. He was speaking with a twinge of disappointment, his eyes lost on the floor between his feet. "There's a lot that goes on at The Raven Room. A lot that shouldn't happen. Promise me you'll never get into any sexual game that can put your life at risk. It doesn't matter if you trust the person you're with. Just don't do it. This includes Thompson." Julian faced her. "And me."

A heavy silence took root between them. "Alana?" Julian insisted.

"I promise."

He leaned closer and rested his forehead on hers.

"Julian, if I asked you to stop going to the club, would you do that?"

"Would you stop going? If I did?"

She wasn't fast to reply and when she did her voice was firm, but marked by sadness. "No."

"If it wasn't for the club we wouldn't be here."

Alana pulled back, just enough to face him and Julian lost himself in her haunted gaze. "The Raven Room gives everything. Takes everything. It will do the same to both of us."

Julian took her into his arms, close to his chest. Even though he would never say it, he knew she was right.

CHAPTER 13

"Where did you meet this one?"

Julian had accepted Peter and Grace's invitation for dinner because Grace had called him, excited about hosting, and he hadn't wanted to disappoint her. Weeks had gone by since his conversation with Peter at Top Notch Beefburgers, and every day since then, when he thought of what Peter was up to and the potential consequences of it, he caught himself closing his hand into a fist. Peter had said he was only seeing one other woman but Julian didn't believe him. There were probably more. Julian's major concern was that Peter's behavior would tear his family apart. He couldn't let that happen to Seth and Eli.

"At the club," he finally replied.

"Really?" Peter was taken aback by Julian's answer. "She doesn't look like the type."

Julian narrowed his eyes. Alana was chatting with Grace at the other end of the room and Peter was sitting across from him, staring at her over Julian's shoulder.

"What do you mean by that?"

Peter grinned, taking the cognac glass to his lips. He didn't take a sip, he lingered, continuing to stare at Alana. "She could have fooled me. Never thought she was a slutmuffin."

Peter's reaction to Alana made Julian uncomfortable and that surprised him. He had never had a problem sharing his lovers. Enthralled by the beauty of Alana's sexuality, Julian had taken pleasure in watching her at the club. Sure, he and Alana hadn't been lovers then and that might have been the reason why seeing her with another man hadn't bothered him as much as witnessing Peter's looks toward Alana. Now, he was fighting with himself not to act like a jealous lover. But he knew what he was feeling wasn't jealousy. It had a different nature. He was fighting the need to protect Alana from what he heard in Peter's voice, what he saw in his eyes.

"Shut your mouth."

"Man, fuck, are you falling for this girl?" Peter was extremely amused.

He raised an eyebrow. "Really? Is that the best you got?"

"I'm just surprised."

"By what?"

"That she's the girl who finally got you to feel something other than your hard-on," Peter said, chuckling. "She doesn't look like your type...at all," he continued, admiring her from his chair. "First, she looks like jailbait, even more than the other chick, what's her name?" Peter rubbed his forehead with his fingers. A large grin crossed his face. "Have to say, until her, I didn't know you had it in you, you know, an appetite for them young. And Alana looks...I don't know, kind? That's it. Kind," he paused, nodding to himself. "I like her. A lot. I'm happy you found her."

Julian wasn't sure how to respond. He regretted bringing Alana along. He had extended the dinner invitation to her because he had wanted to spend more time with her. He was also tired of having Peter and Grace setting him up on dates with women they believed would be a good match, hopefully leading to marriage and kids, things he had never wanted. He had thought that maybe them meeting Alana would put a stop to all of that.

"Well, thanks," Julian tried to smile. He knew he wasn't being successful at it. "I'm glad to hear she has your stamp of approval."

"How does her pussy feel?" Peter continued. "Does she give good head?"

Julian's detached façade started to crack. "Can we stop talking about her?" he asked, his eyes glaring.

"Wow, man, relax." Peter laughed at Julian. "She's the first woman you bring into my home. I'm curious, that's all."

In that moment he realized that was the reason why he had

never noticed Peter's misogyny. Since their university years, Julian hadn't introduced his friend to any of the women in his life. Looking back he wasn't sure why he hadn't. He had a tendency to compartmentalize.

Peter and Grace must have been shocked when he said he was bringing someone with him. They were, understandably, very curious about Alana. In their eyes she had to be different from the other women. His feelings toward her had to be unique. Julian hadn't thought about what inviting Alana would signify.

He cleared his throat. "I'm sorry, Pete. Too much shit in my head right now, that's all."

"That's cool, man."

They all moved into the main floor living room. The warmth coming from the wood-burning fireplace was pleasant; Julian stood by it and absorbed its warmth.

Grace sat comfortably across from them, near her husband. "I was telling Alana we could be interrupted, at any time, by two rambunctious kids." She gave a small laugh, enjoying her red wine.

"Jesus, they have endless energy. It's scary," Peter added.

"It's a good thing there are two of them. They can entertain each other," Julian said.

"Entertain?" Peter grimaced. "Man, it's obvious you don't have kids. More like, I just broke my toy. I'm going to go play with my brother's toy and break it too. Now both of us can cry."

Grace looked at her husband with an expression of outrage. "Neither Seth nor Eli have done that."

"Are you kidding me?" Peter turned to Alana. "My wife is in complete denial that our kids are just like every other kid out there. A fucking nightmare."

Alana chuckled, shaking her head. "I don't have that much experience dealing with babies so I can't say I know what you're talking about."

"Do you have siblings?" Grace asked, folding one of her legs under her body.

As soon as Julian heard Grace's question, he sharpened his

focus. He wanted to hear what Alana would say.

"I don't."

"I guess you and Julian can relate to each other, then," Grace continued.

For the first time since she and Grace had joined them, Alana glanced at Julian. With her hair in a loose side braid, wearing no make-up or jewelry, and dressed in a pair of black jeans and a plain, dark green sweater, she came across as approachable, a no-frills type of person. Julian imagined others always felt at ease around her.

Earlier, when she had removed her shoes at the door, he had noticed her socks had frogs on them. He caught himself smiling. He was starting to enjoy her quirks. The socks with the green frogs had been very fashionable of her. They perfectly matched the color of her sweater.

Julian wondered how Alana was feeling about Grace's curiosity. He hoped, since it wasn't him asking the questions, she would feel compelled to give all of them a glimpse of who she was. He had been trying to understand why it was becoming increasingly important for him to know more about her. Maybe they were growing more familiar and he was uncomfortable bringing someone into his home, over and over again, without even knowing her last name. But deep down Julian knew it went beyond that. She was keeping her identity a secret, unwilling to share anything that would allow him to find her if one day she suddenly disappeared.

At the same time, Alana had seen him at the club and had, afterwards, approached him at the coffee shop. It was clear she had wanted to speak with him. In reality, every time Julian sought her out she had agreed to spend time with him. Alana wanted him, but on her own terms. He had to decide if he could accept that.

"So tell us more about yourself," Grace asked Alana.

"To be honest, I don't have anything very exciting to share about myself. I live on the South side, I work at a bookstore, and I love to read. Mostly fantasy and sci-fi. And I volunteer."

Julian was simultaneously frustrated and impressed by how she handled herself. That had been the same information she had shared with him. Nothing more. Nothing less.

Grace, however, was starting to sympathize with Alana. "You're originally from Chicago?"

"Uh-huh."

That was something she had never shared with him before. That was a start. He wanted to join in and ask Alana several more questions but he decided it would be better to allow Grace and Peter to continue to drive the conversation.

"How did the two of you meet?" Grace directed the question to Alana, who then turned toward Julian. She wanted him to answer.

"At a club," he said without hesitation.

"Since when are you a night club type of guy?" Grace was being ruthless with all of her questions and if the situation had been different, Julian would have gently steered the conversation in a different direction, one where it didn't feel like he and Alana were being interrogated.

"On occasion."

Grace slowly shook her head. "Aren't you always full of surprises?"

From the corner of his eye he saw Alana smirking.

The conversation continued throughout the evening. Peter shared several stories of when he and Julian were in their early twenties, living in a dilapidated apartment in Pilsen, and all they cared about was going to bars and picking up women.

"This one over here always had girls throwing themselves at him," Peter said, scratching the stubble on his chin.

His friend's comment annoyed Julian. "That's not true."

"Don't deny it," Peter scowled at him. "He never had to try half as hard as the rest of us. And, unfortunately, girls went crazy for his I-don't-give-a-shit attitude."

This time Julian didn't say anything.

"I don't know if I believe that." Alana looked amused, something Julian had come to believe happened when she perceived the person speaking sounded like an imbecile. A few times already, Julian had been the target of that amused expression and he took pleasure in knowing she was now directing it at Peter.

"How long have you known Julian?" his friend asked.

She shrugged. "Maybe a month, a month and a half."

"See, sweetheart, I have known this man for almost twenty years. Believe me when I say he usually doesn't put his women first."

Peter's tone was lighthearted and when Alana spoke she was just as cheerful. "You're absolutely right, Peter. I don't know Julian as well as you do." She did not lose her smile. "Maybe no one does. He's very lucky to have you for a friend. A friend who warns the women he brings to dinner of his contempt for the opposite sex. You make sure I don't hold any illusions. I hope he thanks you for the favor."

"You're the first he has brought over," Peter said, winking at her.

"Oh really?" Alana raised an eyebrow. "In that case, I have to thank you."

Peter looked bemused. "Why?"

"Because, as you said, Julian never puts his women first. I can imagine the self-serving reasons why he invited me to join tonight."

"Oh, don't go hard on him. I think he has a soft spot for you," Peter paused, refilling his cognac glass, "and so do I."

The affable expression never left Alana's face. "Thank you, Peter."

"You're welcome, sweetheart. And you can call me Pete."

Julian glanced at Grace and saw she was trying to understand what was happening between her husband and Alana. Since the first day Julian had met her, he felt Grace was always pretending. She had wanted to be a lawyer because that was what her family had expected of her. She had dated a certain type of man because she had been told those were the men who would provide her with what she should need and want. She had married Peter because he fit the image of the ideal husband—a successful young doctor from a stable, wealthy family, who envisioned raising a family in a beautiful house with two cars parked in the garage.

Julian believed Grace genuinely always wanted to be a wife and a mother. But he couldn't tell if she was pretending not to see that her whole life was just one big ugly lie. Not a lie she told to others, but a lie she told to herself. Day after day. Year after year.

Regardless of her being aware of it or not, when Julian met her years ago, he had gravitated toward her because of it. He too pretended. Day after day. Year after year. He considered Peter his best friend, but if he had to stand beside one of them, he would stand by Grace.

"We're both very happy Julian introduced you to us." Julian heard Grace say. She was being her usual lovely self and he was thankful for her poise.

Peter had been wrong. Julian always put the women in his life first. He had remained silent because he didn't trust himself not to make a comment that would start an argument with Peter. His friend had been drinking all night and he suspected it wouldn't take much to set him off. Julian didn't want to upset Grace and Alana.

"And don't listen to my husband," Grace continued, looking at Alana. "He knows Julian is a great guy. He just loves giving him a hard time." She rested her hand on top of Peter's thigh. "It's been like this since the day I met them in university."

Peter nodded, wrapping his arm around his wife's shoulders. "She's right. And believe me, Julian loves giving me shit too. Speaking of university, what school did you go to?" he asked Alana.

She wasn't fast to respond, which made Julian think she wouldn't. When she finally spoke, her voice was low and her words carried some sadness. "I didn't continue after high school."

"Why not?"

Peter was not letting it go. Julian wanted her to answer but at the same time he didn't want her to think that Peter and Grace were asking her so many questions because he had put them up to it.

"In my family, education was never a priority," she said, matter-of-fact.

"Is your family from here?"

"Do you mean, were they immigrants?" Alana's question implied she understood what Peter was thinking. "Yes, they were."

Peter pressed. "From where?"

"Russia."

She had spoken about her family in the past tense and Julian wanted to know what had happened.

"I have always dreamed of visiting Russia. Have you ever been?" Grace was showing true interest, unaware she was again interrogating Alana. "Do you speak the language?"

"I have never been." She tucked a strand of hair behind her ear. "I used to speak it. Not anymore."

"Julian speaks Hungarian," Grace added with enthusiasm. "I'm sure you already knew that, though."

"I did. I have seen his book collection."

"Say something in your first language," Grace asked Julian, with a bright smile.

"I don't know—"

"C'mon, man," Peter jumped in. "You can say anything you want. It's not like any of us will understand."

Alana was now facing him and Julian's eyes searched her face. There was so much he wanted to ask her. So much he wanted to tell her.

Peter was right. They didn't understand Hungarian. So, instead, when he spoke he did so in Russian. He wasn't fluent and he hadn't said a word in that language in a very long time, but he believed he would be able to articulate what he wanted to say. *'Thank you for joining me tonight.'*

As soon as he had started to speak, Julian knew Alana could understand him. Nothing on her body changed. She remained comfortably seated, her body leaning toward the oversized couch pillows. But her eyes reacted to his words. Her wide gaze, full of longing, drew him in. For the first time since he met her, it was like he was looking at the real Alana, the person he saw at the club. No lies. No hidden truths. No questions left unanswered. No persistent doubts. Just the two of them. And his reaction to her was the same—Julian felt connected.

"Do you mind translating that into English?" Peter asked.

Julian didn't want to answer and didn't want to be there. He wished he could take hold of Alana's hand and walk out. "I just said how tired I was of the cold and wish it was summer."

"Really?" Peter sounded disappointed. "We were hoping you would say something dirty."

"Sorry to disappoint you," he managed to say. "Anyway, it's almost nine o'clock. Alana and I should probably leave."

"Are you sure? You guys are more than welcome to stay longer." Grace sounded disappointed.

"Thank you but I still have to do some work this evening. You know how it goes, I spend one hour with a patient and then I have to spend two hours filling out paperwork. I'm also teaching tomorrow."

After they thanked Grace and Peter for the dinner and the enjoyable evening, Julian drove them back downtown. Alana was quiet during the whole drive and Julian decided it was best not to press her for answers. He didn't feel like talking himself. Socializing always drained him, leaving him with the need to just be alone with his thoughts. All he wanted was to be home, in his bed with Alana.

They were nearing North Michigan Avenue and East Ontario Street when she spoke. "Stop the car. I'm taking off from here."

Her request caught him off guard. "What?"

"I want you to stop the car so I can leave. I'm not going to your place tonight."

"If you tell me where you live, I'll drive you to your doorstep. Otherwise you're coming with me."

"Julian, stop the car."

"Are you going to tell me where you live?"

She didn't reply.

"Are you?"

She continued not to answer him. Julian held the steering wheel more firmly. If he wasn't wearing gloves she would have seen his knuckles turn white. "Alana, I'm going to ask you for the last time, where do you live?"

He looked at her but she was silent, not taking her eyes off the road. They were stopped at a red light and the brightness from the storefronts invaded the inside of the car. He saw her trying to open her passenger door. His car's safety mechanism automatically locked all four doors after a few seconds of driving. Realizing she wasn't going to be able to simply walk away, Alana released the door handle.

"You're coming with me." His voice was firm, not leaving room for discussion.

"Let me out of the car," she repeated, sounding calm. Julian knew she was forcing herself not to scream at him.

"No. I told you. You either give me your address or you're coming with me."

Alana remained silent. She didn't turn to face him. Instead, she sat with her back very straight, her hands folded on her lap. Her face was expressionless but she was upset.

Julian continued to drive toward his building and parked the car in the underground garage. He had expected Alana to storm out but she followed him, without saying a word, as he took the elevator to his floor. As soon as he entered his condo, he made his way to his bedroom. Starting to undress, Julian tried to calm down.

"I'm fucking livid," Alana said, joining him in the bedroom. Her voiced sounded low and strained.

"Good. So am I."

Julian continued to move around, opening and closing drawers. There was nothing he needed but he didn't want to look at her. No longer wearing his shirt, he had unbuckled his belt, leaving it loose around his waist.

"How dare you not let me leave your car! And bring me here!"

"I offered to drop you off at your place. You're here because you chose to be." With his back to her, his hands resting on the dresser, he let his head hang forward. He took a deep breath.

"I'm out of here," Alana said.

"No, you're not."

"Are you going to stop me?"

"I don't have to. We both know you want to be here. Otherwise you would have left by now."

"I don't want you to touch me."

Julian turned, locking eyes with her. "I'll be doing much more than just touching you, Alana."

They stared each other down. That fight wouldn't have any winners.

"Don't do this."

"Do what?" he asked, louder than he would have wanted.

His oversized bedroom now felt small. Claustrophobic. Not enough space to contain both of them.

"Punish me, hurt me, humiliate me. All because I'm not giving you what you want."

"I don't know what you're talking about."

"Yes you do. A lot happened tonight at your friend's place."

Julian moved toward her. "Again, I don't know what you're talking about." He stopped, his naked chest touching her body. Alana didn't flinch. She raised her eyes to him and when she spoke, her voice proved she wasn't intimidated.

"Julian, you want me to give you personal information that I don't want to share with you." She tilted her head back to better see his face. "You want me to give to you what you lost a long time ago. I'm not able to do that."

He wasn't sure what she meant but he wasn't going to ask her to explain it to him. There were other things he needed to know. "Is Thompson the reason why you're not telling me more about yourself?"

"Of course not."

"So your strange behavior has nothing to do with him?"

"No, it doesn't."

Julian wanted to believe her but knew that, with Alana, nothing was as it appeared to be.

"Why did you say you were unable to give me what I lost a long time ago?" he asked, making it clear he wasn't ready to drop the subject. "What did you mean by that?"

"I was talking about her."

"Who?"

"You know who."

Julian ran his fingers through his hair and turned away from Alana. He sat on the reading chair by the window.

"She's gone. You have to let her go. No woman is able to give her back to you."

"You have no idea what you're talking about. No idea."

"Sometimes you speak Russian in your sleep, when you dream of her. Earlier you spoke Russian to me. I'm not her, Julian."

He laughed but his face was distorted by hostility. "I loved her. She'll always have a part of me I can't give to anyone else. You?" he said with contempt. "You're just a woman I fuck. You've done a good job at keeping me interested, maybe because you're so full of secrets, but that's it. I'll never think you can give her back to me. Or that you're her," he continued, reveling in the bitterness his words carried. "Never, Alana."

She approached him. She did it slowly, with determination and grace, never taking her somber eyes away from his. She rested her hand on his shoulder and brought her face close to his. Her lips were right by his ear and her breath caressed the side of his neck.

"You can do better than this."

He couldn't see her face but he heard the tone of amusement in her voice.

Sitting completely still, Julian continued to stare straight ahead. He licked his dry lips. He was afraid of what he might do if he moved any muscle in his body.

"Here's the deal, Alana," he whispered, as if there were other people in the room and he wanted only her to hear his words. "You have a choice. You leave now and you leave for good. Or you stay and you do exactly what I tell you to do."

She stayed put. Julian knew what her choice was. "Go stand in the middle of the room."

He watched her move away from him and stop where he told her to. She turned around, facing him. "Start undressing. Do it slowly…don't take your eyes off me."

There was no hesitation on her part. Alana started by removing her green sweater. She continued by unclasping her bra, throwing it on the floor, beside the discarded sweater.

"Slower," he said, almost as a warning.

She unbuttoned her jeans, unzipped them. She did it slowly. Very slowly.

Her eyes were on him.

She rotated her waist, in a gentle motion, to make it easier to slide the jeans over her hips. She bent down, removing them along with her socks.

Alana didn't look away from him.

Julian's gaze lingered on her black cotton panties with a tiny hot pink bow.

Standing up straight, she ran her fingers over the top edge of her panties. She removed them with unhurried movements. Alana stood, naked, in the middle of the bedroom.

He watched her. She was waiting for him to tell her what to do next.

"Undo your braid. I want your hair loose."

Throwing the hair tie on the floor, she started to unfasten her hair. For a short second, she lowered her eyes.

"Eyes on me."

She was quick to follow his order. Running her fingers through her hair, she let it fall over her shoulders. Her hair was long enough to drape over her breasts but Julian could see her erect nipples peeking through it.

"Get on your hands and knees." His voice didn't lose its smooth quality, even when he was being authoritative. "Crawl to me," he continued, when he saw her on the floor. "That's it...keep your eyes on me."

Alana came to him, unhurriedly, like she had decided to make him wait for her. With her hair falling forward, around her face, her body moved in a fluid curve, swaying side to side. She was doing exactly what Julian wanted of her but she wasn't allowing him to demean her. She was beautiful. But more than that, there was a strength to her that made her look powerful. Julian smiled with admiration.

Alana was on her hands and knees, between his opened legs, looking up at him.

Aware of the distinctive silence unfolding between them, Julian didn't move. He stared down at her for several, long minutes. Without warning, he leaned forward and, as he slid two of his fingers inside of her, a small whimper escaped her lips.

"You're wet." Julian had his face in her hair. "You're enjoying this, aren't you? It's turning you on." He closed his eyes, focusing on the arousing sensation of moving his fingers in and out of her. "Tell me, Alana, are you my slut? Huh? Are you my little slut?"

Trying to increase the pleasure he was giving her, she spread her knees further apart. He felt her respond to his question by nodding her head.

"I want to hear you say it."

"Yes….yes," she whispered, pressing her face against his cheek. "I'm your slut."

As soon as she spoke, he removed his fingers from inside of her. He sat back on the chair and brought to his face the hand he had caressed her with. Julian inhaled her scent. "You smell so fucking good, Alana. I love it." He didn't hurry. He continued to sit back and admire her on her hands and knees at his feet.

"Take my belt off my jeans and give it to me."

He observed her as she pulled the belt from around his waist. Before she passed him the belt she met his stare. Her dilated pupils engulfed the color of her eyes and he felt himself drowning in their darkness.

"Reach inside of my jeans and grab my cock," he said, taking charge again. "Suck it."

As soon as she took him into her mouth, his body relaxed against the chair. His breath escaped through his clenched teeth. "That's it…the way I like it…deep in your sweet mouth."

Julian had folded his black leather belt and held it, by both ends. He tenderly caressed her naked back with it.

With his free hand, he took hold of her hair and pulled her head back. "That's enough. Crawl to the bed." He was trying to steady his breathing. "Get on the bed and stay on your hands and knees, right on the edge of it. I want you facing the headboard."

As soon as Alana was on the bed, Julian left the chair and approached her. Standing behind her, she couldn't see him and he used that to his advantage. He wanted to keep her guessing. Julian ran his hands over her lower body, enjoying the smoothness of her skin. With no indication of the anger still surging through his body, his touch was caring. Julian didn't want to stop touching her but he forced himself to.

He had other plans for Alana.

Taking a step back, he lifted his arm, and the first lash of his belt made her scream. Before she could scurry away from him, he caught her ankle and pulled her back toward him. "I'm going to whip you until my arm gets tired. You can't move. And no noise. Do you understand?"

She didn't answer him and he heard her panting. Julian's whole body hurt with the sight of her—on her hands and knees on his bed, completely naked, with a bright red mark left by the first lash of his belt on her pale skin.

"Until I get tired of it. No moving and no noise. Do you understand?" He repeated.

She remained silent.

"Answer me, Alana. Do you understand?"

Still no response from her.

"Alana?" He sounded ominous.

"Yes. I understand," she said, her voice cracking.

"Good."

Unceremoniously he positioned her where he wanted and without any hesitation he resumed whipping her. The loud sound of the belt touching her skin reverberated through the room. Julian wasn't counting the lashes but after a few minutes of it, he felt the sweat dripping down his back and chest. Alana flinched every time the belt touched her skin but she didn't move or try to get away from him again. With her face buried into the comforter, he knew she was crying but her screams were almost completely muffled by the thick fabric.

His erection, free from his jeans, stood imposing, craving release. Julian could hear the loud pumping of the blood through his body. He felt the stiff leather digging into the skin of his closed fist; tasted the blood that came from biting too hard into his lower lip. Julian was close to losing himself in it—the rush, the pleasure of causing pain to a woman.

Taking hold of the little self-control he had left, Julian dropped the belt on the floor. Both he and Alana were gasping for air.

He removed his jeans and, getting closer to her, he was careful not to touch where the bruises were already forming. As when his belt met her flesh, he entered her with a force that made her cry out. He reacted by shouting her name. Her arousal made it easier for him to move inside of her and, bringing his arm around her waist, he touched her. She whimpered.

"Do you like my fingers on you?"

"Yes!" she shouted.

"Come for me, Alana. Be my good slut."

She pressed her body into his, crying and breathing through her mouth.

"Come for me," he ordered, taking large gulps of air. "I want to feel it."

She cried out his name and Julian closed his eyes, his face distorted by the sensation paining him. "I'm going to come so deep in you. So fucking deep. You'll know you belong to me."

She clenched around him and all Julian could do was to let it happen. He felt himself reaching orgasm, the force of it driving his hips to slam against her. From within his trance, Julian was able to pick up on the animalistic sounds that he and Alana were making. The lascivious smell of their perspiring bodies; the heat of her flushed skin against his palms; the taste of closing his lips on her perspiring back; the scraping of his teeth along her flesh; the sight of the numerous, overlapping crimson welts on her skin.

A complete instinctual experience that satisfied all of his senses.

He pulled out of her and, not trusting his legs to hold him up, he sank to the floor. Facing the bedroom windows from his spot by the bed, he stared at the pool of black that was the Chicago River at that time of night.

Julian lost track of time.

He heard the ruffling of the covers and Alana getting up. He couldn't see her from where he was and he couldn't move. He was surprised when he realized she was getting dressed. In the silent bedroom, he was acutely aware of her movements. Fully dressed, she stood in front of him.

Julian lifted his eyes to her and all he could think, at that moment, was how enticing she looked with her untamed hair and flushed complexion.

"Now, Julian, I'm leaving." She gave him a smile that carried no happiness. "And I'm leaving for good."

She turned around and walked out.

Chapter 14

Meredith glanced at her watch. She and Julian had decided to meet during his short break. He was leaving the hospital for the day to start a full afternoon of teaching.

She had visited Hazel a few days ago and she had been simultaneously disappointed and surprised when she saw herself faced with the reality of the old woman's mental state. For Hazel, her son Julian was still a boy and not the complete stranger who visited her almost every day. Meredith had hoped Hazel would be able to tell her more about Julian's childhood and teenage years, but besides repeating over and over again "rather her than him," all she was able to gather through their conversation was how much Hazel loved her adopted son.

Meredith had walked out from the small house in Bridgeport with more questions than when she had when she walked in. She had contemplated not telling Julian about her visit to Hazel but her caregiver would more than likely tell him, so Meredith had decided it would be best if she told him herself.

"Sorry I'm late," Julian said, sitting across from her. He was close to panting.

When he passed her a coffee, she smirked. This was the first time they were seeing each other after the night at The Raven Room. "Trying to bribe me to be your friend again?"

"If I was I wouldn't have bought you coffee. I know you're easy but not that easy."

Meredith scowled at him but quickly burst out in a loud laugh. "You compliment me too much." She noticed that he didn't laugh with her. He merely smiled, and it was not one of his usual light-up-the-room smiles. Something was wrong.

They were sitting in the food court inside the hospital and because it was lunchtime all the tables around them were full. Besides Julian, who had his black coat on and his usual attire of slacks and dress shirt, most people were wearing scrubs. Meredith noticed she was the only female who had makeup on and was not wearing her hair in a bun or in a ponytail.

"I went to visit Hazel," she said, sitting up straighter. She braced herself for an argument.

"Hazel?" he asked, confused. "My Hazel?"

"Yes. I brought her flowers."

Meredith waited for him to speak. When he didn't, she swallowed a large gulp of her coffee. "Are you upset?"

He leaned back, staring at her. "Why?"

"Why did I go?"

He nodded. "And why didn't you tell me?"

Julian wasn't angry. He sounded sad.

"After that one time I was there with you I kept thinking about her all alone in that house and that I had told her I would visit her soon but I never did," Meredith started to say. "And then you and I weren't really talking and I kind of felt bad about how I handled things that night. I did it to make myself feel better, I guess." As the lies poured out of her mouth Meredith wanted to cover her face in shame. Julian was a good time, best sex she ever had, an in to The Raven Room, the club member she was writing about—he had always been a means to an end. But now, sitting across from him, that was not all he was to her. She started to feel guilty. "I'm sorry," she said, unable to face him. She was apologizing for way more than just visiting Hazel but he didn't know that. "I'm sorry I didn't tell you. I should have."

"Just give me the heads-up next time, okay?" he asked, still not angry. "She's not well and she gets distraught over the smallest things. Was she happy to see you?"

"She was super chatty." Meredith smiled, playing with the paper sleeve of her coffee cup. "She loves you beyond belief. And she can't wait for the new fish. A blue one, preferably."

Julian chuckled. "It's amazing, the things she does and doesn't remember."

She raised her eyes to him. "Does this mean we're cool?"

"We'll always be cool, Meredith."

The thought that he wouldn't feel the same way if he found out how she was using him made Meredith feel wretched.

After parting ways, she walked to the subway station on East Chicago Avenue and North State Street. She took the red line south to 79th Street. With thick flurries falling on her hair and face, Meredith covered the three blocks as fast as she could. Her destination was an address given to her by Colton.

Knocking on the front door of a small brick house, she waited. Bungalow style homes lined up the street and besides the piles of dirty snow, the area couldn't have been cleaner. But it was still very different from where she had grown up and that, to Meredith's dismay, made her feel on edge.

She heard the sound of the door unlocking and a head peeked out from the inside.

"Hi, I'm looking for Samantha. I called. She's expecting me. I'm Meredith Dalton."

The woman opened the door and let her in. "I'm Sam."

"Thank you for agreeing to speak to me," Meredith stood by the entrance. She didn't know what to do. "Should I take off my shoes?" she asked, seeing how organized the house looked. Compared to it her apartment was a pigsty.

"Yeah, just leave them by the door."

"I know I've said this to you before but I'm really sorry about what happened to Lena." Meredith was now sitting at a large dining room table, speaking about the woman who had been found dead the day Pam had given her the folder on Julian. "How long did you guys know each other?" Meredith continued.

Samantha was sitting at the opposite end and she gave Meredith a blank stare. "We met at work. We cleaned apartment buildings together. After she quit she stayed in contact. All her family was back in Moldova and she didn't have many friends. She was kind of shy, you know? And too pretty for her own good."

"Why do you say that?"

"She started prostituting herself."

Meredith's hands were folded on the table and her palms started to get sweaty. "On the streets, you mean?"

"Online."

"An escort service?"

"Ruby's Playground. I think it's a website." Samantha reached for a pack of cigarettes. When she offered Meredith one, she gladly took it.

"One of those men killed her. I have no doubts," Samantha added.

"She died of a drug overdose."

That made the other woman angry. "Believe me, that girl didn't do drugs. She was clean. Did they find drugs at her place?"

"I don't think so."

"See? I'm telling you. It doesn't add up."

"Did she ever mention anything about the men she met through Ruby's Playground?"

"She knew I didn't approve so she kept that stuff to herself."

"How about a club? Did she ever say anything about a club? Or going to a club?"

Samantha frowned. "I don't remember. I don't think so."

"When the autopsy results came back it showed that she had sex not long before she died. I know that you said she was prostituting herself, but did she have a boyfriend? Was she seeing anyone?"

"She never mentioned anyone to me." Samantha leaned forward, her elbows on the table. There was conviction in her stance. "Whoever killed Lena took her necklace."

"Sorry?"

"She always wore a gold necklace with a small cross. She had it on the last time I saw her. That was the day before she died. I asked the police for it but they had no idea because it hadn't been on her when they found her."

Their voices were the only sound in the otherwise silent house. There was not even the sound of a clock ticking or the distant noise of a car driving by outside. It was only mid-afternoon but, with the lack of sun, a grey cast came through the window and hit the white walls and beige carpet. It made Meredith want to turn on the lights. The red glow of their burning cigarettes stood out in the shadows.

"The police don't give a shit." Samantha said. "Lena was an illegal. A girl with no money, no family. Who's going to fight for her? I'm a black woman in Chatham, trying to keep my kids out of trouble. I can't take on another fight."

"I told you on the phone, I'm writing an article that will make people want to know what happened to Lena, who killed her. I'll dig as deep as I have to for that to happen." Meredith's eyes bore into Samantha. "I promise you."

Chapter 15

It was well past midnight and Meredith stood on the second floor of The Raven Room.

She still found it astonishing that the club was in the basement of a large, old Chinatown building. At the street level it was divided into three large businesses—two restaurants and a food market. Over the years she had walked past those storefronts several times and not even in her wildest dreams could she have imagined a place like The Raven Room existed right below the dollar sunglasses and hanging roasted ducks.

Turning around, Meredith saw Julian sitting by himself. When she had decided to go watch a scene in the dungeon he hadn't joined her. After what had happened the last time they had been at the club, she was surprised Julian was letting her walk around without him right by her side. They made eye contact and, in his smile toward her, she saw the worry that appeared to be consuming all of his thoughts. She walked up to him and sat on his lap.

"How was the dungeon?" he asked, wrapping his arm around her waist.

"Interesting. There was this woman hanging from the ceiling by chains, cuffs around her wrists. The guy was using spiked vampire gloves on her."

"Nice."

She raised an eyebrow at his comment. "Have you ever done anything like that?"

"I have but not here."

"Why not?"

"It's something that feels very intimate. I wouldn't do it in front of an audience."

Meredith ran her fingers through his hair. "Is that one of the reasons why I've never seen you fuck anyone around here?"

"In the beginning, when I started coming to the club, I was with more women than I'll ever care to admit. It was fun then." Julian tilted his head back, toward her hand. "But the novelty of it wore off."

"I can see how that might happen," Meredith said, noticing how worn-out he looked. "BDSM fascinates me."

"Tell me," he urged her to continue.

"I think BDSM has become a catchall phrase for many different behaviors. Everywhere I turn there's someone telling me what BDSM is and isn't. What it should and shouldn't be about."

"What's BDSM for you? What do you want it to be?"

"Hmm...good question. I don't think anyone ever asked me that..." she paused, staring at his heavy lidded eyes. "For me, it is a medium," she continued, speaking while trying to articulate her thoughts. "A medium through which people communicate with each other."

"Then that's what BDSM is and should be. It doesn't matter what someone else might think. Unless you're planning on using BDSM to communicate with them."

She laughed. "Yeah, good point. And for you? What's BDSM to you?"

Julian had his eyes closed and because his body had relaxed under her, Meredith's own body was melding into his. "BDSM means nothing to me. It's an empty four-letter term. I can't say that I enjoy it or I don't. I'm indifferent. I don't feel anything. That's why I don't scene anymore."

"But I know you get off on being dominant."

"I wouldn't call it that."

"What would you call it, then?"

He lifted his eyes to her and the sorrow and regret she saw in them made it hard for her to continue looking at him. "You don't want to tell me, do you?"

"No."

"Why?"

"I'm not a good man, Meredith. I just do a good job at hiding it."

"Are you referring to your need to be in control?"

"It's because of who I am that I need to be in control."

"I don't understand—"

"Some things are not meant to be understood," he whispered, not letting her finish.

Meredith didn't know what Julian was talking about but she went with it. There had been occasions when the sex between them had been intense, if not downright punishing, but she had never felt threatened. He had always made her feel safe. That was the reason why she was able to fully let go with Julian. She trusted him. "Does it only happen with women?"

"It happens in the dynamic of sexual relationships. Since I'm attracted to women, yes, it only happens with women."

Meredith continued to sit on his lap, running her fingers through his hair in slow movements. She felt the warmth of his hand over her hip bone, saw the glow of the red lighting of the club on his face, heard the soft noises of pleasure coming from all different directions, smelled the sensual and mellow scent that defined The Raven Room. "What are you afraid of?" she asked.

"Myself."

She swallowed hard. She needed to work past the knot in her throat. There was something utterly sad about Julian and if she weren't careful, it would bring her to tears at the most inopportune moments. "What would happen if you lost control?"

"You would see who I really am."

"Would that really be such a bad thing?" she said, trying to sound cheerful but failing. Instead she sounded bitter. "I'm tough as nails. I can handle you."

"You would hate me."

"No I wouldn't."

"Trust me on this. You're self-centered but you're not cruel. You deserve the best I can give."

Meredith studied him for a while. Julian had never before criticized her, and his belief that she was self-centered caught her by surprise. Pam also believed she was self-centered and the knowledge that both saw her as such upset her. Suddenly, Meredith didn't feel like being there anymore. She felt engulfed by the music, the scents, the naked bodies and the moans of pleasure. She felt herself sinking deeper into a reality she couldn't yet fully fathom.

"Do you want to leave?" she asked, rubbing her hand along her sweaty neck. "I won't be sucking any cock tonight."

Maybe genuinely unaware of her discomfort, or simply deciding to ignore it, he gave her a lazy smile. "You don't see anyone you want?"

Meredith allowed her chest to rise and fall a couple of times. With each breath, she regained her composure. "I spotted a hot redhead on my way back from the dungeon," she said, sounding like her buoyant self again. "We've seen her here before."

"So why not try her? She might be game."

"Believe me, I would totally do her but...look, that's her." Meredith glanced at the entrance of the room. "She's hot, right?"

Julian didn't answer but Meredith saw him following the woman with his gaze. She wasn't sure if she was his type, she would have guessed no, but the truth was she wasn't exactly sure what it was about a woman that attracted Julian. The redhead was with an older man and they approached a couple that had been sitting there longer than Meredith and Julian had. She couldn't hear them but it was clear to her the man was introducing the redhead to them.

Meredith liked the dark green dress the woman was wearing. She had picked the perfect shoes to go with it—a pair of black leather high heel boots, matched with sheer black nylons. The shade of her outfit enhanced the color of her hair, which had the perfect I–just-rolled-out-of-bed look to it. The woman was hot but her hair was in a different league. Her hair was gorgeous.

"Fuck, I would kill to have hair like that," Meredith said, more to herself than to Julian. She glanced at him. All his attention was on the woman and even though the expression on his face was hard to read, he didn't look happy.

"Do you know her?"

Julian didn't respond.

Meredith watched the group of four and she got the impression the silver-headed man, the one who had walked into the room with the woman, was the one calling the shots between the two of them.

"I think she's the silver fox's mistress or he's paying her to be here....or maybe both."

At that point the redhead dropped to her knees, opened the slacks of the other man she had just been introduced to, and took him into her mouth. The two men and the other woman continued to talk as if nothing was going on. The woman on the floor was invisible to them.

"Okay...didn't see that one coming," Meredith said with awe. "This place never ceases to amaze me."

Julian remained silent. Meredith felt the muscles in his body tightening up and that made her more interested in watching Julian's reaction to what was unfolding in front of them than the act itself. The hand that had been previously resting on her hip bone was now tense and Julian's fingers dug deep into her flesh. Exhaling through her mouth to help her deal with the pain without complaining out loud, she wondered if Julian was aware of his own strength or even of what he was doing. She slid her fingers under his and tried to ease Julian's grip on her. Realizing he was bruising her, he let Meredith hold his hand instead.

The redhead didn't pleasure the man to orgasm. A couple of minutes after she had begun, he gave her a gentle tap on the side of her head as a sign he was done. Without hesitation and quite gracefully, Meredith thought, she tucked him back inside of his slacks and returned to her feet. She and the older man she had entered the room with spoke to each other as if she hadn't just been on her knees. He said something that made her laugh and she turned her head, looking into the area of the room where Meredith and Julian were sitting. The smile left her face. She was looking straight at Julian. Meredith glanced at Julian and the look on his face made her swallow hard. Meredith didn't see rage. She saw heartache and, more obvious than that, the anticipation in his eyes. Like all he wanted was for the woman across the room to come to him.

Instead, the redhead turned around and left. Meredith could see that the man she was with was surprised by her behavior. Before he turned to follow her, he took a good look at both Meredith and Julian.

Pushing her off his lap, Julian got up. Instinctively, Meredith stood in front of him. "What are you doing?" He intended to follow the woman. "It's time for us to leave," she said seeing the hostile stare the other man shot toward Julian.

"Julian? Let's go." Meredith didn't move until she was certain he had heard her. She placed her hand on the middle of his chest and that caught his attention. He met her anxious gaze. "It's time for us to leave."

In less than five minutes they were out of the club and inside the car they had driven to The Raven Room. Meredith was relieved they hadn't run into the man or the redhead on their way out. She didn't want to find out what would have happened if they had.

It had started to snow again and the weather was not doing anything to help improve her mood. The night was turning out to be a debacle and she felt strung out.

"Where are we going?" she asked.

"To a parking lot near Millennium Park. We can take a cab from there. I'll drop you off at home first and then I'll continue to my place."

"I don't feel like being by myself. You're coming to my place. My roommate is away this week and tomorrow is Sunday."

"Thank you, but—"

"Julian, come over, we can shoot the shit over a couple of drinks. That's it." Her eyes were on the snow-covered road. "I meant it when I said I wasn't going to suck cock tonight."

She was relieved when he didn't try to argue with her. Because of the weather it took them a long time to get to the parking lot and flag down a cab. It was past two in the morning when they entered her apartment.

Kicking off her high heels and dropping her jacket on a chair, she turned on the lamp by the couch. "Make yourself comfortable."

"How many times have I been here before?" Julian asked, also taking off his shoes and throwing his coat on top of hers.

She smiled, lighting the Nag Champa incense. "Once."

"That's what I thought. I also remember your bedroom being the size of my closet."

"Wow, I'm impressed with your memory."

"What can I say, it was a memorable experience," he teased her.

"Red wine or beer? That's all I have." She stood by the kitchen, holding a bottle of wine in one hand and two beers in the other.

"Wine, please."

"Good choice."

She walked back into the living room with the bottle and two glasses. She joined Julian on the small couch.

"Oh, there's something missing," Meredith said, jumping off the couch and picking a record from a pile of vinyl albums. "Nina Simone okay with you?"

"Absolutely. Can't go wrong with her."

She looked at him over her shoulder and winked. "I knew you had good taste when it comes to women."

As the rich and smooth voice of Nina Simone came to life, just loud enough to fill up the silence inside of the apartment, Meredith lit some incense before she returned to the couch and sat facing Julian. Resting his feet on a small stool by the coffee table, he had rolled up the sleeves of his dress shirt, revealing his tattooed arm. The first time she had seen the striking artwork she had been simultaneously mesmerized and taken aback by it. Julian didn't look like the type of man who would mark his body so permanently and with a statement that evoked such curiosity. Contrasting his timeless, elegant style, the vision of his tattoo was jarring. Without a doubt it made him more compelling and Meredith was sure most people who saw it would assume, accurately, that there was a hidden side to Julian. The centerpiece of the tattoo was a raven. It went from right above his wrist and wrapped around his arm, ending at his shoulder. The rest of it, bringing the whole sleeve together, was a realistic and detailed work of shading. It was beautifully done. Every time she had asked him about his reasons for choosing to cover his whole arm with the tattoo of a bird, he had shrugged it off. He had told her it had been his attempt to cover up some street tattoos he had gotten when he was younger. Meredith hadn't been fully convinced but she hadn't pressed further. It wasn't something he liked to discuss and with Julian she would be wise to pick her battles.

"I like your place," he said, looking around. "It's homey."

Meredith glanced at the coffee table, seeing the forgotten magazines, piles of books, bottles of nail polish, pens, candles, an overflowing ashtray and a half-empty box of chocolates. "And messy?"

He grinned. "Yes, and messy."

They enjoyed their wine as they listened to Nina Simone's nostalgic sound. The smoke of the burning incense was floating toward them and Meredith felt herself relax. She loved the smell of it. "Who's the redhead?"

He looked at her like he didn't know to whom she was referring.

"The woman at the club tonight."

"Her name is Alana. And she's not a redhead. She's a blonde."

"No, she's a redhead. But if you want to think she's a blonde, please go right ahead," she replied with a shake of her head. "Alana…fucking amazing hair."

Julian had never spoken to Meredith about another female in his life and that made the redhead important. She wasn't just another woman.

"When you texted me a while back giving me the heads-up you had had unprotected sex, was she the one?"

Julian nodded.

"Okay, so you guys are sleeping together. She didn't look very happy with you earlier. What happened?" she continued. "The guy she was with tonight gave me the creeps."

"That's Thompson."

"Who?" Meredith frowned, resting her feet on the coffee table, beside Julian's. "Who's Thompson?"

"Steven Thompson."

"Holy shit, my dad and stepmom were telling me about him. He goes to The Raven Room? And Alana knows him?"

"You know the answer to both of those questions. You were there. You saw it with your own eyes. She was with him the first night I saw her."

"What is he to her? How do they know each other?"

"She won't tell me. But she's afraid of him. That I am sure of."

"You're sleeping with Thompson's girl and now he knows you and me."

"Why are you saying he knows us?"

"Are you kidding me? Did you see how he looked at us after Alana stormed out?"

"How did he look at us?"

"Like we're on his shit list. You, especially."

Julian rubbed his temples. He looked concerned.

"You didn't answer my question, though. What happened between you and Alana?"

"We got into an argument."

"Details?"

Julian turned to look at her. His expression was inscrutable. Holding the wine glass between her hands, she continued to stare at him. She wasn't ready to let it go.

"Don't, Meredith."

She didn't care if they got into a fight but, at that point, dealing with Julian's brooding mood felt like more than she could handle. Antagonizing him never got her anywhere. She knew better ways of working around his temperament.

"I need a cigarette," she finally said, grabbing the pack on top of the coffee table. He didn't like when she smoked but, at that moment, she didn't care.

"Can I please have one?"

She thought she must have heard him wrong. "What?"

"Can I please have one, too?"

"Since when do you smoke?"

"Meredith, can you just pass me one?"

After lighting hers she passed him a cigarette and the lighter. They smoked in silence.

"I respect you not wanting to tell me what happened between you and Alana." Meredith's voice was firm. "But don't bully me into it. It's abusive and I don't appreciate it."

"I'm sorry. But you can be so difficult…."

"Now it's my fault?"

"No, that's not what I meant. I'm sorry, okay?" He sounded defeated and his eyes appeared to be pleading with her.

"Don't do it again," she said, not dropping the hint of coldness from her words. When it came to push and shove Julian would always revert back to being domineering. She just had to remember to never stop being difficult. "What happened after your fight?"

"Tonight was the first time I saw her since then."

"You have been going to the club every chance you get, hoping to run into her there, haven't you?" Meredith was staring at him but now he was not willing to face her. She refilled their wine glasses.

"She had asked me before not to approach her at The Raven Room so it's not that I was going to talk to her."

"You almost did tonight."

Julian rested his lit cigarette in the ashtray and stood up. "Almost. I'm glad I didn't, though. After our argument that would be the stupidest thing I could do."

"What do you know about her?"

He turned over the vinyl record. "Really nothing."

"What do you mean nothing?"

"I saw her at the club the first time I took you and then I ran into her at a coffee shop. We have hung out since then but she won't tell me much about herself."

Meredith hadn't even noticed the music had stopped. She watched him gently lower the needle onto the record. "What does she know about you?"

Her question made Julian pause. "Almost nothing."

"That's not surprising."

"What's that supposed to mean?"

"You haven't willingly told me anything about yourself."

"What do you want to know?"

"I don't know, everything. What was your childhood like? How did you end up being adopted by Hazel?"

He returned to the couch and Nina Simone's voice came to life again. Julian was silent for so long she didn't think he would answer.

"My mother was pregnant with me when she arrived in America but shortly after I was born, we returned to Hungary, where she was from. Life in Budapest was tough. We were very poor. I don't think I can explain to you how tough it was," he paused, chugging half of his wine, "I don't think I can explain it to anyone. It wasn't just the poverty. It was also the discrimination. No matter what we did, we were always treated like dirty gypsies. To this day I have no idea who my father is. I assume he wasn't Romani, since I think getting pregnant with me was the reason my mother was banished by her family. She never mentioned him. When we were in Hungary she worked as a prostitute. She didn't try to hide it from me. We lived with her boyfriend, who was her pimp. If she were a stray dog he would have treated her better. All he did was beat her up, get drunk and yell. I hated him. When she and I returned to America, I was scared but I thought things were going to get better. Maybe I believed that because that's what she told me. Many times I heard her say she was bringing me back to where I had been born and I was going to have a better life."

Meredith didn't want him to stop talking, so she sat very still, all her attention on him.

"A few months later she vanished," Julian continued with a heavy sigh. "When I was growing up in foster care several people would say, what type of mother would abandon her seven-year-old son in the middle of the night, during wintertime, on the steps of some church. But she had always tried to be a good mother. She loved me. That's why it was so hard for me to accept she had left

147

me. I think it still is."

"Do you think something happened to her?"

"I don't know. Sometimes I hope that's the case. I want to believe she would have come back for me if she could."

"What was her name?"

"Ina."

"Have you ever tried to search for the rest of your mother's family?"

"They were dead to her. They are dead to me."

"What was growing up in foster care like?" she asked, guessing what his answer would be.

"Horrible."

"Was it always horrible?"

"You have to understand, I was only adding to it. I was not a good kid. I was mean, angry, and very aggressive. By the time I was thirteen I was smoking a pack of these a day," he said, looking at the cigarettes on the couch. "And doing hard drugs."

Meredith already knew about his drug addiction from reading it on the file Pam had showed her.

"That's when Hazel came along," Julian said, his hard expression softening. "Social services were desperate to find a home that would take me. No one wanted me. And I didn't want anyone. Finally, she came across a foster family that agreed to take me. They were a last resort. This family had had incidents with previous foster children but Hazel was trying to keep me off the streets. She figured that I was already so out of control, there wasn't anything that could happen to me there that I hadn't already experienced. In some ways she was right."

"Did they live here in Chicago?"

"Yes, Back of the Yards. It was worse then than it is now."

"How long did you stay with this family?"

"Two years."

"Two years?" Meredith was surprised. "That was a long time for you, wasn't it?"

"Considering I ran away every couple of months from every

place I had stayed at until then, yes, that was a very long time."

"Why did you stay that long?"

"Because of Tatiana and Sofia."

"Who were they?" she asked, not failing to notice how the tone of Julian's voice had changed when he said their names. She reached for his hand.

"They were my foster parents' biological daughters. Six-year-old twins."

"What happened?"

"You have to try to imagine how this house looked," Julian ignored her question, staring at her hand on his. He laced his fingers through hers. "It was the top floor of a crumbling, old triplex. I had seen and stayed in condemned buildings that looked better than this place. I remember the first time I walked up the stairs toward the top floor. The smell of mold, the damp filthy carpet, mixed with the smell of stale cigarettes and cooked food coming from the apartments was overwhelming. It was January. Imagine what it smelled like in the summer months, with the heat. There were sounds of people shouting, doors banging, kids crying. For as long as I live I'll never forget that stairwell. Hazel was walking ahead of me and she stopped a few times. I thought she was going to turn around and run." Julian laughed without mirth.

"We entered the house and there was stuff everywhere. You could barely see the walls. There were boxes piled up from floor to ceiling. Every surface had either objects or papers on it. They were what you could call hoarders. Right away I disliked the parents. To me they looked just as filthy as the place they lived in. Hazel stayed for a while but it was late and she needed to leave. I know she wanted to take me with her. If I was disgusted with this place, imagine her. She's one of the most organized and clean people I have ever met. They told me where my room was and all I did was carry my bag with me, drop it on the bedroom floor, and collapse on the bed. Prior to that night I had been living on the streets so I hadn't had a good night's sleep in a while. I was so tired."

It was hard for Meredith to imagine the Julian she knew as

a homeless boy. He was always polished, impeccably dressed and groomed. However, there was a time when he had looked like so many of the panhandling teenagers she passed by when walking around her city.

"When I woke up it was morning. I had slept on top of the covers and I still had my shoes on. My bedroom was not more than a tiny square, with a window facing the wall of another building. The only piece of furniture in it was the bed I was lying on, which was a good thing since it might have been the only place in the whole house that wasn't packed with junk. As I thought how long I could put up with living in this place, I heard my bedroom door open and these two little heads peeked in. I was so surprised I didn't move. I just stared at them. Slowly, they walked into the room and they stood, dressed in blue matching pajamas. They stared back at me. At first I thought I was hallucinating. But then they smiled at me and all I could do was smile back. They became my whole world. Everything started and ended with Sofia and Tatia."

"Can I ask you something?"

He raised an eyebrow. "You're asking me if you can ask me a question?"

She smiled. "I can play nice when I want to, you know?"

"Go ahead."

"Something horrible happened, didn't it?"

Julian refilled their wine glasses.

"You don't want to talk about what happened?" Meredith asked.

"It's not that I don't want to tell you what happened. I never talk about them to anyone. You're the second person I have discussed them with."

"Who else knows about them?"

"Hazel knows. She was somewhat of a witness as the events unfolded. The first person I told about Sofia and Tatiana was my friend Pete. I told him a long time ago."

"Tell me more about them, about the twins."

Julian stared at the wall and his lips curved in a gentle smile. "They were trouble. Very mischievous. Smart. Incredibly smart.

They both had this raspy voice and Russian was their first language, so they spoke English with a heavy accent that made you think they were these two mouthy old women trapped in these tiny bodies. They were hilarious."

"And adorable?" she had to add, now smiling too.

"Very. Tatiana, who I called Tatia, was the most outspoken one. Such an extrovert. She would boss me around and I would let her. I don't think I could ever say no to her, even if I wanted to. Sofia was quieter. More reserved."

"Was Sofia your favorite?"

Julian was silent again.

"It's okay to have a favorite, you know. Nothing to be ashamed of."

"Because she appeared to be more vulnerable, I was more protective of Sofia," he said, lowering his gaze. "She and I had a different connection."

"Were you happy while you stayed with them?"

"No. The house was hell. After being with them for a few months, Hazel found a group home that had agreed to take me, but at that point I couldn't leave. I couldn't leave the twins behind."

"What was going on in that house?"

"A lot of awful things. The worst was the father sexually abusing Sofia. I don't understand how I didn't pick up on it. She was the one who told me. It was a late August afternoon. The father was at work and the mother had left to run some errands and taken Tatia with her. Sofia was sick so she stayed home. The place had no air conditioning and it would always get so hot, like the heat weighed two tons and pressed you down against the ground, making it impossible for you to breathe. That's how it felt. Day and night."

Julian reached for his glass and sipped the wine. He was quiet and Meredith decided it was best not to speak. She was not sure what she should say.

"We were always hungry. That was normal for us. But Sofia looked so hopeless, lying down on the stain-covered couch, that I needed to do something to make her feel better," Julian continued, looking at the light coming from the only lit lamp in the room. "I had no money. So I did the only thing I could think of. Going to any of the convenience stores in the neighborhood was out of the question, they knew me already, so I walked far, maybe thirty minutes. I went into a convenience store I had never been to before and I stole a bunch of popsicles. By the time I got back they had melted so I put them in the freezer and both Sofia and I sat on the kitchen floor, staring at the fridge, waiting for the damn things to freeze again. She was so happy. The look on her face was one of pure delight." He turned his head toward Meredith and she saw in his eyes sorrowful longing for a person that now only existed in his memory.

She was witnessing a side of Julian that was completely unknown to her—he became a different person when he spoke about the twins. Seeing him now, Meredith realized how guarded and cold he always was. To her, this was a disquieting new awareness.

"The parents would hit the twins, you know, good old-school discipline." There was disapproval in Julian's voice. "But Sofia had all of these random bruises on her and I started asking her more about it. That's when she told me. She was so matter of fact about it…she had almost accepted it as being something normal. It was part of her reality. She was just so beaten down. I knew that feeling and I would have done anything so she wouldn't ever have to feel it."

"How about Tatia? Was he sexually abusing her too?"

"When I asked Tatia she said he wasn't. I never believed her."

"What did you do?"

"I didn't know what to do. I told their mother what was going on. She was this ignorant woman, cunning and angry, but regardless of all of her faults I believed she would protect her own daughters from her husband. I was wrong."

"She didn't do anything?"

"Oh she did. She told social services I was the one molesting her daughters."

Meredith gasped. "They didn't believe her, did they?"

"I was a delinquent. My track record made it look like a possible behavior. Hazel was the only one on my side. As soon as the twins found out I was being removed from the house, Tatia blamed her sister for everything, saying if she had kept her mouth shut I wouldn't have had to leave. Sofia just kept repeating I hadn't done it. The mother insisted her daughter was lying and was merely trying to protect me. The father just wanted me gone. The whole situation got really complicated, really quickly."

"I was packing my things when everything happened. Hazel was in the hall with the father when Tatia ran into my room crying, begging for my help. I followed her into the parents' bedroom and I saw Sofia pointing a gun at her mother, asking her over and over again to tell the truth."

Meredith was stunned. "A gun? Where did she find it?"

"The father kept a gun in the house. He would proudly show it off. We all knew where it was."

Meredith squeezed Julian's hand, encouraging him to continue.

"Everyone was screaming. I told Sofia everything was going to be okay, for her to drop the gun and then I heard this loud bang. I moved forward and I felt her body fall against my chest. As I was hugging her close, I looked up. That's when I saw the mother on the floor, blood everywhere."

Meredith covered her mouth. "Oh my God, Julian."

"I don't remember exactly what happened after that. All I could feel was Sofia's body against mine. All I could think was that I had to get her out of that room. I picked her up and I locked myself in the bathroom with her. Sofia was convulsing, throwing up. She was in shock. So much was happening on the other side of the locked door; I heard the voices, the cries, the sirens, Hazel asking me to come out. I sat inside of the bathtub with Sofia and I closed the shower curtain around us. I continued to hug her and I told her everything was going to be okay; that I wasn't going to let anything happen to her. I told her how much I loved her. That I'd never let her go."

"I'm so sorry."

"The firefighters had to remove the door. Hazel was the first to come in. I knew she was telling me they needed to take Sofia, to make sure she wasn't hurt, but I couldn't take my arms from around her. She was holding on to me so tightly. She was terrified. They had to pry her from me," he paused, and Meredith saw he was struggling to speak, "I never saw her again."

Meredith was not expecting such an outcome. "Ever?"

"No. Nor Tatia."

"How come?"

"They were sent to live with her mother's older sister, somewhere in Massachusetts. The father admitted to sexually abusing Sofia but he committed suicide not long after. I spiraled deeper into drugs and almost ended up dying of an overdose. Eventually Hazel adopted me."

"Did you try to contact them?"

"Their aunt wouldn't allow it. Hazel was able to keep tabs on them for a while and she would always tell me they were doing well. I hoped when they turned eighteen we would be able to reconnect. At that point I tried to find them but their aunt had died and there was no trace of them. I'm sure they don't want to be found. Especially by me."

"Why do you say, especially by you?"

"They never reached out."

"So?"

"When they were with their aunt I should have tried harder to see them, to speak with them. Even before that day, before Sofia told me what their father was doing to her, I should have done more. I failed them. I promised Sofia I would never let her go but that's exactly what I did. They have never forgiven me."

"You were sixteen years old, Julian. You did all you could. You were in no better a situation than they were. You can't blame yourself."

"I might agree with you but I feel differently. I always will."

"I think talking to them would change how you feel about it. Have you thought that maybe there were other reasons why they never contacted you? Did they know how to find you?"

"After Hazel adopted me I changed my last name from Lakatos

to Reeve. But if they were trying to find me they would know to search for Julian Reeve."

"Why would they?"

"Superman was my favorite TV show. Their nickname for me was Reeve."

"Maybe they forgot. They were what, eight years old the last time you saw them?"

"They wouldn't forget. Sofia and Tatia were not your average eight-year-old kids."

"Did you search under their full names? Under their nicknames?"

"I did. Nothing came out of it. It has been more than twenty years. I've spent a lot of time thinking of all the different possibilities. Not wanting to be found is the only plausible one."

"I can't believe that these two girls were once so important to you and you're going to go through the rest of your life never seeing or talking to them again. That can't happen. It's," Meredith paused, swallowing hard, "so sad. What was their surname?"

"Dulgorukova."

"Would you recognize them if you saw them now?"

"I'm sure I would."

"Do you have pictures of them? Anything?"

Julian shook his head.

"I have witnessed your nightmares…you always cry out in what I assume is Hungarian. What are they about?"

"Sofia and Tatia. That house. I hear them crying, calling my name. I can't ever find them."

"Part of me wishes you hadn't told me any of this. It's a weight on my soul."

"I'm sorry, Meredith."

"It makes me feel for you."

Suddenly Julian looked angry. "Don't do that."

"How can I not?"

"I didn't tell you about my childhood and about the twins so you could feel for me. Don't be one of those women who are compelled to save wounded men. It won't end well for you."

"I'm an eternal optimist. I want you to have some closure."

"We can't always get what we want, Meredith."

She rested her head on his shoulder and closed her eyes. She felt Julian's face on her hair.

"It's almost six in the morning. We should get some sleep," he said.

"Let's go to bed."

He followed her into the bedroom and Meredith was quick to undress and get under the covers. She hadn't been able to fully process everything she had learned. She hoped she would wake up in a few hours and know how to handle all of it, without feeling emotionally hungover.

It was pitch black and she heard Julian removing his slacks, dropping them on the floor. Soon his naked body was pressed against hers and she relaxed into his arms. He moved her hair away from her neck and touched the spot behind her earlobe with his lips.

"Brunch?"

"Brunch," Meredith repeated. "And then you're going to speak to Alana. You have enough loose ends in your life."

"I will."

Shortly thereafter the cadence of Julian's breathing told her he was asleep. The heat of his body was comforting and she felt safe, held tightly in his embrace. Closing her eyes, Meredith missed how things used to be a few months ago, before The Raven Room, before she knew about the murder, before she knew about Sofia and Tatia.

CHAPTER 16

With his hands deep in the pockets of his black winter coat, Julian walked into Bucket O' Blood Books and Records. It was late, the bookstore would be closing in less than fifteen minutes and there were only two customers browsing the tall bookshelves.

He saw Alana right away.

She was talking to the two people, her back to him. Julian picked up a random book off the display table closest to him. He didn't read fantasy. He had no idea what he was looking at. Flipping the book over he tried to read the back cover blurb. As soon as he came across the word dragon, he put it back down.

He knew the moment Alana had noticed his presence. The feeling she was watching him was hard to ignore. As usual, her expression was difficult to decipher.

"Hi Alana," he said, walking up to the counter. "You once said if I ever wanted to find you, I knew where you worked. So here I am."

"I can see that."

Julian was on a mission and he wasn't inclined to spend time on pleasantries. "Would you join me for dinner?"

"Why should I?"

"Because we need to talk."

It had been almost a month since that evening at his condo. Seeing Alana at the club the night before and now seeing her stand in front of him, Julian realized it had been too long. He should have come to the bookstore the next day.

"We'll go after you finish here. I'll be in the car waiting for you."

"Wait!" He heard her say just as he had turned around to leave.

He looked at her. "You need to buy a book."

"Sorry?"

Alana left her spot behind the counter and came near him. "Those people over there won't buy anything and I feel like selling a book before I close for the day. So you're buying one."

"I'm buying a book," he repeated, sounding uncertain.

She gave him what he would call a top-notch customer service smile. "You are."

He didn't want to risk her not joining him tonight so he chose to humor her. "Very well, what book should I buy?"

"I noticed the expression of blatant wonder on your face when you picked up this one." She went to the display table he had been at and grabbed the book about dragons. "I know you can't wait to read it."

"You're absolutely right. I can't wait."

Alana put the book on the counter. "And, I must say, today is your lucky day. We were sold out of book three in the series, but we just received some copies."

He raised an eyebrow. "Oh, it's part of a series?"

"It's a fantasy book. Of course it's part of a series. I'm assuming you want the complete set."

He watched her pick up a heavy stack of books from one of the shelves and drop it beside the other book. "That's, like, ten books," he said, wide-eyed.

"Twelve actually. By the time you've read them all you'll be a dragon expert."

"Are they really all about dragons?"

"Yes. Every single one."

He rubbed his forehead. "Jesus."

She glanced at the back of one the books. "It's really just about dragons. Beginning to end."

As Alana scanned them and placed the books inside of a paper bag, Julian passed her his credit card. "They will look great on your shelf," she said, as she gave him the bag.

"No doubt they will." He stood, failing to keep a straight face.

Alana was audacious, he had to give her that. "I, and my mighty trove of dragon books, will await you in the car."

Alana continued to give him a flawless smile.

Thirty minutes later he found himself still waiting for her. He started to think he had been wrong. He had convinced himself she would welcome his attempt to have her back in his life but maybe she really didn't want him near her. He had been wondering what to do next when Alana opened the door of his car and sat in the passenger seat. Even though he didn't show it, Julian felt relief and, more than anything else, reassurance.

She was wearing a thick purple scarf and a wool jacket that had seen better days. Alana couldn't have looked more different than the night before at the club. That had been the first time he had seen her wearing make-up and an outfit that didn't look like it had come from a thrift store discount bin. He had been completely stunned. Alana wasn't only pretty. She was also what most men would describe as hot. He was annoyed that it had taken him seeing her in a tight dress, high heels and lipstick to realize that.

"What color is your hair, Alana?"

She gave him a puzzled glance. "Blonde."

"Not red?"

"Maybe strawberry blonde but no, not red."

Meredith had been wrong. Julian wondered if the club's red lighting had been the reason why she thought Alana was a redhead.

"If you don't mind, I'll pick where we'll go for dinner. I'm hungry and need real food," he said.

"Do I sense disapproval of my food choices?"

"No, just fear."

Alana smiled. "Take us somewhere comfortable."

"Define comfortable."

"Non-pretentious."

He considered their options. "We could order room service at my place. It's one of the perks of having paid a fortune to live there."

"When I said non-pretentious I meant non-pretentious food as well."

"If you could go anywhere right now to eat, where would you go?"

"McDonald's."

He turned his head sharply, looking at her with incredulity. "Are you serious?"

"Yeah, dead serious."

"See, I had reasons to be afraid."

"You asked me where I wanted to go and I answered. There's one at Michigan and Chicago Ave."

"Oh my God," Julian paused, shaking his head, "I'm sure I can also get myself a hooker with my big mac and fries."

"You already have me. You just need to get the big mac and the fries."

"If we go there we're buying our food and taking it elsewhere. Would my place be okay with you?"

"Are you trying to get me into bed?"

He couldn't stop himself from smiling at her. "I want to talk to you and I'd rather do it at my place than at McDonald's."

Thirty minutes later they were sitting on a large white rug in front of Julian's living room fireplace. They watched the fire as they lay on several large pillows, the leftovers of their meal still on the floor, next to them. It was the first time he had eaten a burger on the floor of his living room and there was something carefree and youthful about it, which pleased him.

Julian watched Alana enjoy the heat coming from the fireplace. She had been at the club last night and then at work all day. He didn't know how she was managing to stay awake. She had her eyes closed and a soft smile on her lips. Julian wanted to reach out to her, undo her ponytail, and watch her hair fall in waves down her back. He still didn't understand why he was so drawn to Alana but he was determined to find out.

"What are your thoughts on what happened last time we were together?" he asked, studying her profile. They were lying on their stomachs and seeing the glow of the fire on her face, he imagined how radiant she must look during the summer months, with a sun kissed tan.

She was silent and he didn't move or speak. He waited for her response.

"I was really upset when you refused to let me out of the car and you brought us here," she finally said, keeping her eyes closed. "I wanted you to respect my decision not to tell you where I live. That's information that needs to be given, not taken. But I did enjoy the pain and the sex."

Julian was glad she was being candid. He remembered she had never seemed afraid during their argument, just angry. Her acknowledgement that she had enjoyed the pain and the sex brought him a deep and overwhelming feeling of satisfaction.

"I want to apologize to you for not respecting your decision, Alana. It was wrong of me. Did you mean it when you told me you were leaving for good?"

"No. But it felt good to say it. Did you mean it when you told me to choose between leaving for good or doing exactly what you told me to do?"

He couldn't lie to her. "At the time I did."

"Are you happy I am here now?"

He shifted his eyes to the fireplace, watching the blaze. "Yes, I am happy you're here."

"You need to accept that there are things I don't want to share."

When he turned to look at her he found her eyes on him. "Don't ask me to accept your involvement with Thompson, a man you're so clearly afraid of. That will never happen and you should know that," he replied, sounding brusque.

"Julian...we're having a good evening. Why ruin it?"

They were having a good evening but he wasn't pleased with what he had seen at the club and he wasn't going to pretend otherwise.

"Alana, do you go to the club out of your own free will? Is there anything you do there that you are forced to do?"

She didn't reply.

"Are you two in a romantic relationship?" Julian continued, the incredulity in his voice suggesting he didn't believe it himself.

"He's married." She spoke like that should answer his question.

"Did he ask you why you left the room so suddenly? What happened afterwards? Meredith was certain he wasn't happy."

"Who's Meredith? The woman you were with?"

"Yes."

"Is she your girlfriend?"

Julian wasn't expecting her to ask him about Meredith. "No. If she were my girlfriend you and I wouldn't be here right now." He kept his eyes on hers. "You didn't answer my question about Thompson."

She sighed. "Let's make a deal, Julian. Tonight, no more questions."

"Does that mean I'll get answers tomorrow?"

"No." She gave him a playful smile. "I'm trying to be better and not say things I don't mean."

He knew that was her attempt to end the conversation about Thompson and the club. Staring back at her, he didn't hide his desire for her.

"What do I get if I agree to your terms?" he asked, moving closer to her.

"You get me."

"You know I want you." He touched her hair, running between his fingers a strand that had escaped her ponytail. "Now, what I would like to know is why you approached me that day at the coffee shop?"

He watched her close her eyes. When she opened them again he noticed how soulful they were. He liked their ambiguous color. It reflected how he perceived her.

"I thought we agreed to no more questions," she said, gently scolding him.

"I haven't agreed to anything. Yet."

"I can answer this one," she continued, her voice gaining a velvety quality. "There's the obvious answer. You have sex appeal. But I have been with handsome men before." As he undid her ponytail and ran his fingers through her hair, she made a small sound of pleasure. "Then there's the true answer," she whispered, touching his lower lip with the tip of her fingers. "It was the way you looked at me."

"How did I look at you?"

"As if you saw me. Not the Alana who works at a bookstore, likes colorful socks, lives on junk food, has winter as her favorite season."

She turned on her side, facing him, and Julian placed a hand on the small of her back, pulling her closer to his body. His hand moved lower and he made sure he was pressing her tight against his erection. Before she continued, she wrapped her arm around his waist and rested her leg on top of his. Julian wished they had no clothes on. He would have been able to easily slide inside of her.

"But the real Alana," she continued, speaking against his lips. "The Alana with a brain full of useless knowledge, who wishes she still had a family, wants to travel and see the world. Who feels arousal by being physically and emotionally dominated by a man who encourages her to explore what exists beyond the limits she has imposed on herself." She slowly moved the tip of her tongue along the contour of his lips. "You saw me and I knew I would always be understood."

Their faces were so close that they were breathing into each other's mouths.

"Tonight, are you mine?"

"Yes. I'm yours." Her voice was as low as a whisper.

Julian pulled her jeans and underwear down and unzipped his slacks. She was so aroused that she accommodated all of him all at once. They both cried out with the sensation of it.

"We have a deal, then," he said, kissing her.

With one hand still on the back of her neck and the other on her thigh, Julian kept her against his body as he moved in her. Alana wrapped her leg around him and he saw her unbutton his shirt. The sensation of her gentle, yet passionate touch on his bare chest made him close his eyes.

"I love how wet you get," Julian said.

They were moving together. A slow and looped stir of their bodies; the tempo of it was increasing Alana's arousal. Julian looked into her eyes. "You're dripping on me, I can feel it."

"Don't stop." She tried to take him deeper inside of her. "Please don't stop."

"Do you want to come? Do you, Alana?"

"Yes!"

Her nails were on his skin and his breath caught in his chest. He wanted to feel her hands on his whole body. "Tell me how much you want it. Tell me how much you want me…tell me," he whispered, while he kissed her neck.

"I want it. Please don't stop. I want you. All of you. Please."

The husky tone of her voice only intensified his desire, and the heat of her body, together with the scent of her skin, were all that was real to him.

"Who do you belong to? Say it." Julian's focus was on only her and he knew, right at that moment, what she craved. He wanted to give Alana everything.

"You. I'm all yours." He heard her say.

"That's it. You're mine. You're my gorgeous, eager slut. I own you."

Her sounds of agreement almost pushed him over the edge.

With no warning, Julian stopped moving. He continued to hold her against him, remaining very still inside of her.

"Please don't…I'm so close…." Alana whimpered against his chest. The sensation of her scratching and biting him made it almost impossible for Julian not to surrender to his own desire for her.

"Can you feel how much I want you?" he asked, not recognizing his own voice. It sounded guttural, coming from an unknown place within in. "How much I need you?"

He felt her nod.

"Beg for me to let you come. Beg. I want to hear it."

"I'm so close."

"Beg," he demanded, pressing his forehead to hers. They were near the fireplace and the heat from it, added to the elevated temperature of their bodies, was making it hard for them to breathe. They were both sweating profusely. Moving Alana's hair away from her neck, Julian licked the beads of sweat off her skin.

"Please, let me come on your cock. Please. I'm begging you."

Julian felt gratification spread through his body and lifting her shirt up, he tugged on her bra so he could close his mouth on her breast. As he used his lips and teeth on her, he knew he was marking her. Julian heard her cry of pain; felt her pull his hair. He gripped Alana's hips hard.

"I'm all yours," he groaned, his mouth still on her breast.

As soon as he relaxed his grip, she started to move on him.

"That's it…you look so beautiful right now…don't stop…fuck yourself with my cock."

A sob escaped her lips and Julian didn't know if the moisture on her face was sweat or tears. He rubbed his cheeks on hers. He was inside of Alana, her whole frame against his body, but he still wasn't close enough to her.

"I want to feel you come. I need it."

"Julian…."

As she said his name he felt all of her tense up. "There…just let it take you…you're squeezing me so tight," he said, pulling her head back so he could have a clear view of her face. Julian watched the feeling of her orgasm sweep over her. "Fucking beautiful. So amazing. You're my amazing woman."

Alana continued to tremble in his arms and Julian held her, his harsh breathing not different from hers. "I'm not done with you," he whispered in her ear.

He moved her onto her back and kneeled between her open legs.

Julian knew she was still enjoying the pleasure of her release. "You taste so good…so good."

Alana placed her legs over his shoulders and Julian wanted to enjoy all of her. Over and over again. He looked up and saw the angry bruise on her breast. She would probably carry it for a week, if not more, but he hadn't marked her permanently.

Alana caressed Julian's hair with her fingers and he welcomed her hands on him. Soon she was lifting her whole body off the rug to meet his mouth and he brought her closer to him. Julian couldn't imagine a more satisfying taste; Alana's arousal on his tongue, on his lips, on his face.

She was moaning, detailing exactly what she wanted him to do to her. He slid two of his fingers inside of her and pressed upwards. He continued to stroke her and his persistent and repetitive attention was again propelling her toward release. He was close to being as incoherent as she was. The only thought on Julian's mind was that he never wanted to stop tasting her. When her orgasm took hold of her, Alana was loud, shouting his name.

Raising himself over her, he entered her again. He kept her legs over his shoulders and Alana's body molded itself to his.

"Don't stop. I need you." She had her arms stretched above her head and his driving movements were lifting her off the floor. Only her shoulders were touching the rug.

With his hands on her hips Julian leaned forward, not being gentle as he moved in her. "The sight of you...I can't take it." Alana's hair was spread out around her and she licked her lower lip. Her gaze was on him. Julian's breathing escaped him in loud gasps. "Come for me again, Alana."

When Julian's release seized him, the intensity of it drove his body forward, against Alana. He was somewhat aware of her hands on him, her arms enfolding him, her lips on his temple. His throat felt dry and he swallowed several times. His head was tucked under Alana's chin and her arms and legs were wrapped around his quivering body. Julian couldn't shake the realization he was right where he wanted to be. She was again caressing his hair but now her touch had become soothing, gentler. The feeling of it sent shivers down his spine. With her heartbeat against his ear, he didn't want to open his eyes. Julian felt blissful. He was still inside of her and all the muscles in his body were telling him not to move.

"Julian," Alana whispered into his hair, "I want to tell you everything. I want you to know me better than anyone else. But I can't...I can't tell you."

He wasn't expecting her to make such confession. It caught him by surprise. "What would happen if you told me?"

"I wouldn't be able to see you again."

"I don't want that to happen, Alana."

"Neither do I."

"If knowing the truth means not having you," he paused, kissing her lips, "I don't want to know."

Julian closed his arms around Alana and, holding her against him, stood up. He carried her to the walk-in shower of his en suite bathroom. Closing the glass door behind them, he put her down and turned on the hot water. She was standing in front of him, under the stream coming from the large shower-head and, grabbing the bar of soap, Julian ran his hands over her shoulders, down her arms, over her breasts, around her waist. His touch was slow, attentive, with silent reverence. The steam around them was increasing, making the walk-in shower feel smaller. They were shrouded in a thick and heavy cloud of heat.

With water falling on his head and cascading down his face and body, Julian kneeled at her feet, continuing to run his hands down her legs. Moving his wet hair out of his face, he looked up at her.

Alana was watching him.

Flowing down her small body, the water was washing away the rich layer of soap from her skin. That's when he realized she was crying. Getting back on his feet, Julian closed his arms around her. He rested his cheek on her head. Her body weaved with her suppressed sobs and he held her as tightly as he could against his chest.

"Shhh. It's okay. Everything will be okay. I promise. I'll never let you go." As soon as he spoke he finally understood why he was drawn to Alana. He was in trouble.

CHAPTER 17

Meredith stared down at a tall stack of blueberry pancakes. They had sounded good when she was going over the menu, but now she realized she wasn't even hungry.

"I guess I don't have to wonder why you wanted to meet," Pam said.

Pouring maple syrup on the pancakes, Meredith watched the thick, amber colored liquid drip and pool on her plate. "If you thought it was about Julian then you must suck at your job."

Pam slammed her coffee mug on the tabletop, causing Meredith to look up. "Dammit, Meredith, will you ever respect me and my time?"

"When will you believe I'm old enough to make my own decisions and stop acting like I do things just to spite you?" She had managed to get maple syrup on her fingers and now her cutlery was sticking to her hands. Suddenly, she wished she were anywhere but there, sitting across from her sullen stepmother with a large plate of food under her nose that was becoming more unappetizing by the second.

"Listen, what do you want to tell me?" Pam continued to drink her coffee. "I want to get home before midnight."

Meredith reached inside of her purse and passed Pam a piece of paper with two names written on it. "I need you find these two women for me. Sofia and Tatiana Dulgorukova. They might go by Sofia and Tatia."

Taking it from Meredith, Pam frowned. "You know them?"

"You could say that. Please, I just need an address. That's it. But if you can't find an address, I will take whatever you can find." She had first asked Colton but Pam had the power and the connections to get the information she needed faster and more efficiently.

"I don't have time for this, Meredith."

"I know that lately I have been asking you for a lot of favors but they are my friends and I'm worried about them. Please, Pam?" This time, Meredith didn't feel any pangs of guilt for lying.

"I'll see what I can do. I can't promise anything." Pam waved at the waitress and asked for the bill. "You didn't have to bring me here to ask me to do this," she said, turning to Meredith. "A phone call or an email would have done the job."

"Sofia and Tatia were one of the reasons why I asked you to meet me. There's something else," Meredith said.

"Which is...?" Pam stopped talking when the waitress approached the table with the bill.

"I saw someone at The Raven Room," Meredith continued. "I think he's a member."

"Who?" Pam asked impatiently. "Just tell me."

"Thompson. Steven Thompson."

Meredith saw the shock on Pam's face.

"He was with a woman and the way he was interacting with her, I don't know, it just looked off."

"Do you know this woman? Is she one of these?" Pam asked, looking at the piece of paper Meredith had given her.

"No, she's not. All I know is her first name, Alana. And that she works at a bookstore called Bucket O' Blood." Meredith didn't tell her stepmother that she got that information through Julian. She hoped that Pam would uncover more on Alana.

"Can you describe her to me?"

"I would say early twenties, petite, long red hair...that's all I can remember. Are you surprised Thompson goes to The Raven Room?"

"Thompson is the least of my worries." She cleared her throat. "So what's going on with you? You haven't stopped by the house in a while."

"Been busy with school."

"Are you still seeing Reeve?"

Meredith took a piece of pancake into her mouth. She had

been expecting her stepmother to make a comment about Julian so she was prepared with an answer. "When it comes to Julian, you and I will never see eye to eye," Meredith said with a resolute expression. "Nothing I or anyone else says will ever change your opinion."

"I know you have your mind set on writing that article but you need to reconsider. It's a bad idea."

"Where are the files on Julian before he was adopted?"

He had told Meredith about his past but she still wanted Pam to give her the remaining information on him. Maybe she would find something that he hadn't shared with her.

"I have been too busy working on a case. But I'll make sure to get the files, don't worry."

Meredith concentrated on eating her pancakes. "Which case?"

"You know I don't talk about the cases I work on." Pam replied. "Did you hear what I said about you writing the article on Reeve and The Raven Room?"

"I did. But I don't want to talk about work either."

"I think it's time for me to go," Pam finally said, grabbing her jacket and purse.

"Please keep me posted on what you find on those women." Meredith dipped a piece of her pancakes in the maple syrup. "And good luck with your case."

"As I said before, can't promise anything but I'll see what I can do." Pam was now standing by the table, getting ready to leave. "Sometimes I worry...what type of people are you associating yourself with?"

Meredith laughed. "People like you, Pam. Real people."

Finally by herself, Meredith took a deep breath. She sat back in her seat and she noticed the bill was still on the table. It seemed that Pam thought she should pay for her coffee.

At that moment her phone buzzed. The head of her program had emailed her—she had spoken to Isaac Croswell, an editor friend of hers at the *Chicago Tribune*, about her investigative piece on The Raven Room and he wanted to meet with her. As she stared at Isaac Croswell's contact information, Meredith felt conflicted. Turning down that opportunity would be counterproductive but if she did go ahead and contact him, she would be undeniably betraying Julian. Discussing him and The Raven Room with Pam was one thing; revealing to the world private details about Julian's life and her experiences at The Raven Room was something completely different.

When a text from Julian came up on screen, Meredith almost gasped. He wanted to know if she was free. For Julian to be contacting her at that time, it could only mean two things. He either wanted sex or he needed to talk. Regardless, she was up for both. She texted Julian back, telling him she was at Little Goat Diner eating a bottomless plate of pancakes. He quickly responded that he would be joining her.

In less than twenty minutes she saw Julian walk through the door.

"Why are you here at this time eating pancakes by yourself?"

"I could ask you why you are here at this time, watching me eat pancakes, couldn't I?"

Julian smiled, sitting across from her in the booth. "Good point."

Since she had known Julian he had always kept his hair short but it was obvious he hadn't gotten a hair cut in a while. The dark stubble covering his jaw suggested he had also skipped shaving that morning. Julian had always looked older than he was but right now he appeared haggard. "Sorry to be so blunt, but you look like shit."

Julian rubbed his eyes. "I'm afraid I'll have to agree with you."

"Too much work? Not eating? What's going on?"

Running his hand through his already disheveled hair, he yawned. "A mix of both. I have been working long hours at the hospital."

"Nothing else?"

"I haven't been sleeping well."

"The nightmares?"

He nodded. "Pretty bad."

"Have you ever thought about seeking help? I know you're a shrink but when it comes to that, I don't think you can do much for yourself."

"I have in the past. Not recently."

"What triggered the nightmares to become so bad?"

Julian shook his head.

"Really?" she said, realizing he wasn't planning on giving her an answer. "You're going to show up here at almost midnight looking the way you do, interrupting my special pancake moment, and refuse to answer my simple question?"

"C'mon, why are you here?" he asked with a scowl, shifting the focus of the conversation back to her.

Meredith groaned and sunk further into her seat. "I came here to meet my stepmom."

"Ah…I see. Hence the pancakes."

"Yes, hence the pancakes."

"Is everything okay?"

"Don't turn the tables on me, Julian. We were talking about you."

"Right now I don't feel like talking about myself."

"Too bad. You joined me here, didn't you?"

With his forearms on the table he let his head fall between his shoulders. Neither of them spoke for a while. When Julian lifted his eyes to Meredith, he was smiling. "You should consider becoming a psychologist. You would be amazing at it."

"Don't try to distract me with compliments. What's going on?"

It was his turn to groan. Waiting for him to reply, she continued to work on her plate of pancakes.

"Alana is what's going on," Julian finally said, his voice low and full of frustration.

"Alana, huh?"

"Yes…listen, I don't want to talk about her."

"Because you're also sleeping with me and you happen to have feelings for her?"

"I never said I had feelings for her…and why did you just say that?"

"You know why."

"I actually don't."

"You believe it's unfair to me for you to sit here and talk to me about another woman. Please don't deny it."

"I don't want to disrespect you."

"That might be true. But more than that, you believe I have feelings for you and you're afraid I'll turn into a bunny boiler."

"Do you have feelings for me?" he asked, watching her closely.

Meredith continued to focus on eating her pancakes. "I do care for you. Do I love you? I don't know." She licked some maple syrup from her lower lip. "You're a man easy to fall in love with but a hard one to love," she added, raising her eyes to meet his.

Julian didn't reply.

"I always want you to be part of my life," Meredith continued. "But I'm young. I have a lot of people to meet, a lot of places to see, a lot of experiences to embrace…a lot of plates of pancakes to eat."

They both laughed.

"Here, let me help you with that." Julian reached for his cutlery and took a big piece of a pancake with his fork.

As they were eating, the waitress brought them coffee and while Meredith had hers with cream and sugar, Julian drank his black.

"The whole time you and I've known each other we've had sex with other people. We both know that," she said, holding her mug with both hands. "The only reason you're now uncomfortable discussing Alana with me is because there are feelings involved. To you, it's not just fucking. You care for her."

Julian lifted his eyes to her and it looked like he was thinking about what to say. "I care for you, Meredith."

"I know you do," she replied, her tone matter of fact. "Alana won't change that. Because of her, you and I have become closer."

"I believe we would have become closer, regardless. It's only normal for people who sleep together for a long period of time."

"Or, you might start to hate them."

"Sure, but regardless of the nature of your feelings you have grown closer."

"Is that happening between you and Alana? You're growing closer?"

"Yes…I'm also growing more aware of certain things."

"Which things?"

"It's complicated."

"Explain complicated…and while you're at it, can you put your back into eating these? You've taken, like," Meredith paused, waving her fork in the air, "two bites. It's pitiful."

"Jesus, you're so bossy." Julian removed his sweater and rolled up the sleeves of his dress shirt. He grabbed his fork again and started to eat. "I'm not even hungry."

"You should be. You look like you haven't eaten in days."

"I'm trying to help you finish these. Otherwise you'll be here all night."

Meredith rolled her eyes. "Oh please, I'm putting you out of your misery by sharing my food with you. Pancakes make everything better."

"I have to admit, these are damn good." He spoke as he chewed. "Delicious."

"See? I know what I'm talking about. You look perkier already." She grinned, winking at him.

"It's the blueberries. My favorite."

"Now tell me, what's complicated?"

"She reminds me of someone…of them."

That caught Meredith's attention. "The twins, you mean?"

"Yes, Sofia and Tatia."

"Did something happen?"

"Yes and no. I've realized that I'm projecting."

Meredith couldn't stop herself from looking confused. "I'm trying to understand what you're saying. In your mind Alana is the twins and that's why you are sleeping with her…and that's why the nightmares have become worse? You feel guilty or something?"

"I'm not sleeping with her because she reminds me of Sofia and Tatia. I'm sleeping with her because I'm physically attracted to her. You were also attracted to her when you saw her at the club, no?"

"I was. But for some reason, she's not the type of woman I ever imagined you with."

"My friend Pete said the same thing when he met her." Julian reached for the maple syrup and poured more of it on the pancakes.

174

"But going back to your question, I care for her because she reminds me of them. But, at the same time, her presence in my life is making the nightmares worse."

Meredith watched Julian put half a pancake in his mouth and gulp down half of the coffee in his mug. For someone who wasn't hungry he was doing a very good job at cleaning up her plate.

"Julian, sorry to break it to you, but you'll only be able to care for women who, in one way or another, remind you of Sofia and Tatia. You need to come to terms with that."

Meredith's comment made him chew slower. "Are you saying I care for you because, somehow, you also remind me of them?"

"Yes. Something about me, could be really small, like the way I scrunch up my nose when I'm unhappy or the way I tilt my head when I am trying to focus. Anything. But with Alana it's stronger because of whatever is going on between her and Thompson you perceive her to be in a vulnerable situation." She lifted her hands up in the air. "Congratulations! That's what I call a strike of good luck."

Julian didn't look pleased with her sarcasm. "I think now is a good time for you to stop analyzing me."

"I'm not analyzing you. I'm just telling you how it is."

"Forgive me if I fail to see the difference."

"So, what are you going to do about her?"

He sighed. "I don't know."

"Have you told her about the twins?"

"I haven't."

"You should."

"I believe Alana has enough problems in her life. She doesn't need to hear mine."

"I doubt you told me about the twins because you thought my life needed some extra misery. It's about you sharing with Alana something very important to you. Something that has shaped who you are today."

He didn't reply and Meredith took the opportunity to continue. "Look at yourself, Julian. I'm worried about you. Clearly you can't go about things the way you have been up until now. It'll put you in your grave."

"I don't want you to worry. I just need time to deal with it. All will be fine."

"Did you have a chance to ask Alana about Steven Thompson?"

"She won't tell me anything."

"That's not a good sign."

"I know."

"I have never asked you this, but how did The Raven Room come to be?"

Julian shook his head. "Meredith, I'm just a guy with a membership."

"How did you get one?" she asked, watching him eat.

"I can't tell you that. There are rules…rules I cannot break."

"You can't tell me how you became a member? How come I'm allowed there? Is Alana a member as well or is she taken there, the same way you take me?"

"Why are you asking me these questions?" Julian didn't try to hide his frustration.

"Because I should know, don't you think?" she asked, lifting an eyebrow. "I've been to The Raven Room several times, was dragged up a set of stairs by a scary looking asshole and I don't know anything about the damn place. That night, it looked like you knew those men. You were even speaking to them in Mandarin. What's down there, Julian? Don't tell me it's another entrance because that's a lie. It either has to do with drugs or sex. Or maybe both. And it's fucked up shit, isn't it? The woman that was found dead was young and beautiful. Just like Alana. Do you want her to end up dead too?"

Meredith could see she had succeeded at bringing out Julian's least pleasant side. "Don't ever say that again." His tone was cold and his green eyes had become hard. "I would never want anything to happen to Alana, to you, or to any other woman. Do you understand? I saw both my mother and the twins being abused and I was powerless to stop it."

"You might not know who killed her, or even if the club is involved, but do you think it is a possibility for her death to be linked to The Raven Room?" Meredith asked.

"Of course it's a possibility. You bring together a group of bored people with too much money and power under one roof; you tell them—*please feel free to mingle, fuck and fulfill all of your kinks and fantasies*. What do you think is going to happen?"

"Do you know who owns The Raven Room?"

Julian placed his fork down and looked straight at her. Meredith saw him clenching his jaw and if this had been six months ago, she would have retreated from him with apprehension. Sleeping together over an extended period of time may bring people closer together. It also made one worry less about the consequences of their words and actions.

"I don't think anyone really knows who owns The Raven Room."

"Do you have any ideas who might?" she continued.

"I don't. It's not my business and neither is it yours."

They stared at each other for what felt to Meredith like a very long time. He was angry but she wasn't bothered by it. She knew how to handle Julian when he was angry. What made her truly uncomfortable was Julian's ability to act like he was in control of himself, while giving the impression that if he loosened the grip on his iron clad self-restraint, his menacing temper would be released and cause a great deal of destruction in its path. She had never seen him display a large degree of emotion but she knew it was there, held in check beneath his steely exterior.

Before she could say anything else, his phone, which was on the table, started to vibrate. They both glanced at the bright screen and saw Grace's name. Frowning, he held his phone as it vibrated a few more times. "Sorry, I have to take this call."

As soon as he answered, Meredith could hear a distressed female voice on the other side. She assumed it was the same Grace married to Julian's friend, Peter. Meredith couldn't make out what the woman was saying, but by the tone of her voice and Julian's attempts to get her to calm down, it was clear that something was wrong. She didn't want to eavesdrop but at the same time she couldn't ignore it. As soon as Julian ended the call, he got up from the booth and started to put on his sweater and coat.

"I have to go," he said, holding his car keys and his phone. Reaching inside his pocket he dropped a fifty-dollar bill on the table. "It's on me."

Meredith glanced at the money. "What happened?"

"Pete's wife is on her way to my place with the boys. I need to get home." Julian leaned toward Meredith and, before he could stop himself, he kissed the top of her head and breathed in the scent of her hair. He noticed the gesture caught Meredith by surprise and, in some ways, he was surprised by it as well.

Meredith looked up at him. "Call me if you need anything."

"Thanks," Julian said, his hand gently cradling her nape, "I will."

Chapter 18

Julian was thankful that the streets were clear of snow and he was able to drive home faster than usual. Grace had sounded frantic on the phone. As he was about to reach his condo building, Julian's phone started to vibrate. It was Peter. Julian tucked the phone back into his pocket. Before anything else, he wanted to speak with Grace. Peter left him a voicemail and he listened to it while he was in the elevator from the underground parking garage. His friend wanted to know if his wife and sons were with him. Stopping in the large lobby, Julian saw Grace sitting on one of the couches with both Seth and Eli on her lap.

"I got here as soon as I could," he said, approaching her.

Holding both boys, Grace tried to stand up. By the trail of used tissues on the table in front of her, Julian could tell she was struggling to keep herself together. He took one of the twins from Grace and instantly got hit in the face with a small hand. They were sturdy babies, hard to control if they decided they weren't in the mood to be held.

With Seth in his arms, Julian took the large baby bag from Grace. "Let's get upstairs."

"I'm sorry to show up like this," she said, her head low.

"Don't apologize. We'll get Seth and Eli comfortable."

An hour later, the boys were asleep on a thick blanket on Julian's bedroom floor and he and Grace were sitting in the dimly lit kitchen, each with a large glass of red wine in front of them.

"Grace, what happened?"

"Pete and I got in a huge fight. There's something wrong, Julian. I don't know what it is but I know there's something wrong."

"With him? Did he do or say something?"

"We've both been so busy with work, you know, sometimes our schedules don't line up and trying to raise two boys…it's hard. We don't spend that much time together but I've noticed he's always on his computer, or his phone…he's online a lot."

"Do you suspect he's—"

"Cheating on me?" she said, finishing the question for him. "He might be, I don't know. He probably is."

"Have you asked him?"

"I have, Julian, several times but he continues to give me the same answer. That he isn't and I'm just acting crazy. He accuses me of resenting him for cheating on me in the past."

"Do you resent him?"

"I don't trust him."

"He called me as I was driving home," Julian explained, watching her carefully as he spoke. "I didn't pick up but he left me a voicemail asking if you and the boys were with me. Does he know you're here?"

"I didn't tell him where I was going. I just grabbed the kids and left."

"You need to tell him you and the boys are safe. He needs to know."

"I don't want to talk to him. At least not yet."

"I'll have to call him then."

"I don't want him coming here."

"I agree that Pete coming here now is not a good idea. I'll ask him to give you some space."

Julian took his phone from his pocket and saw that, since leaving the voicemail, Peter had tried calling him three more times. He was probably frantic by now.

Alone in his office, Julian made the call. Peter answered the phone on the second ring and, as Julian suspected, he was worried and extremely irate. Julian had left the kitchen because he didn't want Grace hearing Peter shouting. He found out that Grace had slapped her husband during their argument. It took a long time to calm Peter down. Until they were thinking more clearly and in control of their emotions, he wanted to keep Grace and Peter away from each other.

Julian promised his friend he would call him first thing in the morning to let him know how Grace and the boys were doing and that, until then, they should get some sleep. He reminded Pete that there were two young children whose well-being needed to come first.

After hanging up, Julian returned to the kitchen and sat on the tall stool beside Grace. Wrapped in a throw, she was nursing her glass of wine.

"What did he say?" she asked without looking at Julian.

"He was very worried and he's angry." Holding his glass, he was quiet for a while. "Did you hit him?"

"I did. And right now, if he walked through that door, I would slap him again."

"Grace, you and Pete can't go around hitting each other. I had no idea your relationship had deteriorated this much."

"Really, Julian, you of all people had no idea? After everything Pete has done, after everything I've done, you didn't think our relationship was this fucked-up?"

"I guess I refused to see it."

"I don't know what to do. I'm so unhappy." Grace rested her head on her hand and Julian continued to sit still, listening to her. "It's everything...you know?" she continued, wiping away the fresh tears with her hands. "Working at the law firm is so stressful. I hate it. And then there's the house, the cars, the trips...sustaining our lifestyle is not cheap and I see myself almost forced to work harder. Just so I can continue to afford what I have. God, I feel insecure. Since having the twins I don't like the way I look. I went to see a dietician so I can eat healthier, I have a personal trainer but I loathe working out. I'm so sick of it. All of it. I feel like I've lost myself, that I'm trapped in a life I never wanted. I don't know what to do."

Julian wrapped his arm around her shoulders and brought her closer to him.

"How can I stop feeling this way?" she whispered, her face

buried in his chest.

"I wish I had an answer." Reaching for the glass of wine with his other hand, he took a sip. "Many people feel the way you do."

"Aren't you supposed to know what's wrong with me?" Grace said, her voice made rough by the tears.

"It's not a matter of right or wrong."

"I want you to tell me," she paused, taking a steadying breath, "is Pete cheating on me? If he is you'd know."

Continuing to hold Grace, Julian rested his chin on top of her head. She was right, Peter had told him about the woman he had met online but he couldn't share that with her. He couldn't tell her the truth because if he did she would walk away from her marriage hating Peter and Julian didn't want that for Seth and Eli. Above it all he needed to protect them.

"He hasn't told me anything," he said, holding her more tightly.

Hearing him speak, Grace pulled out of his embrace. "Are you telling me the truth?"

Meeting her gaze, he replied without hesitation. "I am."

She took the bottle of wine and refilled her glass. "He's changed. It's like I don't know him anymore." Her stare was lost on the kitchen wall. "I feel like I'm living with a stranger. It scares me. I wonder who I'm married to, really."

"We both know there have been times in the past when he hurt you and disappointed you, but he loves you and the twins very much. Of that I have no doubt. You're his family."

Grace turned to him. "You're still seeing Alana?"

Her unexpected question caught Julian by surprise.

"I like her," she said, while drinking her wine.

"You speak like you didn't expect to."

"I guess that's true. All of these years I've been listening to Pete describe the type of women you associate with. Meanwhile, I've been trying to set you up on dates with my friends and colleagues and nothing ever seemed to stick. Then all of a sudden, you waltz into my home with Alana…pretty, can hold an intelligent conversation, not too young. I was expecting less or nothing at all from you."

"Because I wasn't interested in dating your friends and Pete thinks every woman I spend time with is a whore?"

She remained silent.

"Tell me why, Grace."

"Because you rejected Seth and Eli. You rejected your own kids."

For several long minutes Julian didn't reply. He ran his hand through hair and inhaled loudly. "I don't think we should talk about that right now—"

"Why not?" Grace asked, not letting him finish.

"Because you've a lot in your mind. It's a bad time."

"It should never be a bad time for us to discuss Seth and Eli."

"What do you want to discuss?"

"Don't you hate yourself? I've lost count of the many times I've laid awake beside my husband going over in my head what happened that night. I lie to him every day. The guilt is a horrible burden and it's destroying me and my marriage."

"At the time we made a decision that was best for everyone. Now all we can do is deal with the consequences of it."

"Today, right now, do you still think it was the best decision for everyone?"

Julian locked eyes with her. "Yes, I do."

"I don't."

"What do you want from me?" he asked, quietly.

"I don't know. I don't. I'm so confused."

"Grace, we had sex one time while you and Pete were broken up. We were both drunk. When you found out you were pregnant, you were already back with Pete. You were happy to be with him and wanted to work on your relationship." Julian was trying to keep his voice low and impassive. "You wanted to be married and have a family. I couldn't give you what you wanted but he could. If you had told Pete he wasn't the father none of that would have been possible."

"If I had, would you have been there for me and the boys?"

"I have never wanted kids and I still don't. I was honest with you."

Grace got up from the kitchen stool and went to stand against the counter. She kept her eyes on the floor. "You know what breaks my heart?"

Julian turned to face her. "No, tell me."

"You would have been a better father."

"You don't know that."

"Yes I do. I do because tonight you dropped everything so you could be here for me and them."

"It's one night. Not a lifetime. I'll always be there for you when you need me but Seth and Eli need a father; someone who's there every day. I'm sorry, Grace."

"Even with all your flaws you're a better man than Pete."

"You've no idea what type of man I am."

"No, you've no idea what type of man your best friend is. If you do, you're refusing to see it. I don't know if I want him raising my kids."

"You want a divorce? Do you want to tell him he's not the biological father of the boys?"

In a gesture of hopelessness, she threw her head back. "I don't know. I kept thinking that if I dedicated myself to my career, if I kept a more beautiful home, if I ate healthier, if I exercised more, I would somehow become a better wife, a better mother and my life would stop spiraling out of control. And then you showed up with Alana and you guys appeared to be so in sync with each other that it made me angry, you know? How dare you show up at my house with your charming new girlfriend? How dare you be happy when I'm not? How dare you move on when I'm left lying to my husband and my kids every hour of every single day?"

Julian made his way to Grace but stopped before he got too close. "Look at me," he asked. She met his eyes. "This is not about me. It's about you," he continued, his voice gentle. "You're a lawyer in a high profile law firm. You're a new mother of twins. Your marriage is in crisis. You're overwhelmed and you're exhausted," he said, taking a step closer to her. "You're going to get through this, though. You're brilliant and strong. Never doubt yourself." Julian stretched his hand to Grace and waited for her to take it. When she wrapped her fingers around his palm, he took another step forward and closed his arms around her, hugging her. "I'm here for you and I'll help you get through it."

"Do you think Pete suspects?" she asked, hugging him back.

"He doesn't."

"How are you so sure?"

"If he did he would have punched me in the face or tried to ruin my life."

Grace remained silent, like she was thinking about what Julian had said. "It would destroy him to find out Seth and Eli aren't his and that you and I lied. He wouldn't be able to cope with such betrayal."

"I know," Julian replied, closing his eyes. "I know."

Grace removed her arms from around Julian's waist and rubbed her temple. "I think I should get some sleep…I can barely stand up anymore. My head is killing me."

With his hands still on her shoulders, he studied her face and saw how tired she looked. "Please make yourself comfortable in the guest room at the end of the hall."

"I need to get Seth and Eli."

"I'll watch them. You go get some sleep."

"They wake up throughout the night—"

"Grace?" he interrupted, "I got it. Just go lie down."

She nodded. "If they get fussy, just bring them to me."

"I will. Don't worry."

He watched her walk out of the kitchen and disappear down the hall. Turning off the lights behind him, Julian went into his bedroom. The nightstand lamp was on and the large room appeared cozier because of the warm, soft glow. He glanced at the twins in their improvised bed on the floor and he realized Eli was awake and staring at him with interest. Hoping he wouldn't feel scared and start crying, Julian walked up to him and crouched down by the edge of the blanket.

"Hey you…wide awake, huh?"

Julian didn't fully understand why, but he spoke to Eli in

Hungarian. It felt natural to him to speak to the boys in his first language. Eli continued to look at Julian, his face serious. "I have problems sleeping myself, so I can relate," he continued in Hungarian.

At that point Seth rolled over and soon enough he was also staring up at Julian with curiosity. "Now both of you are up," he whispered, shaking his head. "No crying, okay? Your mom needs to sleep. She's going through a rough time and we all need to work together to make sure she feels better."

He quickly changed into a t-shirt and a pair of track pants. Opening the curtains, he moved the boys closer to the expansive window and, grabbing a pillow and some extra blankets, joined them on the floor.

While Eli was entertained playing with one of his toys over Julian's legs, Seth started to cry and he held the distressed boy in his arms. Not knowing what to do, Julian did what his mother used to do when he was growing up—he brought Eli's face to rest on his cheek and started to point out constellations in the night sky. Not long after, he was holding both boys in his arms. Julian knew it was merely the sound of his low-pitched voice that had lulled them to lie peacefully against his chest. But he was enjoying giving the twins their first astronomy lesson, one that they would not understand, let alone remember.

After talking at great lengths about the Orion constellation, his favorite, he looked down at the boys. "I'm undeserving of you," Julian said, almost to himself, as he caressed their heads. "And I gave you up to a man just as undeserving. I'm so sorry."

Chapter 19

With sweaty palms and her breathing shallow, Pam waited. Steven Thompson was thirty minutes late. As usual, they were supposed to meet at the Asian art gallery, inside the Art Institute. Meeting in public was safer but every time they did, she was afraid someone would see them together. Thompson hated that particular area of the Art Institute. He said it made him feel like Pam and her ancestors were conspiring to bring him down. Because she wanted to make him pay for the uneasiness that their meetings caused her, Pam continued to choose that spot. She took pleasure in watching Thompson, a paranoid man, behave like a caged animal.

"What's the reason for our little date?"

Pam didn't bother turning around. "I don't have anything. I can't make a move."

"Did you drag me here to tell me this bullshit?"

"Don't press my patience, Steven."

"Why don't you ask your stepdaughter, who has been busy spreading her legs to the nice folks at the club? I'm sure she could help you."

Pam silently counted to five before she answered. She didn't want to lose her temper. "Leave Meredith out of this."

"Why don't you have anything on him? It's impossible. Four women, Pamela. Four."

She hated when he called her by her full name. "Shut up. You don't think I've done everything to find evidence I can use to link him, at least, to one of the deaths?"

"He did it."

"That doesn't help me. I need hard evidence."

Thompson was silent. "So what do we do?" he finally asked.

"I'm going to speak again with everyone who might know or have seen something. If I end up empty handed, there's nothing more we can do." Pam didn't take her eyes away from the ancient woodblock text on display in front of her. "The thought that he might get away with it makes me so mad."

"He won't stop. There will be more women. Sooner or later he'll fuck up."

"He's got a type. Young, Eastern European, blonde, shorter than five-foot-four, ingénue looking. Can you get me a list of every woman who goes to The Raven Room and fits that description?"

"What you're asking me is near impossible. I don't think that information exists and if it does only the fuckers who manage the club have access to it." Thompson shook his head. "I've been having problems with them."

"Bribe, blackmail, threaten. Do whatever you have to do to find out."

"We're talking about some of the most dangerous people in Chicago. Do you want me to end up with a bullet between my eyes?"

Pam raised an eyebrow and Thompson chuckled. "Always such a cold bitch."

The Art Institute was about to close and they were the only ones in that gallery. They were standing side by side but they still hadn't looked at each other. From the corner of her eye, Pam saw Thompson's black leather shoes. After all those years he still wore the same style of shoes.

She backed away from the glass box and turned without looking at Thompson. With her back to him, she stopped. They were less than two steps away from each other. "I'll call you if I come across anything. Meanwhile, find out if there's a list."

The air between them had shifted and she knew he was now looking at her.

"We're doing the right thing, Pamela."

She wished what they were doing was only about justice but they both knew it went beyond that. "It's not about right or wrong," she said, not sure he could hear her. "It's about stopping a killer and keeping The Raven Room out of the spotlight."

"Besides being a cold bitch you're also the smartest woman I know."

Pam continued to walk away from him, eyes straight ahead. "Don't let me turn you on."

She was already in the hall when she heard Thompson's laugh. They could have had that conversation over the phone and, like her, he was aware of the risk of them meeting in person. But regardless of whether it was him or her who asked to meet, neither of them ever said no.

She exited the Art Institute, hands deep inside her coat pockets. She had forgotten her gloves at her desk and it was so cold she couldn't stand the strong wind touching her exposed skin. As soon as she entered her car, she turned on the heat, rubbed her hands together and pressed her palms against her red cheeks. She caught a whiff of the air freshener she had clipped to the car vent a few weeks ago. Tropical breeze. The sweet, fruity scent reminded her of fine, white sand and turquoise ocean water but also made her want to pound her fists against her frozen windshield. Instead, she hit the steering wheel over and over again. While she was at it, she swore, screaming as loud as she could.

She took her phone out of her coat pocket, knowing exactly what she would see when she looked at the screen—the icon of a little Christmas tree. As he always did after their meetings, Thompson had texted her. She had saved his contact under that icon because it brought her memories she was foolish enough to hold on to. She also knew exactly what his text would say. She deleted it without reading it.

Pam started the car and drove toward the police station. It was close to six o'clock and the sky was already pitch black but she had work to do before she could go home. It would be another evening of her running to the twenty-four-hour deli across the street and eating a sandwich at her desk.

It was past midnight and Pam was still at the station. She had turned off the overhead florescent lighting and only the lamp on her wood veneer desk, with its wobbly shade, remained on. Pam opened the bottom drawer and grabbed a large folder. Inside there were large pictures of four women. All of them had been found in their homes, naked in their beds. And in the same position—on their backs, head turned to the right, both legs bent at the knees and turned to the left, the right arm stretched out and the left arm bent over the head. She knew that pose held meaning but so far she hadn't been able to decipher it. She would have Colton search pictures, images, sculptures of females, hoping he would come across something that resembled the position in which the women had been found.

No matter how hardened a homicide detective she was, she always took consolation knowing the victim hadn't suffered. It helped her get through the job. People are not afraid of dying. They are afraid of pain. She was relieved that the women had been killed by heroin overdose. Compared to what she was used to seeing, it was the perfect death.

Pam went through her notes on the last victim and wrote down the address of the woman who had identified the body. She had already spoken with her but maybe she had remembered something since then. Returning to her car, she drove away from the station and turned on the radio. It was the beginning of April and they were still calling for snow.

Chapter 20

"What kind of camera is that?"

Julian and Alana were walking around in the Lakeview neighborhood. It was a clear day and, for the first time in several months, the temperature wasn't freezing. After spending the night together and lounging in bed all morning, they had elected that Sunday was Alana's day, which meant it would be up to her to decide what they were going to do. Julian had been enticed by the prospect of using that as a means to get to know her better.

"It's a Holga." She passed it to him. "You've never seen one?"

"First time." He held it with his gloved hands and admired it for a while. "Looks like a toy."

Alana laughed. "It's a medium format film camera. You never know how your pictures will look when you take them with a Holga. It's unpredictable. Colors tend to be very saturated, you get beautiful vignettes…it almost forces you to see the world in a completely different way."

"Like *They Live?*"

"What?" She stared at him confused.

"You've never seen the movie *They Live?*" he asked, his eyes wide.

"You look shocked."

"How could I not be? It's a great movie."

"What's it about?"

"It's about a guy who discovers this pair of sunglasses and, while he's wearing them, he's able to see that the world is being taken over by aliens…." He smiled.

"Aliens?" she asked, raising her eyebrows as she tried to contain her laughter.

"What's wrong with aliens?"

"There's nothing wrong with them. I'm just surprised you're into aliens, that's all."

Alana took the camera back and pointed it at him. He raised his hands to his face. "What are you doing?"

"I'm taking a picture of you," she said from behind the Holga. "I'll name it, *Julian and the Aliens*."

She was fast, and before he could say no, she pressed the shutter and got her picture. Julian dropped his head, his eyes on the pavement.

Putting the camera back inside her purse, she approached him and rested her hands on his chest. "Are you embarrassed?" Her tone was light and joyful.

"Not embarrassed. I'm just not used to having my picture taken, that's all."

Alana got on her tiptoes and dropped a small kiss on his chin. Julian was quick to wrap his arms around her waist and, keeping her close to him, brought his lips to hers. He didn't care that they were standing on the middle of the sidewalk. The feeling of her tongue caressing his, the way she moaned softly when he deepened the kiss, made it too pleasurable for him to consider his usual need for privacy. In that moment, Julian's world consisted only of Alana. He lifted her off the ground and with one of her hands on the back of his neck and the other grasping his shoulder, she held on to him tightly.

The close proximity of a dog barking at its owner made them break the kiss. Julian lowered her to her feet but was hesitant to let her go. Looking down at Alana, he brought her infinity scarf closer to her neck and adjusted the winter hat she was wearing. He enjoyed feeling her body against his and he didn't want to stop touching her.

"That look...tell me what you're thinking," Alana whispered.

"Do you really want to know what I'm thinking?"

"Uh-huh."

Julian ran his gloved thumb along her jaw until it came to rest it on her still-moist lips. "I'm thinking how this morning it felt unbelievably good to have my cock deep inside of your tight ass. How I loved watching my come drip out of you while you were still panting and your body was trembling in front of me."

She closed her eyes. "You're making me wet."

"I don't believe you."

Alana grabbed his hand and started to cross the street.

"Where are we going?"

"You'll see."

She took them to small coffee shop, on the other side of the road.

"Here." She passed him some money. "Can you buy me a coffee? I'll be right back."

Taking off his gloves, Julian shook his head. "I'm not taking your money. I'll buy us coffee."

"I'll get the next round, then." Alana turned around and walked toward the end of the coffee shop. "Black, please, no sugar," she said over her shoulder.

As he watched her disappear through the large door, he got in line to order, wondering what Alana was up to. The place was packed, the usual scene for a Chicago coffee shop on a sunny winter Sunday afternoon.

Julian was standing by the door holding their coffees, with his back to a family sitting by the window, and when Alana returned he felt her put something inside his jacket pocket. She took one of the cups from him with a smile.

"Check for yourself," she said, sipping her coffee but not taking her eyes away from his face.

Julian reached inside of his pocket. His expression shifted from curiosity to surprise and then to approval. Slowly, he took his hand out of his pocket and, in a casual gesture, rubbed it over his nose and mouth. He moved to stand behind Alana.

"I've your panties in my pocket and your scent all over my face," he spoke so only she could hear.

"Is it turning you on?" she said, still facing the room.

"Check for yourself."

In a fluid motion, as Alana turned to face him, she reached for his crotch and fondled him. It all happened very fast and for a brief moment their eyes met.

"You've no idea what I'll do to you when I get my hands on you later today," he said to her as they were again outside of the coffee shop.

"Is that a threat?"

They were walking side by side, enjoying their hot coffees.

"I don't threaten. I simply do."

"I guess I'll just have to wait and see, won't I?" Her tone was serious but full of mischief.

"Alana, you'll beg."

"For?" she asked, glancing at him with desire in her eyes.

"For me to stop."

"That will never happen."

"Oh really?"

"Not when it comes to you."

"We shall see if you continue to think that way once I stop holding back."

Admiring the bare tree branches swaying above them in the light wind, she smiled. "We shall."

They wandered around for several hours and Julian found himself laughing and enjoying himself more than he had in a very long time. Alana's happy demeanor was a positive influence on him. Julian let go of the thoughts that persistently weighed on him. It had been a week since Grace had come to him and revealed the true state of her marriage with Peter. After spending the night at Julian's condo, Grace had left Seth and Eli in his care while she had returned home to have a conversation with her husband. Watching over the boys for several hours had been exasperating. Julian had to constantly stop them from putting anything they could get their hands on into their mouths. He had to change more diapers than he ever thought he would. To entertain them, Julian had showed them every kid-friendly video he could find on the Internet and, through all of that, Seth and Eli had stirred within Julian a sense of wonder. When Grace had arrived to take them back home with her, he had experienced a mix of strong emotions. But he hadn't shared them with Grace. Julian knew he had, a long time ago, relinquished his right to have such feelings toward the boys.

"Should I even ask why we ended up at the cemetery?"

They were at Graceland Cemetery and, because the weather was still too cold for most people to wander outside for long periods of time, it appeared they were the only ones there. The sky had changed from a cheerful, clear blue to a deep, depressing grey. The wind, which had picked up, was the only sound breaking the eerie silence.

"I love cemeteries," she replied softly, not standing far from Julian. "You don't?"

"Not particularly."

"I've been fascinated by them since I was a kid."

"What do you like about them?"

Without a destination in mind, they were wandering amidst the graves throughout the barren grounds.

"The dead. I read the names on the graves, how long they were alive, and I try to imagine what kind of life they might have had, the happy and sad events they experienced, who they might have loved and who might have loved them, who they left behind…like they're the characters of an epic novel created by my imagination."

When a strong gust of wind moved Alana's long hair off her shoulders and made it flutter around her face, Julian took a moment to admire how she stood out against such a stark and poignant background.

"If you walked in here today and you saw a grave with the name Julian Reeve on it, what type of person would you make him to be? What life would you give him?" he asked, pulling up the collar of his black wool coat to better protect himself from the cold wind.

"I'd say he lived a short life. A linguistics professor, he was an intellectual who wore thick tortoiseshell frames and had an extensive collection of blazers. He loved books. Even more than

I do." Alana winked at him. "He had a wife, a nice woman, and a couple of children. But he wasn't in love with her so when he met Rosalind, who he called Rosa and who happened to be a few years older than him and an accomplished poet, he couldn't stop himself from being attracted to her. The two of them started an intense and life-changing affair. While his sweet wife stayed at home raising the kids, he and Rosa traveled the world together. But Rosa died of a mysterious disease. He was by her side until the end. Losing her broke his heart and plundered his soul into a silent despair that couldn't be expressed through words. He died five years later, hit by a car while crossing the street. In his pocket there was a note Rosa had written for him when they had just met and their hearts were ablaze with a fervor only love can create—*My dear Julian, my silly Reeve. Do you remember when I said you were my Superman?*" Alana turned to Julian, a carefree smile on her face. "With Reeve for a surname I had to mention Superman."

Before he could speak, Julian cleared his throat. "I don't know what to say…does that sound like a good life to you?"

"Absolutely. He got to experience an all-consuming love that, because of death's merciful intervention, didn't wither under the cruelty and relentlessness of time. He died in love and she died loving him. Not many have that."

Julian wanted to move closer to Alana but he was having a hard time doing anything else that wasn't surrendering himself to the memories her words had stirred.

"You're such a romantic," he finally said, his gaze lost in the empty air in front of him.

"No, I'm a pragmatist."

At that point Julian was able to smile. "You made a love affair the highlight of my short life. Isn't that a perfect example of a romantic?"

"Imagine you're on your deathbed and reminiscing about your life. What do you think will jump out at you? How you should have treated more troubled kids? How you should have made more money? Unlikely."

"If you were on your death bed right now, who would you think about?" Julian asked, his voice almost drowned out by the wailing sound of the wind.

Walking a few feet to her right Alana sat down on a wooden bench. Julian joined her, sitting so close that his leg touched hers.

"My family."

"You mentioned before you wish you still had a family...are they dead?"

She nodded. "Yours?"

"I don't know for sure but I would guess that they are."

They were both staring at the muddy ground and Alana was the first one to speak. "I'm sorry they're gone."

"What happened to yours?" he asked, forgetting that by asking that question he was nearing dangerous territory with her.

Alana shook her head.

"You don't want to talk about it?"

"It hurts too much."

Julian wrapped his arm around her and Alana rested her head on his shoulder. They sat for a while, in silence. He didn't know what she was thinking but he imagined it was about her family. He rarely allowed himself to think about his but there was a melancholy to their surroundings that awoke in him memories of his childhood. There was a time in his life when Julian had felt so lonely that he wished he had a sibling, someone he could trust and confide in, but knowing his brother or sister would have probably gone through what he did after his mother abandoned him, was too overwhelming. He found comfort in knowing all the pain he had felt hadn't been mirrored by someone he cared about.

Julian's gaze wandered. The scattered rows of dark tombstones, some of them tilted, went on for as far as he could see. An unexpected feeling of tranquility started to take shape in him and regardless of the damp cold seeping into his core, his body relaxed against Alana's.

"Have you ever loved?" she asked, leaning closer to him. Her movement had been almost imperceptible but he had noticed it.

"A long time ago."

"The girl from your nightmares? Tatia?"

Julian lay his cheek on her head and felt the cheap fabric of her winter hat against his skin. Looking down he noticed her naked hands on her lap. Taking his gloved hand out of his pocket, he covered both of her hands.

"She and someone else," he replied, his stare still on her icy hands.

"I hope you told them."

"Not enough times."

"If you saw them today what would you say?"

He felt the tender touch of the falling snowflakes on his face and a shiver of contentment ran through his body. He inhaled deeply. His nose and mouth were so close to Alana that the scent of her took hold of his senses. "That I remember."

By the time they walked out of the cemetery, there was a layer of fresh snow on the ground. The temperature started to drop, which meant the city was in for a winter storm.

"I really wish I had my car with me," Julian said, as he ran his fingers though his now white hair.

"Why? You're not enjoying getting around on foot as the sky dumps snow on your head?"

He gave her an amused look. "Do you even need to ask?"

"Have you always been this high maintenance?"

"I have lived in poverty and in wealth. Let me tell you, I choose wealth any day."

"I can't say I blame you."

"Where are you taking us?"

"It's okay, Julian."

"What's okay?"

"To not always be in control. There's relief to be found when you allow someone else to take charge."

Alana's comment wasn't inaccurate. Julian understood the solace relinquishing control could bring. But for him there was no relief being vulnerable around someone else, especially someone he was intimate with. The possible negative consequences were just too great for him not to fear.

"I thought you were excited about calling the shots today," he said.

"I am. And even though you started the day being excited about it too, for some reason, it's now causing you serious anxiety."

He sighed, smiling. "That obvious, huh?"

"Glaringly."

They got on at Sheridan subway station and took the Red Line to Belmont. When they got to street level the sidewalks were slippery and Julian reached for Alana's hand. She was so light that if she slipped she would fall easily.

"So…where are we going?" he asked again.

Alana looked up at him and groaned. They both burst out laughing.

"A bookstore. Happy now?"

"Which one?" Julian pressed.

"You're something else. I told you where we're going."

"And I asked you the name of the bookstore. What's wrong with that?"

"There's nothing wrong with you asking but I'm not telling you."

"Why?"

"Because you have to let go and we have to start somewhere," she said.

"Really? It sounds childish to me."

"To be honest, I don't care if you find it childish or not. Don't listen to the chatter in your brain. Give yourself to the moment and flow with it."

Julian shook his head in frustration but didn't speak. He allowed Alana to lead the way and soon they were entering Elliot's.

Alana greeted the man behind the counter with a friendly smile and Julian followed her up the narrow wood stairs to the second floor.

"Don't let the grumpy looking man downstairs fool you. He's actually very nice. I call him Bubbles," she whispered, leaning closer to Julian as they made their way upstairs.

Julian laughed, leaning forward and kissing her neck just as she removed her scarf and jacket. "Am I starting to see the real Alana?"

"Who would that be?"

"Trouble. Lots and lots of trouble."

Turning around, she winked. "You have no idea."

The bookstore was almost empty and they spent several hours browsing its three floors filled with books. Julian wished he had visited the bookstore sooner. With its creaky floors, narrow corridors and a smell that reminded him of a dusty old house, the place had the charm of a hidden, forgotten library. It was impossible not to be seduced by it.

After spending some time on the bottom floor, Julian finally found Alana on the third floor, sitting by the small stained-glass window, wearing her thick-framed reading glasses and her nose buried deep in a large book.

"Anything that interests you?" he asked, keeping his voice low even though they were the only ones on that floor.

"I always find something that interests me."

Speaking to her from his standing position made Julian feel unnecessarily domineering so he sat on a pile of books, across from her. "I can't believe I haven't been here before. It's quite a gem."

"I knew you would like it. It's my favorite used bookstore in the city. It's been here for fifteen years. I believe only soulless people don't love books with a past…what do you have there?" she asked, looking at the book Julian was holding. "Let me guess, it's about aliens?"

"Funny," he sneered at her teasing tone. "It's about the Ottoman Empire."

"Sounds like an easy read."

"You?"

She lifted the book she was holding so he could see the cover.

"*Sex and Punishment, Four Thousand Years of Judging Desire.*" Julian read the title out loud. "Sounds like an easy read."

Alana laughed, closing the book. "I'll be done in less

than a week."

"Why did you choose it?"

"It looked interesting."

"How so?"

She raised an eyebrow. "Trying to analyze me, Dr. Reeve?"

"Just curious, that's all."

"We saw each other for the first time at a sex club. I'm sure you can understand why I would find the topic of society attempting to control sexuality through the law interesting." She tucked a strand of her hair behind her ear. "You might be more educated and wealthier than me, but I'm not a vapid little thing."

"You haven't shared much about yourself, but from day one it has been clear to me how intelligent you are."

She smiled at him and Julian leaned back, admiring her. She was in her element and he couldn't remember seeing her more at ease.

"Pass me your Holga," he instructed.

"Why?"

"Who's afraid to let go now, huh?"

Alana rolled her eyes. She grabbed the camera and passed it to Julian. He pressed the shutter. As soon as he had taken the picture, Alana returned to the book she had been holding.

"Can you look at the camera again?"

"You had one shot," she replied, not looking up from the page.

Julian wasn't bothered by her refusal to cooperate. She looked even more beautiful when she wasn't facing the camera and her attention was on something she visibly loved.

"Alana?" Julian called out to her. "I want you to know if you ever wanted to lay low for a while, you could take time off from work and stay at my place. I'd be more than willing to help you out. If you ever wanted a different job, a different address, a fresh start...I could give you that."

"Why would you do that for me?" She didn't sound upset by his offer. Merely surprised.

"Because I care for you and I don't want anyone to harm you. I want you to know you have options."

"Thank you. Thank you for giving me an option and for leaving it up to me to decide."

"I know if I tell you I want you to stop going to the club, quit your job, and stay at my place, you'll say no."

"You're right on that."

"Will you think about it, though, and then tell me what you want to do?"

"I will, Julian. I promise."

Removing her glasses, she kneeled on the floor, between his legs. Julian caressed her cheek with his hand and kissed her lips, affectionately at first. Soon the kiss became eager, more assertive and he cradled her nape on his open palm, keeping her face close to his. Alana broke the kiss and while she held his gaze, he felt her hands slide down his torso and stop over his erection. She fondled him over the thick fabric of his jeans and Julian bit his lower lip.

"There aren't security cameras on the third floor," she said, unbuckling his jeans.

As he felt her mouth on him, Julian threw his head back and knocked over a large pile of books. He cursed under his breath but Alana didn't stop. Gathering all of her hair with his hand, he held it in his closed fist as her head moved up and down. Julian usually used his hold on her hair to control her movements. Enjoying it deep and rough, her gagging sounds and the tears spilling down her cheeks from the strain always fueled his arousal. But this time he simply held her hair up for her, allowing her to be in control.

Pulling him out of her mouth, she looked up, saliva dripping down her chin and onto him.

"You're so fucking good at this," he whispered, breathing hard.

He saw Alana pick up the forgotten camera from the floor and, while she continued to stroke his erection with her tight fist, she began to take pictures of him.

"Don't."

Julian became aware of the voices on the floor below and Alana placed a finger to her lips, a warning sign for him to stay quiet. Leaning closer, she kissed him. "We'll hear if they come up the stairs. Close your eyes and enjoy. I want you to come in my mouth. I want to swallow you."

In his sprawled position over the toppled books, with his briefs by his ankles and dust sprinkled all over his coat, Julian wanted to abandon himself to the feeling of her lips and tongue on him. The voices downstairs continued and he hoped they didn't decide to climb the stairs to the top floor. Should they do so, he wouldn't have the strength to move. They would be caught.

He desperately wanted to shout and vocalize the satisfaction he was feeling. Julian was so immersed in his own pleasure that when she pressed her saliva covered finger inside of him, Julian didn't flinch. He took a series of deep breaths, coercing his body to relax. As Alana kept him deep in her mouth, he felt her finger move forward, slowly, until it was as far as possible inside of him. The pressure of it, laced with the insinuation of pain, propelled Julian into a dense haze where Alana, the bookstore, the voices downstairs and even his own body ceased to exist. His orgasm hit him so violently that he experienced an unadulterated state of deliverance.

With the last spasms rolling over his body, Julian opened his eyes and saw Alana still kneeling at his feet, her tongue licking him and her finger hidden in him. The dress shirt he wore under the V-neck sweater was glued to his body by a thick layer of sweat.

Standing up, Alana stared down at him. "Now I want you to take me to your place and show me exactly what you've been thinking of doing to me all day."

Julian looked up at Alana and a violent surge of dominance ran through him. "I'm never letting you go." They were the same words he had told her in the shower a few weeks ago.

"Why?" she whispered, her eyes never leaving his.

"Because since the day I saw you, you've always been mine."

· · ·

By the time they crossed the doorstep of his condo it was nighttime. Having removed her boots and jacket, Alana stood in the foyer in knee-high black wool stockings over a pair of sheer nylons. Julian wasn't sure if her oversized sweater was meant to be a dress or if she had just decided that she should wear it as one.

He still couldn't believe she was as old as she said she was and part of him wondered if she had lied to him about her age.

"Come here," he said, leaning against the wall.

She moved toward him, stopping when the tips of her toes touched his.

"Look at me."

She lifted her eyes to him. Julian didn't move. The top of her head didn't even reach his collarbone. Suddenly their difference in size scared him. Without warning, Julian closed his hand around her neck. His grip wasn't strong enough to prevent her from breathing, but he was exerting enough pressure to make her uncomfortable. As he lowered his head toward her, he pulled her up slightly, their faces a mere few inches apart. Alana didn't say anything but he felt her swallow hard.

"Do you understand what I can do to you?"

She continued to stare back at him and he could feel her breath fan his face.

"Do you?" he repeated.

"Why are you doing this? To scare me? To get off?"

"So you understand how vulnerable you really are. Remember, Alana? You need to protect yourself." Julian brought her face even closer to his and that made her grasp the hand he had around her throat. "From me, Thompson and every other man at The Raven Room."

"This is not about me. Never was. This is about you."

"I'm doing this because I care for you."

"You care for me? You're saying all of this because you hope I can stop you from hurting me. But guess what? It's not on me to stop you. It's on you."

"Yes, I want to control you. I want to hurt you. I want to tie you up, blindfold you, gag you, spank you, hear your screams, see your tears, smell your arousal, feel the sweat on your skin, taste your blood. I want you, Alana. All of you."

"Why?"

"I told you."

"Why Julian?"

"Because that's who I am."

"Show me."

"Show you?" he repeated, not letting go of her neck. He was looking at her like he was in agony.

"Yes. Show me who you are."

"Don't, Alana."

"Please, Reeve, I need this as much you do."

Julian felt her hands on his hair, on his face, and he wasn't sure if it was the look in her eyes or the way she said his name, but placing both of his hands under her thighs, he lifted her up and carried her to the bedroom. He threw Alana in the middle of his bed. With one swift movement, together with her knee-high stockings, he removed her nylons and discarded them on the floor. He did the same thing to her bra and oversized sweater. She was fully naked in front of him. Pressing her face into the mattress, Julian pulled her onto all fours, her knees on the edge of the bed. Unbuckling his belt, he unzipped his jeans and brought her lower body closer to his. He held on to her hips, driving himself fully inside of her. She cried out.

"Is this what you want, huh?" he asked, aware he was hurting her. She wasn't ready.

"No. And it's not what you want. More. I want more."

The cadence of their bodies coming together was the only sound in the otherwise silent bedroom. Julian grabbed Alana's hair with one hand and, wrapping the long stands around his fingers, he tugged. "Why? Tell me."

"Tell you what?"

He tugged again, making her head jerk back. "Why did you come into my life?"

Alana spread her legs further apart and that made him slide deeper inside of her.

"You came into mine," she said, her voice breaking. "You did."

Without warning, Julian stepped back and turned her so she was facing him. With his body hovering over hers, he brushed her hair away from her eyes and held her face between his hands.

"Remember the first time I saw you at the club? Thompson had his cock inside of you but you weren't giving him any part of you. You were making it your own experience. Your pleasure was your own. It was beautiful. You are beautiful."

"Julian…" Tears fell from the corners of her eyes, rolling over his hands.

"I'm right here," he whispered, caressing her cheek, running his fingers in slow circles over her tear-streaked skin. "Right here." Removing his clothes, he joined her. When he entered her again, Alana's body didn't fight him.

"Give into it," she said, wrapping her arms and legs around him.

"Alana…" Julian's voice carried a warning.

"Give into me."

Suddenly, Julian stopped moving inside of her. He got up and went to stand by the large window, his chest heaving with his laborious breathing. He stared at her on the bed.

"Face me, on your knees, legs open," he demanded, his voice harsh.

She kept her eyes on his face for a minute longer. Propping herself up on her elbows, Alana was breathing just as hard as he was. She followed his instructions.

"Touch yourself." Julian licked his dry lips. "That's it, make it feel good." Remaining very still, he continued to watch her. "Three fingers. I want to see them go inside of you."

She tilted her head, making her long hair fall over her shoulder, touching the curve of her breast.

"Tell me when you're about to come."

He stood, not touching his erection. All of Julian's attention was on her. The bedroom wasn't overly warm but beads of sweat covered his chest, droplets sliding over his stomach.

"I'm close," Alana said, trying to stay upright.

Hearing her, he got back on the bed, kneeling in front of her.

Julian slapped her hand aside. "Stop touching yourself."

There was a mix of confusion and expectation on Alana's face. He stroked her hair. "Open the drawer on the nightstand to your left." Julian's eyes never left her.

"What am I looking for?" she asked.

"You'll see."

As she searched inside of the drawer, Julian took in the shape of her naked back. He imagined running his hands up and down the sides of her torso, absorbing her warmth through his open palms.

Alana turned to face him, holding in her hand the only object he kept in the drawer. She didn't say anything but she didn't have to.

"Use it on me," he demanded.

Looking down at the razor blade in her hand, and then up again at Julian, she shook her head. "I can't."

"I need it. I want you to be the one to give it to me."

"Not this."

"Do it, Alana."

"I can't."

"Do it," he repeated. "Right here." He touched his upper arm.

"I've noticed the scars hidden under your tattoo. You used to be a cutter."

"Yes."

"But you don't have any recent scars."

"It's either you or me."

"Why?"

"Alana, do as I tell you."

"I can't do it."

"Alana—"

"Listen to me, Julian—"

Moving fast, he took a hold of her hand with the razor and brought it closer to his arm. Alana screamed, turning her body away from Julian and forcing him to use his own body to immobilize her. Just as he was about to close his arms tightly around her, she elbowed him in the groin. Julian winced in pain and Alana took the opportunity to escape across the room.

"What are you doing?" Julian asked, narrowing his eyes. He didn't move but his body was ready to act. His muscles were taut, strained by the tension running though him.

In a succession of quick and short movements, she started to cut along her arm. "How does it feel, huh? Watching me cut myself? Does it hurt?"

"Alana, don't!" Julian jumped from the bed and closed the space between them with large strides. He seized her hand and squeezed her wrist. "Drop the razor."

"Feel it, Julian!" She was shouting, trying to keep the razor close to her skin. Some of the cuts had started to bleed and, as they struggled, Julian's naked body became covered in red smears. "I want you to feel it!"

"Stop it, Alana! Drop the fucking razor."

They both fell to the floor. Holding her from behind, he threw his legs over hers and as he held one of her arms close to her chest, he kept the hand with the blade away from her.

"It hurts, huh? It fucking hurts when someone you love hurts themselves, doesn't it?"

"Drop it," he repeated, holding her against the floor. He squeezed her wrist tighter and Alana yelped in pain. "Let go of the razor. Do it."

Julian was panting. With his body covering hers, he could feel Alana's sobs shaking her frame. He saw her open her fingers and drop the razor. Not hesitating, he threw it across the room. He didn't try to move away from Alana or to lessen his hold on her.

"Let me go." She was the first to speak and her throat sounded raw.

Julian pressed his forehead against her temple. "Are you done hurting yourself?"

"Yes! Let me go."

He took a deep breath, his lips on the curve of her jaw. He waited a bit longer but eventually he moved his arms and legs away from her. As soon as he eased his hold, Alana got up and went to pick up her sweater, putting it on as fast as she could.

"You're bleeding. Let me look at your cuts."

"Stay where you are," she said, seeing him get up from the floor.

"Alana, where are you going?"

He followed her and she turned around, facing him. "I'm leaving, do you understand?"

"Before you leave, I have to look at your cuts."

She closed her eyes and took a steadying breath. Turning her back on him, she walked toward the front door, leaving her stockings and nylons behind.

Julian watched her grab her purse, her jacket and her boots. Not stopping to put them on, she opened the door and, before closing it behind her, she glanced at him. "We can't be together. If we do one of us will die."

After she left, Julian continued to stand in the hall, naked, with Alana's blood on his body.

CHAPTER 21

Meredith hadn't heard from Julian so she decided show up on his doorstep. It wouldn't be the first time she knocked on his door unannounced. Julian was the only person she didn't mind showing her irrational side to. He had many faults, but he always seemed to understand where she was coming from, even when her behavior reflected her more embarrassing flaws.

After taking a shower and putting on a pair of comfortable jeans, t-shirt and a hoodie, Meredith took a cab to Julian's condo. There was no way she was going to drive. The mix of snow and rain was a dangerous combination. It took her twice as long to get there and by the time she stepped up to his front door, she was ready for a tall glass of wine. She knocked, waiting to see if he was home. After a few seconds, she knocked again. Putting her ear to the door, she had heard a noise coming from the other side. She knocked a third time.

"Julian? It's me, open the door," Meredith said, pounding on the door. "I know you're in there."

Frustrated by the lack of response, she banged her palm on the door. "The cab ride to get here cost me more than twenty dollars. I had to give my phone number to the concierge so he would let me up and now your neighbors are about to find out how batshit crazy the women in your life are," she shouted, not ceasing to bang on the door. "I'm not leaving until you speak to me."

Meredith put more effort into slamming both of her hands on the door, expecting at any second to see security stepping out of the elevator. "Goddammit—"

Catching her hands midair, the door opened and she found

herself staring at Julian. "What the hell, why aren't you getting back to me?"

"Go away, Meredith."

"What?"

"Go away."

"Fuck that." She walked past him, entering his condo. "I come all the way here because I'm worried about you and this is how you talk to me?"

Facing her, he held the door open. "Please leave."

She stood with her hands on her waist, looking at him with determination. "No."

Julian grabbed her by the arm and started to push her toward the door.

"What do you think you're doing?"

"Getting you to leave."

"Stop it. You don't get to treat me this way."

As she felt Julian tightening his grasp on her, she stopped thinking and instinct took over. Putting all of her body weight into it, she slapped him. As soon as her hand made contact with his cheek, Julian let go of her and took a few steps back. With his back touching the wall, he slid to the floor. Elbows on his knees, head hanging forward, he closed his hands on the back of his neck.

Meredith stood, her palm stinging. She watched him on the floor and when he didn't move or look up at her, she closed the door. Getting rid of her jacket, she approached Julian and extended her hand out to him.

"C'mon, get up," she said, her voice firm but kind.

He didn't react but Meredith didn't waver.

Several seconds went by before he grabbed her hand and came to stand. Wearing only a pair of old sweats, she noticed his unkempt hair, the dark circles under his eyes and the several days' worth of facial hair growth that had almost become a full beard. She frowned when the odor of his unwashed body hit her and it made her wonder how long Julian had been locked up in his condo. Seeing the small streaks of dried-up blood on his body made Meredith pause.

Not letting go of Julian's hand, she led the way into the bedroom. All the lights were off but the curtains were pulled back, opening up the room to the breathtaking view of the city. Meredith saw the pile of large pillows and blankets on the floor by the window. That's where he had been when she had showed up at his doorstep.

Sitting on the large pillows, Meredith wrapped herself with one of the soft blankets. She and Julian were side by side, their shoulders almost touching, facing the downtown skyline as a heavy fog began to form and obscure the tallest buildings.

"I'm sorry I grabbed your arm."

Meredith nodded, continuing to look straight ahead. "I'm sorry I slapped you."

"I needed it."

"When was the last time you stepped outside?"

"A week ago, I think."

"Shit. Why didn't you reply to any of my texts or phone calls?"

"Maybe I wanted you to come."

She sighed, rubbing her forehead. "You're lucky to have me, you know that?"

He nodded.

Glancing at the red smears on his chest, she decided it was time to ask him. "Whose blood is that?"

"Alana's."

"Alana's?"

"Uh-huh."

"What the hell happened, Julian? Is she here?"

"Not anymore."

"Tell me what happened."

For a while the only sound in the room was Julian's deep voice as he described to Meredith what had taken place between him and Alana. He never took his eyes away from the lights sprawled below them and by the time he finished speaking, Meredith couldn't take her eyes away from his face.

The silence between them was as thick as the fog descending upon the city and while she searched for the best thing to say, she reached for Julian's hand and wrapped her fingers though his. She felt him holding on tightly.

"I'm not well, Meredith," he said, his face in his hands. "There's something very wrong with me."

She swallowed hard. She didn't know how to handle whatever it was he was dealing with but turning her back on him felt wrong. All she could do was make him talk to her.

"Because you asked Alana to cut you? I've never done it but there are a lot of people who are into it. I wouldn't say that makes you crazy...hey, sometimes I get off on hate-fucking douchebags. No one is perfect."

With his face still in his hands Julian shook his head. "I wanted to cut her. Not me. Her. But I couldn't get myself to do it so I forced her to cut me."

Meredith squeezed his hand. "Why couldn't you?"

Julian didn't reply.

"Is that why you go to The Raven Room?" Meredith continued, touching the back of Julian's head. She started to caress his hair. "Is that what you do down there? You cut women?"

"Please, Meredith. Please don't."

"While you're doing it, how do you feel? Explain it to me so I can understand."

"I can't explain it."

She insisted. "Try."

Julian didn't move and he took a while to answer.

"The look of pain and satisfaction on their faces, the sight of blood seeping out of their bodies...I feel a mix of arousal, guilt, and release. All at once." His voice was thick with shame.

"They want you to do that to them?"

That question made him lift his face from his hands and look at her. "Yes, of course. That's why I go to The Raven Room. So I can have willing partners."

Meredith was mesmerized by what Julian was sharing with her. "How old are they?"

"Some are younger than you."

"How do you feel if you don't do it?"

"The need for it keeps growing and it's all I can think about. It's all I want. I can go a few weeks without it but then it takes over. I can't function. I feel like I'm going mad. I started to self-harm when I was a kid. It helped me cope. I continued throughout my adolescence, especially when things got really rough." It sounded like Julian was remembering a time in his life he wanted to forget. "Cutting is not something you do in front of others but when I was living with the Dulgorukova family, Sofia and Tatia were always around. I started doing it in front of them." The expression on Julian's face transformed to reveal nothing less than profound regret. "Now, as an adult, I can see how wrong and destructive it was for them to witness it, but at the time I just knew I needed to cut myself. I didn't think about the consequences. That's what changed it for me. Them watching."

"Did you ever cut them?"

"I would never hurt them. Ever, Meredith."

She brought the back of his hand to her lips and kissed it. "I believe you."

"After adopting me, Hazel sent me into therapy. I was trying to stop and one day I was having sex with this girl and I asked her if I could cut her. She said yes," Julian lowered his eyes. "After that, I couldn't turn back. I felt like I had finally come face-to-face with something that had always been there, inside of me. Before I just didn't have the courage to embrace it."

They were speaking softly, as if they both feared there was someone hiding in the shadows who could overhear their words. "I know you're afraid," Meredith said. "But you're not alone. I'm here." She looked at the low, heavy clouds on the night sky and she imagined how it would feel to be Julian. "You take pleasure from engaging in blood-play with women who want it as much as you do. That doesn't make you a bad man." She stared further up into the sky. "You're ashamed of who you are. The day you embrace yourself, you'll be strong. Until then you're weak."

They continued to sit side by side, holding hands.

"Are you worried about Alana?" Meredith asked.

"She walked out of here without half of her clothes, bleeding… she wouldn't let me make sure she was okay."

"Have you talked since?"

"The next day I drove to her work but she wasn't there. I've called several times since but they always tell me she's not in."

"She's probably avoiding you. I'm sure she's okay, Julian."

When he didn't say anything, Meredith turned her head to look at him. He was sitting with his eyes closed.

She watched him for a while. Julian was the type of man who appeared to have everything. But beneath it all there was so much misfortune, pain, and destruction that she believed most people would either pity him or simply want to stay as far from him as possible.

"I shouldn't have asked her to cut me," he said, breaking the silence.

Meredith sighed. "You shouldn't have asked the way you did."

"When she started to cut herself…I felt scared. For her. I was so scared for her."

"Listen, would it help if I stopped at her work to make sure she's okay? I won't approach her."

Julian looked stunned by her offer. "Would you do that?"

"Right now it's clear to me that not knowing if she's okay is harming you more than anything else. We need to get you to be able to function again. I'll go."

Julian rested his head on her shoulder. His blatant need for comfort caught Meredith by surprise. The Julian she knew wouldn't have showed such vulnerability but, then again, one of the things she now realized was that no one, including her, truly knew Julian.

"Outside of the club, who else is aware of this about you?" she asked, feeling his hair rub against her cheek.

"Pete. No one else."

Meredith wrapped her arms around him, covering both of them with the blanket she had been holding. "If the truth becomes known your career is over."

"I know, Meredith."

"Everything you have worked to achieve will be taken away from you. You're a child psychologist and an Associate Professor who goes to an underground sex club to cut women while you get off. Your past involving Tatia and Sofia will come out. The fact you were once accused of sexually abusing an eight-year-old girl will be in everyone's mind. It won't matter that her father, in the end, admitted to it. Your life will be destroyed."

"I think of that every day."

Julian sounded defeated and, because there wasn't anything else for her to say about it, she changed the subject. "You're going to shower, shave, put on some clean clothes and eat half of the pizza I'm about to order for us."

"Only half, huh?"

Meredith smiled. He was trying to lighten the mood and she was thankful for it. They both needed it. "Yes, and that's if you're lucky."

Twenty-minutes later, Julian came out of the shower looking more like the man Meredith was used to. When the party-size pizza arrived they sat on the bed, eating slice after slice.

They emptied a bottle of red wine and afterwards they were both too full and tired to move.

Meredith was falling asleep beside the empty pizza box and dirty napkins when she felt Julian tuck her in under the covers. He caressed her hair and Meredith kept her eyes closed, feeling her body sink even further into the soft bed. Julian hid his face in her hair, something he always did when they slept together, and Meredith found relief in that small gesture. It made her believe that no matter how much she came to learn about Julian, there were things that would never change between the two of them.

Chapter 22

A loud sound woke Meredith. Lifting her head off the pillow, she struggled to open her eyes.

"What's that noise?" she asked, looking at Julian, who was lying beside her.

"Someone is at the door."

"Are you expecting anyone?"

"No."

She reached for her phone as Julian was getting out of bed. "It's eight AM on a Sunday morning. Who's crazy enough to be out and about at this time?"

"You have a sister I don't know about?" he asked, glancing at her over his shoulder.

"Must be one of your other crazy bitches."

Julian left the bedroom and Meredith rolled over, covering her head. She was too tired to get up.

When Meredith woke up again she looked around the room and saw how much brighter it was. She had slept longer than she had wanted. Wondering where Julian was, Meredith sat up, making the empty pizza box fall to the floor. She cursed, rubbing her eyes. Used to sleeping in the nude, she had a vague memory of removing her clothes at some point throughout the night but she had no idea where they had ended up. Not bothering to spend more time looking for them, she stood in front of the mirror—her hair was out of control and she had pillow marks on her face. She needed coffee.

Meredith walked out of the bedroom and made her way down the hall, toward the living room. What she saw as she turned the corner made her stop.

Standing naked, his back to her, Julian was swaying his hips in a languorous movement. Resting on the opposite wall, a tall mirror allowed Meredith a full view of what was taking place in front of him. On the couch, prone on her hands and knees, moaning softly, was a woman Meredith did not recognize.

Julian was deep inside of her. With one hand on her hip and the other caressing her where their bodies met, he was slowly propelling her toward orgasm. Leaning forward, moving her long hair to the side of her neck, Julian began to cover her back in small kisses. There was a tenderness to his touch that made Meredith's breath catch in her chest. Never before had she witnessed such a display of adoration from Julian. Everything Julian was doing, the way he kissed the woman's skin, the way he stroked her, the way he moved within her, was all to bring her pleasure. In light of how Meredith had seen him act in the past and considering what he had told her the previous night, she hadn't been prepared to come face-to-face with loving and affectionate Julian.

Her eyes returned to the woman and Meredith suddenly realized who she was. It was Alana. Without her makeup and sexy outfit, she looked like a different person from the one she had seen at The Raven Room. Even her hair appeared to be lighter. She had been attracted to Alana when she had seen her at the club. Now watching her under Julian, making soft panting sounds of desire, her attraction toward Alana only intensified.

She and Julian looked beautiful together. The sight of them had an effect on Meredith but her feelings couldn't be described as jealousy, anger, or disappointment. In fact, she was too enthralled by what she was witnessing to process her emotions or even try to understand why Alana was there.

Julian brought his lips closer to Alana's face and even though she could barely hear it, Meredith knew he was whispering endearments to her. Alana turned her head toward Julian and caressed his cheek, giving him a smile brimming with contentment, arousal, and emotion. Whatever secrets she was keeping from Julian, whatever lies she had told him, Julian's feelings for Alana were reciprocated.

Straightening his back, he continued to move inside of her. Standing tall, with every muscle in his naked body taut, his striking tattoo sleeve adorning his arm, the feeling of ecstasy hatched on his features, he looked tantalizing. For the first time Meredith was watching him have sex with someone else and the vision of it was awakening all of her senses.

Her eyes shifted back to Alana and the contrast of her feminine shape, the sight of her small breasts, the fairness of her skin against Julian's darker and harder frame, sent a wave of desire through Meredith's body. Arousal blossomed within her and soon her nipples were hungry for someone's touch. The familiar sensation in her core proved she was ready for the only thing that could satiate her need.

In that moment, Julian looked at the tall mirror standing behind the couch. His eyes, heavy-lidded with pleasure, met hers. Meredith didn't shy away. As he continued to thrust, his gaze drew her in, immersed her in the erotic experience he and Alana were sharing.

Julian wasn't telling her to leave. He was inviting her to be part of it.

Meredith swallowed hard and a smile formed on Julian's face. He knew how aroused she was. For a few more moments nothing changed. While Julian and Alana savored the gratification that could only be achieved through the experience of unguarded intimacy, Meredith stood, admiring them.

She watched Julian lean forward again and whisper into Alana's ear. She nodded in response and looked up, catching Meredith's eyes in the mirror. There was a silent exchange between the two of them. Alana was acknowledging her. She stood up and walked toward Meredith.

As Meredith opened her mouth to speak, Alana placed her fingertips against her lips, silencing her.

"I know who you are," Alana whispered, her seductive gaze lingering on Meredith's face.

Meredith felt herself being pulled into Alana's eyes. She didn't know how to describe their color. At first glance they appeared to be brown but the longer she stared at them, the greener they became.

Glancing at the bandages on Alana's arm, Meredith understood why she had hurt herself when Julian had asked her to cut him. The person in front of her, the beautiful and arousing woman Julian had come to love, was just as lost as he was.

It wasn't clear who moved first, her or Alana. Their mouths came together and Meredith quivered against Alana's soft lips. One of the things Meredith appreciated most about the female body was its subtle power to trigger the most consuming desire. The feeling of Alana's tongue caressing hers made Meredith moan. When she had initially seen her at The Raven Room, Meredith had fantasized about Alana's hair and now, as she buried her hands in it, a small sound of pleasure escaped from the back of Alana's throat. Meredith couldn't believe her fantasy was coming true.

Alana brought her hands to cradle Meredith's face and while both of them were immersed in their kiss, Meredith became aware of someone else's proximity. Another set of hands, bigger, stronger, caressed her shoulders. Julian was standing behind her and soon his mouth was against her skin, adding to the sensual touch of his hands. His attention, together with Alana's, was stimulating Meredith to the point she was no longer sure she could sustain her own weight. She felt weak, wanting to collapse to the floor and let the waves of pleasure wash over her. The sensation of her arousal seeping out of her and dripping, little by little, down her leg, never failed to validate what she thought was magnificent about her own sexuality. She had always drawn power from her ability to embrace what she desired but, in that moment, for reasons she didn't understand, she felt vulnerable. When Alana's eager mouth closed between her legs, Meredith cried out.

"How does it feel?" She heard Julian ask by her ear. "To have her tongue on you, to drip right onto her lips?" Kissing her neck, he gripped her breast.

"Good…too good." Meredith let her head fall back toward Julian.

"Never too good," he whispered.

Meredith found herself caressing Alana's head and the insistent strokes of Alana's tongue made Meredith's whole body swing forward. If Julian didn't have his arms around her, she would have slumped to the floor. With her back pressed firmly against Julian, she let him hold her. Glancing downwards, Meredith watched Alana kneeling at her feet, and the need to taste her in the same way brought a renewed sense of urgency to the elation building within her.

Julian was right—never too good.

What she felt next made Meredith moan loudly. Entering her from behind, with slow indulgence, Julian was now inside of her. Alana didn't stop, continuing to stimulate her, licking and kissing her. She was running the tip of her tongue along Meredith's entrance, where she and Julian were joined, and she knew he too could feel Alana's mouth on him. He had slightly bent her at the waist, his muscular thighs coming under hers to help support her overwhelmed body, and all Meredith wanted was to capture the release she so desperately needed. It was close, teetering between cruel allusiveness and her voracious reach. Before it possessed her, Julian stopped. He told Alana to lie on the couch, on her back, and directed Meredith to kneel between her legs. She didn't hesitate. Abandoning herself to pleasure Alana, she made a small sound of approval when Julian joined her on the floor, on his knees, and entered her again. Alana was no less aroused than she was and tasting her sent a burst of desire through her whole frame, transporting Meredith to a frenzy nearing physical release.

With her mouth and hands on Alana's body, she kissed the inside of her thighs and licked the sweat off her skin. Meredith caressed her stomach, her breasts, sucked on her erect nipples. Hearing her lustful pants, feeling Alana's hands holding on to her, she penetrated her with her fingers and Alana's body lifted off the couch, meeting her giving mouth.

Meredith's eyes were closed and Julian felt impossibly hard inside of her, his palms pressed so tightly to her waist they were searing her skin. His groans were mingling with Alana's loud breathing, adding a rougher edge to the animalistic sounds coming from Meredith.

The pleasure building within Meredith and the certainty that both Alana and Julian, through their own pending release, were right there with her, carried Meredith over the threshold into an orgasm that forced her to let go of the already frail hold she had on all that existed outside of her own body.

Meredith's first fully rational thought was that she was lying on the floor, naked, with the soft area rug tickling her skin. She blinked, her eyes refocusing on the white ceiling. She shifted, knowing she couldn't get up just yet. From the corner of her eye she saw Julian, on the floor as well, his back resting against the couch. He had his eyes closed and his hand was around Alana's ankle, who was still on the couch, with one leg draped over Julian's shoulder. Meredith sat up and she let her head fall into her hand.

"You okay?"

Looking ahead, she found Julian's eyes on her.

"Yeah, the room is just spinning." It was a half-truth. The room was spinning but she was far from well as the realization of what she had just done was becoming clear to her. She just had sex with both Julian and Alana.

He caressed Meredith's knee. "Stay here. I'm going to get you some water. Can I bring you some?" he asked, turning to Alana.

"Please." Meredith heard her say.

As Julian was leaving toward the kitchen, Meredith glanced at Alana. "I saw you at The Raven Room before," she said, running her hands through her tangled hair.

"I remember," Alana answered. "Wait, you have a huge knot in your hair. Let me help you."

Meredith remained very still, aware of Alana's body close to hers. "One of the drawbacks of having long hair."

"All worth it, I would say. You have beautiful hair."

"Are you kidding me?" Meredith laughed. "I would kill for hair like yours."

"Stop talking nonsense. You're a knockout, Meredith, from head to toe."

Before she was aware of what she was doing, she touched the

discolored line along Alana's shoulder.

"Like my scar?" she asked, smiling.

"Sorry," Meredith removed her hand. "That was rude."

"Why is it rude? It's just a scar. A love bite from a twelve-year-old Golden Retriever I had just adopted from a shelter."

"Did you take him back to the shelter?"

"If I had taken him back they would have put him down." There was sadness in Alana's voice. "His longtime owner had died and he had nowhere to go." She reached for Meredith's hand and put it back on her shoulder. Encouraged by Alana's gesture, Meredith caressed the scar with her fingers. "When he bit me I had had him for only a few hours. He was scared," Alana continued. "He and I became the best of friends. I was heartbroken when he died."

Meredith was impressed with Alana. She appeared genuinely friendly toward her.

At that moment Julian returned with two glasses of water, passing them to Meredith and Alana. "Both of you have wild hair right now."

"So do you," Meredith replied, not waiting to drink the cold water he had brought them. She took a couple of large gulps, enjoying the refreshing feel of it.

With a boyish grin, Julian ran his hand through his messy hair. "I guess that means I should go take a shower. I'll be right back."

Watching him leave the room, Meredith had the sinking suspicion he was trying to give her and Alana some alone time.

"He's hoping that by the time he comes back we'll have become best friends and I'll have told you all my secrets."

Meredith chuckled. "I think you're totally right."

"What do you know about me?"

The question caught Meredith by surprise. Alana was still trying to work through the knot in her hair and her proximity was making it hard for Meredith to think.

"Alana," she paused, not daring to look at her, "the truth is that Julian told me everything. I'm aware of what happened the last time you saw each other."

They were both silent. When she was getting ready to speak again, Alana got off the couch and sat on the floor in front of her. Not knowing what Alana was thinking, Meredith allowed herself to stare into Alana's eyes. As soon as she did, she knew her attraction for Alana hadn't dissipated when her orgasm was over. It was still there and now it felt more authentic. Alana wasn't just the woman she had seen with Thompson at The Raven Room and she certainly wasn't just a woman who reminded Julian of his past. Up until now all she knew about Alana had been through Julian and, somehow, that had made her appear less real to Meredith. But that had just changed.

"I came here because I was worried about him—"

"You don't have to tell me anything," Meredith interrupted her gently, shaking her head.

"I want to. After I left I kept thinking about what he had asked me to do and I found myself feeling less angry."

Meredith glanced in the direction of the bedroom, where Julian was showering in the bathroom. Certain she wouldn't be overheard, she turned back to Alana. "There are reasons why I haven't walked away from him and one of those is that, to this day, no man has treated me as well as Julian has. At the same time he makes me feel like a woman, he makes me feel like his equal. I love that."

She wasn't sure why she was telling that to Alana. Maybe it was because Alana was the first person she met who also knew Julian. "He believes he's the scum of the earth because part of him wants to protect us and the other part wants to hurt us."

Alana's expression changed. She was now looking at Meredith with a mix of sadness and resignation. "Do you trust him?"

"He's the only person I trust completely."

"Protect yourself." Alana reached for Meredith's hand and held it between hers. "From everyone and everything. The Raven Room destroys all within its reach."

"What are you trying to tell me?"

Alana didn't reply.

"You were at the club with a man, Steven Thompson. Are you referring to him?" Meredith continued.

"Stay away from Thompson," Alana said, a hint of panic in her voice.

"Why? Has he done anything to you?"

Alana was about to answer when Julian reappeared, wearing a pair of fitted jeans and a t-shirt under a dark pullover. His hair was still damp from the shower and Meredith smelled the faint hint of masculine cologne. He sat on the large reading chair by the couch and looked at both of them with an amused expression.

"Do you mind sharing with us whatever is making you smirk?" Alana asked, not moving away from Meredith.

"You know, me sitting here with two beautiful, naked women at my feet. Does it get any better than this?"

Meredith groaned as she got up. "I'm putting an end to your enjoyment. I'm getting dressed."

She returned to the bedroom and dove under the bed, looking for her missing clothes. After a few minutes of crawling on the floor on her hands and knees, she found them. Without bothering to take a shower, she got dressed, grabbed her phone and walked down the hall. She stopped by the living room entrance. "I'm leaving. I've a lot to get done today." She turned to face Alana. "I'm sure I'll see you around."

Alana nodded, her gaze nothing less than a plea for caution. "Remember. From everyone and everything."

Before she turned her attention to Julian, Meredith's eyes lingered on Alana. She wished she had more time alone with her.

Julian offered to walk her out.

"What was she talking about?" he asked, as soon as they got to the foyer. He kept his voice low.

"No idea." She didn't want to share Alana's warning with Julian. "I'm glad you both are fine now, though." She wasn't sure how much she believed that last part. Nothing was fine. No one inside of that condo was fine.

"How are you feeling about what happened between the three of us?"

"It's not my first time. You know that better than anyone else."

"I don't care about all the group sex you've had. I care about how you're feeling right now."

The urge to slap Julian, like she had done the night before, shot through Meredith's body like an electric current. She smiled. It wasn't a happy smile. It was full of bitterness. A little voice in the back of her head kept whispering to her she was angry with herself and not with him but she ignored it. One thing had become more important to her than writing a piece on The Raven Room—her relationship with Julian. And that was the reason why she still hadn't contacted Isaac Croswell. Meredith finally understood the extent of the power Julian had over her. She had never felt more afraid.

"I can't do this."

With those words she left.

Chapter 23

Meredith crossed the street, toward White Palace Grill, the diner in University Village Pam had chosen for their meeting. Staring at the business sign, she couldn't understand why, of all places, Pam had picked this one.

"Why are we meeting here?" she asked, sitting across from Pam.

"Best coffee; in my books, that's a good enough reason."

Meredith glanced at the large mug, filled with steaming black coffee that Pam had in front of her. "I hope you called me because you have some information for me?" She didn't want to be there and the sooner she got what she wanted from Pam, the sooner she could meet up with her friends, get drunk, and forget all the things in her life that were haunting her.

"I do have some information for you." Pam reached inside of her messenger bag and dropped a folder on top of the table. "I also would like you to explain to me how you got the address of that woman in Chatham, Samantha Michaels."

Meredith opened her mouth to speak but Pam cut her off. "I know you stopped by and asked her many questions about her friend, Lena."

There was no point for her to deny it. "Yes, I did."

"Why?"

"I don't have to explain myself to you."

Pam hit the table with her open hand. "Samantha mentioned that the woman who visited her said she was writing an article that would make people want to know what had happened to Lena and who had killed her."

Meredith couldn't deny it but she was ready to spin the truth.

"That was just something I said to get her to speak to me. You know that I'm writing a piece on the club and not about some women's death."

Pam looked like she was about to jump across the table and shake her. "Don't lie to me. What do you know, Meredith?"

"I don't know anything."

"You think The Raven Room had something to do with that woman's death, don't you?" Pam asked.

"You know what I think? Lena didn't kill herself and she didn't die of an accidental overdose. But you can't prove it so there's nothing you can do about it."

Meredith and Pam stared each other down.

"Do you understand why I want you stay away from that place? From Julian Reeve?"

Meredith didn't reply.

"What made you think of the club?" Pam continued.

Meredith shrugged. "I'm not telling you anything."

Pam took a deep breath. She was trying to compose herself. "I was able to find an address for the woman you saw at The Raven Room with Thompson. Alana."

Pam had shifted gears and that put Meredith on alert. She stared at the piece of paper her stepmother had laid on the table. "What's that?"

"An address."

"Of where Alana lives?"

"Don't know if she lives there full-time but she might."

Meredith took the white piece of paper and, unfolding it, read the address. "Are you kidding me? New Jackson Hotel?"

Pam took a sip of her coffee. "That's what I got."

"That place is a dump."

"That place is home to several permanent tenants, likely to this Alana woman as well, so stop being your judgmental self," Pam replied, her disapproving tone making clear what she thought of Meredith's comment. "It may not be the high class establishment you're accustomed to but it serves a purpose."

"You could say that about almost anything."

"I'm not getting into an argument with you about how a place like the New Jackson might be a necessary evil." Pam crossed her arms over her chest. "I wasn't able to find anything on the other two."

"You didn't get anything on Sofia and Tatia?"

"That's what I said. The type of search required to lead to useful information would take months."

Meredith could tell Pam was holding back. "You found out they're connected to Julian."

Pam leaned closer, her elbows on the table. "I hope you didn't think I wouldn't."

"I thought finding out what happened to the twins was worth it."

"Or did you hope it would make me feel bad for Reeve?" Pam asked with sarcasm in her voice. "You should know sob stories don't work on me."

Meredith closed her eyes and pinched the bridge of her nose with her fingers. "I really wish I could understand why you hate the man so much. It almost feels like a personal vendetta."

"He shot Olga Dulgorukova."

Meredith blinked a few times. "Excuse me?"

"One of the cops who was at the scene was convinced Reeve was the one who pulled the trigger. Not Sofia. Reeve."

"Why would the cop think that?"

"His fingerprints were on the gun."

"So? Maybe he touched it afterwards. Maybe he had touched the gun prior to that day."

"That's why it couldn't be proven that Reeve was the one who pulled the trigger."

"Even if he did it, even if he was the one that shot Olga, is that the only reason why you want to bring him down?"

"If he cared for that girl why would he allow her and everyone else to believe she killed her mother? Why would he allow an eight-year-old to carry that burden for the rest of her life? I'll tell you why," Pam paused, tapping the tabletop with her finger, "he's a sick person. I've been in this line of work long enough to recognize a sociopath when I come across one. I'll tell you what I know about Julian Reeve's main personality traits." Pam's eyes didn't leave Meredith's face. "He manipulates people. He uses them and when he no longer has a use for them, he discards them without a hint of remorse. Do you understand what I'm telling you?"

Meredith moved away from Pam, sitting back in her chair. She was still holding the piece of paper in her hand and she felt her fingers closing tightly on it, crumpling it. "How could I not? You're making it very clear." Meredith took the folder Pam had put on the table. "I should get going."

"How well do you know her?" Pam asked.

"Who?"

"Alana."

"Not well. As I told you before, I saw her at the club with Thompson and someone there told me about her. Why do you ask?"

"I did a little bit of further digging on her," Pam paused, her serious eyes on Meredith.

"Okay…can you elaborate?"

"If she's a stranger to you then why do you want to know?"

"Really?" Meredith asked. "You either tell me or you don't. Your choice."

Meredith knew that Pam was considering what to do. She didn't move or look away. "Her last name is Stewart, Alana Stewart. But Alana Stewart doesn't exist."

"What do you mean, Alana Stewart doesn't exist?"

"She did exist but she died of leukemia five years ago. She would be thirty if she were alive today. Alana Stewart has been dead for a long time."

"What?" Meredith couldn't hide her astonishment. "How is that possible?"

"It's called identity theft. A very common crime."

"I don't believe it."

Meredith saw Pam reach inside her bag and bring out a black file folder. She opened it, laying its contents on the table. "Is this the

Alana you know?" Pam asked, her finger pointing to a large color photo of a young woman.

Meredith took the photo, looking at it more closely. It was of a brunette with large brown eyes. "No, that's not Alana."

"What I would like to know is who the woman at The Raven Room really is."

"Why did she steal this woman's identity?" Meredith asked, bewildered.

"Because she's hiding. People only hide when they're running from something."

"No shit. I was wondering if you knew anything else."

"She quit her job at the bookstore more than two weeks ago and she's no longer volunteering. She has no emergency contact either."

"Are you going to arrest her?"

Pam didn't reply but she didn't need too. Meredith straightened her back, all of her attention on Pam. "Why are you wasting your time on her?"

"Identity theft is a crime."

"Don't lie. That's not why you're interested in Alana."

Meredith realized that just like her, Pam was refusing to tell the truth. She needed to get to Alana before Pam did.

"Do what you've got to do," Meredith finally said, sounding disinterested. "I'm sure Chicago will become a safer city as soon as you throw that girl in jail." She reached for her purse and stood up, bringing the collar of her jacket closer to her neck.

"Meredith?" that made her face Pam. "I need you to stay away from Reeve."

"Because you think he shot someone as a teenager and he's a sociopath?"

Without waiting for a reply, Meredith walked out of White Palace Grill. She had made her way two blocks west when she grabbed her phone and did what she didn't think she would do anytime soon—she called Julian.

He picked up by the second ring. "It's me," Meredith said, her phone pressed tightly against her cheek. "I know you're pissed I have been avoiding you for three weeks but this is serious. Listen to me carefully. Is Alana with you?" She closed her eyes, hoping the answer would be yes.

"No, she's not," she heard Julian say. "What's going on, Meredith?"

A curse escaped her lips. "Have you seen her recently?"

"She has been staying at my place but I don't know where she is right now."

"You need to call her."

"I can't. She doesn't have a mobile phone."

Meredith shook her head in disbelief. "You need to find her and bring her back to your place."

"You need to tell me what's going on."

"The police are looking for her. They're going to arrest her."

"What? Why?"

She ignored Julian's urgent tone. "There isn't time to get into details right now. Apparently she lives at the New Jackson Hotel, on Jackson and Halsted Street."

"New Jackson? Are you sure?"

"That's the info the cops have."

"How do you know all this?"

"Later. I'll explain everything to you later. Not right now." Meredith lowered her voice. "You need to find Alana."

"You've been ignoring my calls and my texts and now you call me to tell me I need to get Alana because the cops are after her. Do you have any idea how crazy all of this sounds?"

Meredith didn't answer his question. She knew better than anyone else how fast everything was unraveling. "Don't bother looking for her at the bookstore. She quit. If you go to the New Jackson you need to be very careful. Dress down, blend in. Look like someone who might be staying there."

"I'm at work but I have my gym clothes with me. I'll change."

"Good. If my stepmom wasn't involved I'd be looking for her myself."

"Your stepmom is involved? Why?"

She wondered how she was going to tell him all the things she had kept from him. "Julian, you need to find Alana."

"You better have answers. Go to my place and wait for Alana and me there. I'll tell the concierge to let you in."

"I will. You'll find her and everything will be fine. You just need to get Alana."

Meredith hung up and waved down a passing taxi. As soon as the car stopped, she got in and told the driver Julian's address. Sitting in the back seat, she held her phone tightly between her hands. She kept telling herself that Julian was going to find Alana, bring her to his place, and they would be able to make sense of what was going on. Alana would tell them why she was using someone else's identity and, hopefully, they would come up with a plan that would work to their advantage.

Less than an hour later Meredith was in Julian's living room. She texted him, asking for an update, but he didn't reply. Unable to sit still, she approached the window. The sun was setting and the view was beautiful. Pressing her palms to the glass, she let her eyes take in the array of red, yellow, and purple tones across the sky. Meredith stood, losing herself in the purity of the moment. There was no murder, no club, no Alana, no Julian. Just her and the cold glass against her skin, the city beneath her, the blend of bright colors slowly changing around her. The sound of footsteps pulled her out of her trance and threw her back into everything she wanted to run away from.

"Meredith? Are you here?"

The urgency in Julian's voice confirmed her fears.

She met him in the hall. They hadn't seen each other for a while and Meredith couldn't stop herself from taking a moment to take in his appearance. He was wearing track pants, a grey hoodie and a pair of running shoes. His face was unshaven and his dark hair, longer than she had ever seen before, was starting to curl at the base of his neck. There was now a palpable grittiness to him that she hadn't noticed before.

"I couldn't find her," he replied, almost out of breath. "I drove through the whole area. No sign of her."

"Goddammit." Meredith walked past Julian and sat on the bed. She stared at the floor for a while, trying to think. When she looked up, Julian was standing in front of her. She saw confusion and anger in his eyes. She prepared herself for what would come next.

"Start talking," he demanded.

"Alana is using someone else's identity. The real Alana died of leukemia five years ago and, let me tell you, she doesn't look at all like the Alana you and I both know," she paused, trying not to sound nervous, "the police are going to arrest her on identity theft charges."

"How did you find out?"

"My stepmom."

"And how the fuck does your stepmom know about Alana? Why did she tell you?"

"Because I told her about Alana."

For a brief moment neither of them spoke.

"You told her about Alana?" Julian repeated.

"I wanted to find out more about you and I told my stepmom you were a member of The Raven Room and you were going to take me." Meredith was speaking calmly, her steady voice not more than a desperate attempt not to look pitiful. "I wanted to find out where Sofia and Tatia might be so I asked her to look into their whereabouts," she added, not avoiding his seething gaze. "I told her I had seen Alana with Steven Thompson at the club, knowing she would look into her and come across an address. I wanted to pass that address on to you."

When Julian glared at her instead of speaking, Meredith took the opportunity to continue. "I never revealed to her your relationship with Alana. Or what happened when I made my way into the basement of the club or why you really go there." She couldn't tell what Julian was thinking, but his tight jaw and threatening stare made her believe he was ready to lash out at her. She would not dare mention the piece she was writing on him and The Raven Room.

There was heavy silence again. "It was a mistake," she added, sounding regretful. "I should have never told her anything. I'm sorry."

Julian's eyes, fixed on hers, were deepening her uneasiness. Instead of filling the silence with a slew of apologies, Meredith remained quiet, staring at him from the bed.

Julian walked toward her, only stopping when her knees were digging into his thighs. He touched her hair and then moved his hand along her neck, to caress her cheek. She didn't take her eyes away from his but all of her attention was on his fingers, stroking her.

"You lied to me. You betrayed my trust."

Meredith chose not to reply. Julian spoke in a smooth tone that sent a chill down her spine. She hadn't flinched or backed away but her whole body was tense, waiting for a gesture or movement from him that would make her react.

"You're afraid of me."

She was barely breathing. "I'm not afraid of you, Julian. What could you possibly do to me? Hit me? Cut me?" Her voiced was now as smooth as his. "I would like to see you try."

"I won't do any of those things to you, Meredith. But I'm going to break your heart. Like you just broke mine."

Her eyes never left his. She felt his warm breath on her hair, their faces unbearably close together. Now was not the time for her to cry. "We have to find Alana. The club…she might be there tonight."

Julian didn't reply. He continued to caress her cheek.

"I'll go with you," Meredith added.

He laughed, a bitter and hollow sound. "After everything you told me, do you think I would take you?" He shook his head. "I can't."

Meredith pulled back, her intense blue eyes meeting his. "You don't want to take me?" she asked, trying to take pleasure in her words. "Then don't. It doesn't matter how many times we hurt each other. Right now, I'm still the only one who can help you."

CHAPTER 24

Julian scanned his key and entered his four-digit code on the keypad. Hearing the sound of the door unlocking, he made his way inside. He was now in the lowest underground level, the birthplace of the club, The Raven Room.

It was busy, several people sitting in the main area, chatting and laughing. A man, dressed in a dark blue suit, was holding a glass of wine in one hand and a leash in the other. Julian glanced behind him and as soon as he looked at the floor he saw the woman. Fully naked, with her buzzed haircut. She was sitting on her heels, with her hands folded on her lap and downcast eyes. The thin chain was attached to a metal loop on the leather collar around her neck. With the collar against her striking pale skin, and several red welts on her breasts and thighs, the woman was impossible to miss. She probably hadn't been outside for months. Julian had to turn away. She no longer looked human to him.

Someone had decided to use the vintage vinyl record player in the corner and the music coming from it was both soft and somber. It was an old blues song and it made Julian think of the many rainy Sunday afternoons he had spent in his condo admiring Chicago's skyline, wondering if, once it got dark, he would find the resolve to stay away from The Raven Room.

Julian hadn't seen Alana in the other areas of the club and although he had never seen her down there, it was the last place for him to search. Desperate to locate her, part of him wanted her to be there but a bigger part of him hoped that she wasn't.

Walking down the corridor awash in red light, he found the doors to many of the soundproof rooms locked shut. He wondered if Alana was behind one of them. But unless he waited to see who came out, there was no way to know. Reaching the end, he turned around and decided to return to the main area, figuring that anyone coming or going would have to come past him. He was about to exit the corridor when one of the first doors opened and a woman emerged. A few steps behind her, Julian was unable to see her face, but he didn't have to. With the long, wild hair he was certain it was Alana. He reached for her arm, turning her around to face him. She had made Julian promise to never approach her at the club but he wouldn't be able to honor that promise any longer.

She stared up at him with a shocked look. Julian took in the tangled hair, the black mascara smudged around her eyes, the sheer lace dress she wore with nothing underneath. "You're leaving with me. Right now," he said, keeping his voice as low as possible. He didn't let go of her arm.

"Take your fucking hands off me," she replied, in the same tone as him. "I'm not going anywhere with you."

She tried to move away from him but Julian tightened his grip. He knew he was bruising her. "Stop," he warned, bringing his body closer to hers. "If you don't, you'll end up in jail."

"What are you talking about?"

"I don't care what your real name is but the police know you stole someone's identity. They know you come to the club. It's not safe." Julian was whispering, not wanting the others around then to overhear.

"Go to hell, Reeve."

Julian was about to drag her toward one the empty rooms, so he could talk to her and calm her down, when the door of the room she had walked out of opened and he suddenly found himself face–to-face with Steven Thompson.

"Did you find...?" Thompson started to say, but stopped himself when he saw Julian and Alana. His eyes moved between the two.

Alana took the opportunity to escape Julian's grasp. "Let's get back inside," she said to Thompson as she rested both of her hands on his chest and gently pushed him.

"She's leaving with me." Julian took a step forward and grabbed Alana's arm again.

"What the fuck is going on, huh? Did you lie to me?" Thompson asked, looking at Alana.

"I don't know what you're talking about," she replied, giving him a nervous smile.

The image of Alana trying to dissipate Thompson's anger made Julian clench his jaw. He tugged on Alana, pulling her away from Thompson. But the other man didn't hesitate; lifting his right hand he slapped Alana so hard that, even in Julian's grasp, she was thrown in the opposite direction. Her body made an ugly, hollow sound as it hit the wall. Seeing Alana crumpled to the ground, Julian's anger took over.

He launched himself at Thompson, punching him repeatedly. Thompson was older than Julian and, not expecting the attack, tried to protect himself from the onslaught. Lost in his rage and no longer aware of his surroundings, Julian continued to pummel Thompson until three security guards physically pulled him off the man. As the guards dragged Julian away from the corridor toward one of the emergency exits, Julian struggled against them.

"I can't leave her behind…No! He's going to hurt her," he screamed. "Alana!"

The guards ignored his cries and it didn't matter how hard Julian fought. He couldn't overcome them. Before being dragged out of The Raven Room, he glanced over his shoulder and saw Alana trying to stand up, using the wall for support. There was a fourth security guard standing by her. Thompson had his eyes on Julian.

"She's mine," Thompson yelled, wiping the blood off of his chin. "You hear me? She's mine to do whatever the fuck I want."

Julian continued to shout, calling out for Alana but it was no use. Before he knew it he was outside, in one of Chinatown's many dark back alleys. The security guards threw him against a brick wall and one of them had him by the throat.

"You know this type of behavior is not accepted."

As soon as the guard said that his fist met Julian's face multiple times. Before Julian could react, he felt a couple of punches to his side. The pain of his ribs cracking made him heave. When the two other men let him go, he slumped to the snow-covered ground. On his hands and knees Julian coughed, spitting out blood. He touched his cheek and winced, feeling the deep cut. The burning pain in his side made Julian take a series of shallow breaths.

He could still hear the sound of Thompson's hand coming in contact with Alana's face and her body hitting the wall. The images of her on the floor, struggling to stand up, would be forever imprinted on his mind. Julian clenched his fists. No matter what, he was going to take Alana away from Thompson and make sure she never went to The Raven Room again.

• • •

Meredith had just opened a beer when she heard someone struggling to open the front door. After Julian had refused to take her with him to the club, they had agreed she should stay over at his place, in case Alana were to show up. She had chain-smoked for hours, pacing back and forth. Now, at almost three in the morning, she hoped it was Julian and Alana coming through the front door.

She entered the foyer just as Julian managed to step inside the condo. She gasped. "What the fuck happened?" Meredith ran toward him, helping him into the living room and onto the couch. "Julian, speak to me. What happened?"

"I'm fine. Just looks bad."

"Are you kidding me? You're not fine. You have to tell me what happened." Julian's clothes were ruined, especially his shirt. It was covered in blood. "Now!" she added, sitting on the edge of the coffee table, across from him.

"Alana was at The Raven Room with Thompson. She wouldn't leave with me. He hit her and I fucking lost it on him. As security was taking me out they did this to my face. I went to the New Jackson again but she never showed up. I couldn't stay because of the police."

Meredith ran both of her hands through her hair. "Fucker! I hope you bashed Thompson's face in."

"Don't worry, he looks worse than I do."

"We have to go look for her," she said. "We'll drive around the club and the New Jackson. Maybe we'll spot her."

"I'll go by myself."

"Don't be stupid. One of your eyes is so swollen you can barely see and, by the way you're sitting, it looks like you might have a couple of cracked ribs. I'm coming with you and that's the end of it."

Julian didn't try to argue with her and Meredith sprung to action, helping him change into a pair of jeans and a sweater. She gave him two extra-strength painkillers and tended to his face, cleaning the deep cut on his cheek. They both figured he had a couple of broken ribs but couldn't come to a consensus on whether his nose was also broken.

They were out the door and inside of his car in less than twenty minutes.

"I'm sure she's okay," Meredith said, glancing at Julian, who was sitting very still in the passenger seat. "Alana is tougher than she looks."

"She's five-foot-one and less than a hundred pounds. That's how tough she is."

Meredith wrapped her hands tightly around the steering wheel. "We'll find her, Julian."

"I hope you're right."

"Why did she refuse to leave the club with you?"

"I had promised her I would never approach her there. I broke my promise."

"You had a good reason to."

"That's not how she saw it."

They were driving west, toward the hotel. "She's going to tell us everything," Meredith paused, her attention on the sidewalk, "holy shit! I think that's her...yes! That's her."

"What?" Julian asked, shifting on his seat. "Where?"

"Right there." Meredith pointed toward the lone figure walking on the sidewalk.

"What the fuck…?" he started to say. "Pull over!"

Meredith quickly pulled the car to the curb. Without turning off the engine, they both got out and made their way toward Alana. Julian was the first to get close to her and as soon as she saw him she started to back away.

"It's me," Julian said, his hands outstretched in front of him.

It was dark and Meredith only saw Alana's face when Alana stepped back and the light from a storefront made it visible. The image caused Meredith to cover her mouth with her hand. She heard Julian curse violently.

Alana's face was bloodied and swollen. She was struggling to hold herself up and the closer Julian got to her, the more scared she became.

Meredith touched his shoulder. "Let me try," she whispered.

He nodded, glancing away.

"It's me, sweetheart, Meredith." She kept her voice low, trying to sound non-threatening. "Please let us help you. We just want to help you. No one is going to hurt you. I promise."

Alana was now almost on the ground, with one arm against the wall and the other folded over her stomach. She wanted to stay upright but her body was not cooperating.

"We're going to help you, okay?" Tentatively, Meredith got close enough to her that she was able to touch Alana's hair. "Can you hear me? We just want to help you."

"No hospital," Alana said, almost choking on the words. "Don't take me to the hospital."

"We won't. But we need you to come with us so you're no longer on the street, alright? We'll get you out of those clothes, clean you up and give you something to ease the pain. No hospital, though. We promise."

Meredith extended her hand to Alana and she took it. She turned to Julian and, with a small gesture of her head, summoned him closer. She watched as he put one arm around Alana's shoulders and the other one under her legs, scooping her up against his chest.

As he lifted her, Meredith heard Julian grunt with pain from his broken ribs.

"She's out," he said as Meredith opened the car door so Julian could lay Alana down on the backseat. "She needs to been seen by a doctor."

"We can't take her to the hospital," Meredith replied, walking around the car. "If we do they'll call the cops and she'll be arrested."

"We don't know how badly she's hurt." Julian had joined Alana on the back seat, her head resting on his lap.

"Your friend," Meredith said, merging into the road and then turning right onto the next street. "Isn't he a doctor? Call him and tell him to meet us at your place."

"I can't involve Pete in this."

"Julian," Meredith paused, banging her hand on the steering wheel and looking at him through the rear-view mirror, "we can't take Alana to the hospital and we don't know how to help her ourselves. There's no option. Pick up the fucking phone and call him. Right now."

She saw Julian consider what she had just said.

"My phone is at the club. I need yours," he finally said.

"It's in here." She passed him her large tote.

Meredith heard Julian digging frantically inside her bag and spilling half of the contents onto the floor.

"Fucking hell. Why can't you carry a normal sized bag?"

"Are you for real?" She was close to screaming. "If I wasn't driving right now, I'd kick your ass." She switched on the car's overhead light. "Here!"

With the help of the added brightness, Julian found the phone and he dialed Peter. Meredith tried to calm down, hoping Julian's friend would pick up. After a heated back and forth, ridden with curses, promises and threats from both sides, Peter agreed to come over to Julian's place.

Meredith turned off the overhead light. "Are you sure he's your friend? He didn't sound happy to hear from you."

"Lately we haven't been seeing eye to eye on a couple of things."

"Can you trust him?"

Julian didn't reply and Meredith turned her attention to the road. She hoped they hadn't made a mistake by calling Peter. She glanced in the rear-view mirror and saw Julian looking down at Alana, tenderly caressing her head.

"How's she doing?" she asked, tilting the mirror so she could get a better view of Alana.

"She's in and out." Julian tucked her hair behind her ear. "I'm afraid to touch her."

"Where do you think she was going when we found her?"

"The hotel, I would think." He looked at her body. "She's still wearing the dress I saw her in at The Raven Room. No shoes, no jacket…in this weather." Julian rested his head on the back of his seat.

"She hadn't been out there for too long. We got to her in time."

Meredith heard Julian picking up her personal belongings and putting them back into her bag.

"Meredith," Julian called out.

"What?" she replied, glancing at the rear-view mirror. Something in Julian's tone made her apprehensive. "What's wrong?"

"I don't know if I'll ever forgive you."

"I can't take it back, Julian."

He was quiet for a while. "Would you? If you could?"

"Yes."

"I don't believe you."

"Why?"

"You put your needs and wants before everyone else around you."

Julian's words made her tighten her grip on the steering wheel. "Is that how you see me?"

"I'm being honest. I've always been honest with you."

Meredith was silent. She didn't want to show how much his words hurt her. She focused on the road. She didn't know if she could stop herself from saying something she would regret. "You either accept my apology or you can go fuck yourself."

"Meredith."

Ignoring him, she felt Julian kick the back of her seat with his foot. He was trying to get her attention. She continued to ignore him and Julian kicked her seat again, harder this time.

"What?" she shouted, lifting her eyes to the rear-view mirror.

"I'd have told you all the things you went to your stepmother for. All you had to do was ask."

"Bullshit. You kept me in the dark. I might have betrayed your trust, but your secrecy pushed me to it."

They didn't speak for the rest of the trip.

After parking the car in the underground garage, they made their way toward the elevator. Julian was again carrying Alana and she had her arms loosely wrapped around his neck and her eyes closed. Leaning against the wall, Julian rested his cheek on the top of Alana's head. Meredith could hear him tell Alana, over and over again, that she would be okay; that he would never allow anyone else to hurt her.

Unlocking the front door, she followed Julian into the bedroom. As Meredith went to close the curtains and turn on the lamp in the corner, he lowered Alana onto the bed.

"We need to get her out of that dress," Julian said, grabbing a blanket.

"Where are your scissors? It'll be easier if we just cut it off."

"They're in the kitchen, right by the pile of mail."

Moments later, Meredith returned with the scissors. She found Julian sitting on the bed, looking down at Alana. She had moved into a fetal position. Julian was rubbing his hand up and down her back.

When Meredith tried to pass him the scissors he shook his head. "I can't. You'll have to do it."

Meredith leaned toward Alana, a knee resting on the bed, and she pressed the side of the scissors against her skin. Feeling Julian's eyes on her, Meredith cut the flimsy, tight dress, moving from the bottom hem all the way up to the neck.

As soon as she lifted the sides of the dress off Alana, her first instinct was to cover her up again. Meredith didn't want Julian to see what had been hiding under that dress but he already had.

"Do you think Thompson was the one who did this to her?" Meredith asked, fearful. She continued to stare at Alana's back.

"It was him. I'm sure."

Meredith was afraid of what she was going to find as she continued to remove the rest of the dress. The sight of Alana's battered body validated Meredith's fears and made her recoil in horror.

"What type of object leaves cuts like these?" she asked, almost to herself. "Her body will be covered in scars."

Meredith felt Julian get closer to her and rest his hand on her shoulder.

"You don't have to. I'll do it." She heard Julian say. His voice sounded pained.

"You didn't answer my question."

Julian squeezed her shoulder. "A bullwhip."

Alana was not wearing underwear and Meredith continued to stare at her marked body. Suddenly, she was afraid and she tried to steady her trembling hands. Julian approached Alana, and very carefully, turned her around so he could finish removing her dress. The front of her body carried the same bruises and cuts. Julian kneeled on the floor, cradling her naked body against his chest. He had his face tucked into Alana's neck and Meredith saw Julian's whole frame sway.

He was crying.

Unable to continue watching, she lowered her eyes. Witnessing Julian's sorrow made her chest feel like it was about to burst.

The sound of the doorbell made her jump. "Your friend is here," she whispered. "Go. I'll stay with Alana."

Without speaking, he covered Alana with a blanket. As he was about to exit the bedroom, he locked eyes with Meredith. "Let me handle Pete. Don't tell him more than he needs to know. Even if he asks."

She nodded. The last thing she wanted was to discuss what was happening with someone she had never met before.

After about fifteen minutes, Julian entered the bedroom with his friend. Both Meredith and Peter didn't say anything to each other. She realized that Julian had already explained the situation. Peter was quiet and, with Meredith sitting at the end of the bed and Julian standing right by him, they were not giving him much space to work. Meredith wasn't sure how aware Alana was but she wanted to stay close in case Alana became scared again.

Meredith stared at Julian. A whole side of his face was now swollen and the skin had become a deep red. His eyes showed the same emotion she was feeling—fear.

Peter spent a long time cleaning the cuts on Alana's torso. There had been no words exchanged in the bedroom for more than half an hour and when Peter spoke, his voice was restrained. "She doesn't appear to have any broken bones or a concussion, but without taking her to the ER, I can't be sure."

"She's not very responsive. Why do you think that is?" Julian asked.

"She's under the influence of some drug. Could be K, but who knows."

"Is there anything I should or shouldn't do?"

"Just let her rest. When she wakes up she's going to be in a lot of pain, mostly because of the deeper cuts and bruises on her back. I'm going to give you a prescription for some strong painkillers and an antibiotic cream. She'll be lucky if the cuts don't get infected." Peter glanced at Julian. "You should get stitches on that cheek."

"Can you do it?" Julian asked, his arms folded across his chest.

"Not here."

"Then I'm sure a Band-Aid will do the trick."

"Seriously, man, the kinky shit you're into has to stop. Cutting women? Beating them up?"

"Not now, Pete," Julian said, shaking his head.

"Then when?" he asked, angry. "Things are spinning out of control—"

"I said not now," Julian interrupted him, raising his voice.

"You never want to hear what I have to say but this is serious. I'm not okay with any of this, man. Regardless if it's consensual, it's not right."

"If there's nothing else you can do for Alana I'd like you to leave."

"Leave?" Peter asked, approaching Julian. "You wake me up in the middle of the night to treat your mangled, drugged-up girlfriend. I'll have to lie to my wife when I get home because if she found out what you're capable of she'd never allow you around her or our kids. And you've got the balls to talk to me this way?" Peter said, close to shouting. "Kick me out of your home?"

Meredith moved toward them and wrapped her fingers around Julian's closed fist. She squeezed hard. If they were to start hitting each other she wouldn't know what to do.

"Fuck you, you sick piece of shit," Peter said, stabbing Julian in the chest with his finger as he enunciated each word.

Meredith watched Peter grab the medical bag he had brought with him and walk out without saying another word. The whole time he had been there he had acted like she didn't exist.

"Why didn't you tell him the truth?" she asked Julian.

"It's easier this way."

Meredith knew he was right. Explaining to Peter what had happened would only raise questions Julian wouldn't be able to answer.

She tucked the blanket around Alana. Meredith dimmed the light in the bedroom and pulled the reading chair closer to the bed. She sat on it with her feet folded under her.

"What are we going to do?"

"I don't know." Julian stood for a while, watching her and Alana. "But I'm relieved that both of you are here. Safe."

"Are you wondering who Alana really is?"

"I've wondered that from the first day I met her."

"I feel foolish calling her by a name I know is not her own," Meredith said.

"She might never tell us her real name."

Meredith leaned forward and caressed Alana's hair. "Regardless of who she might be, the secrets she might be keeping, or the lies she might have told you, she cares for you. I saw it when I watched the two of you together that day in the living room. I hope you never forget that."

Julian didn't reply and Meredith continued to caress Alana.

"I'm going to run to the drugstore to pick up the medication," he finally said. "I'll be back as soon as I can."

"No, I'll go. You're in bad shape too. Stay here with her."

"She freaked out when I approached her on the street but you made her feel safe. In case she comes around it's best if it's you who she sees."

Julian left and Meredith settled back into her chair. She buried her face in her hands and shuddered at the thought of all that had happened that night.

She woke up to Julian covering her with a large, soft blanket. "What time is it?" Meredith asked, yawning.

"Almost six. Are you okay in that chair?"

"I'm fine."

"Go back to sleep. I'll watch over Alana," he said, sitting on the bed.

They were speaking in a hushed tone.

"How are you feeling? A lot of pain?" she asked, looking at him.

"It's not the first time I've had broken ribs and a mangled face. Nothing to worry about."

Meredith wanted to remain awake but her eyelids felt heavy and she couldn't keep her eyes open. The last thing she remembered, before she fell asleep, was the blanket slipping off of her and a careful set of hands covering her with it again, making sure she was warm.

She woke up with Julian gently shaking her.

"Meredith?"

"What's wrong?" she asked, disoriented. He was crouching by her chair, his bruised face close to hers.

"Your stepmom is on her way up."

"What?" she sat up quickly. "Why is she here?"

"She said it was urgent. I couldn't turn her away."

Meredith caught herself holding her breath. "Do you think she knows Alana is here?"

"I don't know."

"Fuck."

They heard the doorbell and they both turned to face the entrance of the bedroom.

"That's her." Julian stood up. "I don't think it's a good idea for her to know you're here."

"Besides berating me for my choices, there's nothing she can do to me." Meredith left her chair and tried to fix her hair with her hands. Her heart was pounding. "How's Alana?" she asked, looking at the sleeping form on the bed.

"Still out."

"Do you have a brush or something that I can use? My hair is a mess."

Julian pointed toward his en suite bathroom. "Bottom drawer."

Meredith ran into the bathroom and searched for the brush. Her fingers touched something and she pulled it out. In her hand was a gold chain with a small cross.

Hearing Julian call her name, Meredith debated whether she should return the necklace to where she found it. The police were at Julian's doorstep. What if they started looking around, she thought. She couldn't think of a reason she'd want to believe as to why Julian had such piece of jewelry hidden in the back of a drawer. Taking a steadying breath, Meredith reminded herself she trusted Julian and that was the feeling she was choosing to listen to. Certain that the necklace was safer with her than anywhere in the condo, she slid it inside her front pocket and exited the bathroom.

"My hair is fine," she said to Julian, almost choking on her own saliva. Her whole body was shaking. "Let's go."

Closing the bedroom door behind them, they walked toward the other end of the condo. Meredith stood in the foyer as Julian opened the front door.

"Good morning, Doctor Reeve. I'm detective Pam Sung and this is my partner, detective Luke Colton."

Meredith saw Colton standing beside her stepmother. He looked surprised to see her but was trying to hide it.

"Good morning," Julian said. "How can I help you?"

"I have a couple of questions I would like to ask you. May we come in?"

Julian moved to the side, allowing Pam and Colton to enter his home. When she spotted Meredith the expression on her face changed. She was angry.

"Hi, Pam," Meredith said, trying to steady her voice. "What's going on?"

Pam ignored her question and turned to Julian. "Where were you last night?"

He pointed to his face. "Getting myself a good beating, as you can see."

"Where were you, Doctor Reeve?" she insisted.

Julian folded his arms across his chest. "Why do want to know?"

"Answer my question."

Meredith took a step forward, her heart still beating fast. It became obvious to her why her stepmother was there. "What happened last night, Pam?"

Continuing to ignore Meredith, she focused on Julian. "Remember Alana Stewart? The woman you've been having an intimate relationship with?"

Julian didn't waver. He stood, silent.

"She was found dead this morning," Pam added.

"You're lying," Julian said, his tone clipped.

Pam reached for the file she had under her arm, opened it and passed a series of photos to Julian. "It's quite obvious you knew her, Doctor Reeve."

Meredith watched Julian flip through the photos. "How did you get these?" he asked, lifting his incredulous eyes to Pam.

"They were in her room, amongst her things."

Meredith snatched the photos from Julian's hands, flipping through them herself. It was a series of bright images, one showing Alana reading a book, one of Julian by a park, a few of them together, smiling, and a sexually explicit one of Julian, lying on the floor, surrounded by books.

Meredith passed the photos back to Pam. "She's not dead."

Pam took another photo from inside the folder. "I don't know about you, but she certainly looks dead to me."

Meredith took the photo from her stepmother. When she saw the face of the woman lying on the bed she looked at Julian.

"Meredith?" she heard him say. "Who's in that photo?"

She had to swallow several times before she could answer. "It's Alana."

He came closer and grabbed the photo from her. As soon as he saw the image his expression changed. "It can't be," Julian finally said, shaking his head in disbelief. "It can't be."

"I'm going to ask you again, Doctor Reeve," Pam paused, narrowing her eyes on Julian, "where were you last night?"

"With her," he replied, still staring at the photo he held tightly in his hands.

Meredith remembered Julian telling her the night before that he had waited at the New Jackson for Alana. "It doesn't matter," Meredith whispered. "Alana is safe. She's in the bedroom."

"What are you saying?" Pam asked, frowning. "I have her body in—" she stopped mid-sentence, staring past Meredith and Julian. She looked perplexed.

They both turned around and, standing behind them, completely naked, was the person they were all talking about.

Julian was the first one to speak. "Alana…what's going on?"

"He's telling the truth. I was with him last night."

Alana wavered on her feet, unsteady.

"Then who's the dead woman?" Pam asked.

"My sister."

Julian looked as if his world was spinning uncontrollably and he didn't know how to stop it. "You have an identical twin?"

"I do." Alana reached toward the wall, trying to support herself. "But she's gone now."

Julian's expression was of complete shock but he rushed to Alana's side.

"Should we take him down to the station for questioning?"

Colton asked Pam, trying to take charge.

Pam nodded, too lost in thought to speak.

"I have to ask you to accompany us," Colton said to Julian. "There are a lot of questions that need answers."

Julian let go of Alana. Before he walked out of the condo with Colton he passed Meredith and quickly leaned in, giving her a kiss on the cheek. "Her shoulder," he whispered.

"Did he do that to you?" Pam asked Alana, looking at the marks on her body.

She shook her head in response.

"Then who?" Pam pressed.

Alana slid to the floor in tears. She didn't reply.

"Calm her down," Pam said to Meredith, disgust in her voice. Her eyes lingered on Alana before she turned toward the door and followed Colton and Julian out of the condo.

Meredith was about to curse at Pam but stopped herself. She was relieved Pam was leaving without Alana and didn't want to give her any excuse to turn around.

She crouched down to a sobbing Alana. Meredith wanted to hug her but was afraid doing so would hurt her. Alana now looked even worse than she had the night before.

Meredith kneeled on the floor. "I'm so sorry about your sister. I really am."

She moved the hair away from Alana's neck. Suddenly, Meredith understood what Julian was trying to tell her. There was no scar.

Meredith cupped Alana's face with both her hands and tilted her head up, so they were facing each other. "You're not Alana," Meredith said as gently as she was able to. "Alana was murdered last night. I want to know your name."

END OF BOOK ONE

7529

CPSIA information can be obtained at www.ICGtesting.com
Printed in the USA
BVOW08s2334111115

426712BV00007BA/175/P